blUrred

a Kissed by Death novel

Other books by Tara Fuller

inbetween

blurred

a Kissed by Death novel

tara fuller

Entangled Publishing, LLC
2614 South Timberline Road
Suite 109
Fort Collins, CO 80525
Visit our website at www.entangledpublishing.com.

Edited by Heather Howland and Kaleen Harding
Cover design by Heather Howland

Print ISBN   978-1-62061-085-5
Ebook ISBN   978-1-62061-086-2

Manufactured in the United States of America

First Edition July 2013

For Jared, Colten, and Caden.
You are the reason my heart beats. You are the reason I have
stories to tell.
I love you.

Prologue

Anaya

The flames closed in, each lick of heat a tick of the clock. My scythe pulsed at my side and warmth spread down my arms and into my fingertips. Six seconds. I could have his soul out in six seconds. Just one swipe of my blade and he could have peace.

Not this one, Anaya. This one is special. No matter what, you will ensure that he stays in his flesh.

Balthazar's words echoed in my mind and my palms shook, just inches above his chest. His soul was already seeping through. Almighty...if only the rest of them weren't here. Finn, Scout...they were going to see.

"She made it!" Finn's voice was nothing but static. A distraction I didn't need. His human was safe, but I wasn't here for her. I was here for Cash.

Heat exploded in my chest. The glittering soul was so

ready to escape its flesh that it wasn't even waiting for my blade. Oh, God. This felt wrong.

"I can't do this," I said to no one.

You will.

Balthazar's whispered voice extinguished the heat, the doubt, the reason. All that existed was this moment. This boy. This baffling connection silently blooming between us. I placed my palms over his chest. His soul pushed against my hands and his body shuddered, fighting what I was trying to give back to him.

"Shhh…" I leaned over him, my braids brushing his pale cheeks. "It's not over for you, Cash. Not yet." I settled my weight over my palms and pressed the last bit of his soul back into his flesh.

"Anaya!" I flinched at the sound of Scout's voice. "What in God's name are you doing? Take him already."

I didn't possess one, but in that moment it felt like my heart was in my throat, refusing to let me breathe or speak. I realized that I was giving something back to this boy, but it didn't feel like it. It felt like I was taking everything away. I tucked a braid behind my ear and watched Cash's face like it was the last one I'd ever see. He was so beautiful, so still.

A shadow hissed behind me, closing in, looking at the boy beneath me as if he were nothing more than another meal. I leaned in closer to protect him, to lend him my warmth.

"Breathe," I whispered. "Please, breathe."

Smoke swirled between us, but even through the darkness I could see the color bleeding back into his lips. His skin. A sliver of breath and smoke slipped through his mouth, and his face contorted in pain. I felt that pain. I felt it to the depths of my soul. He didn't have to be feeling this. He could be at peace. Instead he was alive. He was...*alive*. Guilt rushed through me, mixing with the selfish relief I felt at seeing him breathe.

I smoothed the wet hair back from his forehead and leaned down until my lips grazed his ear. Sparks danced across my lips. "I'm so sorry," I whispered.

"Aren't you going to take him?" Finn asked from behind me.

Fire crackled around us and I reached out to touch the tip of Cash's nose. "No. Not this time."

Before Finn could question me, a fireman rushed in from the hall and scooped Cash up into his arms.

In an instant a flash of cold and light consumed me. I closed my eyes and let it pull me into the sky. Balthazar was calling. When the world went still, I caught myself before I accidentally stumbled over the edge of a valley.

What had I done? My hands shook with the force of my decision. My *mistake*. The driving force in my existence as a reaper was to take, to reap, to end. For a thousand years, it had come as easy as breathing, and now...I'd denied it. I could still feel his soul on my palms, warm and vibrant. I could smell him all over me, clinging to me like a dream. My scythe burned angrily at my side, wanting the soul we'd been dispatched to take.

"I trust everything went well."

Balthazar emerged from a shadow and stepped into the muted gray light. I couldn't look at him. If I looked at him, I'd feel the enormity of what I'd done. Instead, I focused my gaze on the empty gray riverbank of the Inbetween below us, where souls searched for something they'd never find. Home. Their pale faces tilted toward the sky, eyes swirling with impending darkness as they wandered through the forever frozen twilight. Most would soon be shadow-bound, never to see Heaven or the second life they sought.

"Why didn't you allow me to take him?" My voice trembled. "He earned the peace that waited for him. I…I just stole that from him."

"Because he has a purpose. You cannot comprehend how valuable he is," Balthazar said, turning to me. "That human… that soul has been a thousand years in the making, Anaya. I did what was necessary."

His cold eyes raked over me once before settling on my face with the weight of a decision. "And now I'm going to ask *you* to do what is necessary. One *last* task."

Hope flared to life inside me. I'd been waiting a thousand years to hear those words. "Last task?"

"I need your help securing that soul. If he is who I think he is, I can't risk him falling into the hands of our enemies." Balthazar's jaw clenched and a breeze ruffled the edge of his robe. "You guard him, deliver him to me when the time comes, and I'll give you what I promised."

I attempted to organize my thoughts enough to reply. This was unheard of. Souls bound for Hell were sometimes intercepted to be recruited as reapers, yes, but a Heaven-bound? Never. "Deliver him to *you*? Not the Almighty? Not to the place of peace that he has worked lifetimes to earn?" My insides burned with the force of how wrong this felt. After shoving that vibrant soul back into its wilting body, I wasn't sure anything would ever feel right again. "You are asking me to deny his eternal happiness in exchange for my own?"

In response, Balthazar swept his hand through the air, clearing the mist around us. An image rippled out in front of me. The sea lapped up onto the sand, pulling layers of it back out with the tide. The sky was so bright and blue that the image burned my eyes. My head rested in Tarik's lap. He took one of my braids, dipped it in the surf, and tickled my nose with the tip. I laughed and he leaned down to capture the sound with his lips. His dark hair was wet from our swim and dripped onto my closed eyelids.

I gasped, overwhelmed by the pain and longing that swept through me. Even now, a thousand years later, I could taste him. Feel the water, cool and perfect against my skin. Balthazar had chosen the memory well. It had been the day I'd fallen in love. The day that altered the course of my existence forever. Old wounds fractured inside my chest and the loss scorched my throat, fresh and fiery. I reached out to touch the image, but it swirled away like smoke.

"I am offering you salvation, Anaya," he said. "A chance to cross over. All I ask in return is that you succeed in the task I have provided for you. You wouldn't throw away the chance to be with the ones you love again, would you?"

I shut my eyes, trying to cling to the image of Tarik. In that moment, I would have done anything. Even if it was as awful as denying a soul as beautiful as Cash's the eternal home he deserved. If the path led me back to my family, back into Tarik's arms and away from the call of the dead, I would take it.

Balthazar touched my shoulder and cold seeped through my pores, warring with the warmth inside me. I opened my eyes, clutching the scythe at my hip to calm it.

"Tell me what I have to do."

Chapter 1

Cash

There isn't a handbook for cheating death.

It would have been nice if there was one. Anything would have been more helpful than these fluffy stories about white tunnels of light, angels, and perfect peace. I didn't get any of that. What I got was this. Not life. Not death. A freaking nightmare.

"Smile!" The flash popped and flames sparked behind my eyes. I was back in that house again, being swallowed by smoke and heat and panic. Sunset-gold eyes blinked down at me. *I'm so sorry*. Crap.

I rubbed my eyes and refocused on the big black shadow dripping from the gym rafters. There was only one for now, but it wouldn't stay that way. More would come. They always did. They'd creep in through the cracks and corners until darkness consumed every square inch of this gym. Until all I could feel was cold filling up my insides and fear throbbing behind my ribs. The shadow above me hissed and I watched as it swirled like smoke around the big silver ductwork, coming closer with every pass. The air around me felt like cold venom, crawling across my mouth, trying to find a way in. I pressed my lips together and closed my eyes.

"Cash?" The photographer with curly saffron hair piled on top of her head peeked around her camera and frowned. "You weren't smiling, hun. You weren't even looking at the lens. Let's try one more."

I scrubbed my palms over my face and someone behind me adjusted my cap. This was so stupid. They could paste a picture of Mr. Rogers in my place in the yearbook for all I cared. All I knew was that I didn't want to be here for this. I didn't really want to be here for anything anymore. What I *wanted* was my life back.

I forced my mouth into a fake grin, but a second shadow slithered over the shoulder of the photographer, and the smile disintegrated on my lips. The shadow's tar-like tongue reached out to taste the silver bangles on the photographer's wrist. I stumbled backward off the stool at the same moment the camera flashed, and my back hit the ground hard, forcing the air from my lungs. After living off an inhaler the past week, that shit hurt. I winced and sat up, trying to catch my breath and failing.

"Oh my God, are you okay?" The photographer stood up, holding the camera at arm's length. Students piled up behind her, whispering and trying to see what had happened. Great. More fuel for the gossip queens. Just what I needed.

Ms. Moyer tried to help me to my feet, but I waved her off. I had to get the hell out of here. Not just away from the way they were all looking at me like I was a nut job. Away from the shadows. Senior pictures were the least of my worries. Besides, the longer I stayed here, the worse my chances got of avoiding Em. And I wasn't ready to face her. Not yet.

I tore off the cheesy blue graduation gown and picked up my cap. "Can I do this later? I need to get my inhaler out of my locker."

The photographer nodded and Ms. Moyer looked me over with sympathy in her eyes. "Come right back. We need to get these done today."

"Okay." I grabbed my bag and the crowd of seniors split down the middle to let me through. It didn't take much to be kicked off the popularity podium at Lone Pine High, and the look in each person's eyes said they were watching my hellacious fall. As if I cared. I wasn't coming back. I was going home. It's not like Ms. Moyer wasn't expecting it. They should have been used to my disappearing acts by now.

I got halfway down the hall and skidded to a stop. Shadows seeped out of the air vents on the ceiling, melting down the sky-blue lockers like sludge. They pooled across the tile until the darkness closed around my boots, and my heart thundered in my ears.

I shoved my hands into my hair and pulled until my eyes watered. Anything to take this shit away. They were freaking *everywhere*. Dark and cold like a nightmare come to life.

My head snapped up at the sound of someone laughing. A guy about my age wearing a gray wool coat stood across the hall, a chunk of pale blond hair falling over one eye. In a town a small as Lone Pine, it wasn't hard to pick out someone who didn't belong. And this guy didn't belong. As if to prove my point, he eyed the shadows around me with interest, his mouth twisting into a grin as one swirled around the base of my boot and up my pant leg. Other than the tremor rolling down my spine, I stood completely still, afraid to breathe.

"Back off!"

I flinched at the unexpected sound of his voice splitting the silence and stared in awe as the shadows around my legs parted. They didn't leave, but even the few feet of space gave me room to breathe again. When I looked up, the guy was still watching me. As if he were waiting to see how I'd react.

"Who are you?" I asked. He didn't answer. Just winked and backed around the corner, disappearing behind a row of lockers. The second he was out of sight, the shadows closed back in. I pulled my boots out of their darkness and barreled though the hall.

"Hey!" I patted my jeans for my inhaler, my lungs burning with the want for air. "Stop!" I braced myself on the edge of the lockers where he'd been standing and the metal seared my hand with cold.

What the hell?

I spun in a circle, searching the empty halls. He was gone.

I backed down the hall toward the exit. I was fucking losing it. Had he even been real? Did the things circling my ankles even exist or was I just my own brand of crazy now? I wasn't ready to answer that, so I turned around and ran until my feet hit the gravel parking lot. The sunshine felt good against the frosty sting of my skin, so I kept going until I was in my Bronco, speeding down Main Street. I prayed to God I didn't get pulled over. If I had to stop, they'd catch me. What happened if they did? I stepped on the pedal a little harder. I didn't want to find out.

I didn't know how long I'd been home. Long enough for the light in the windows to fade and the neighbor's dog to stop barking. Long enough for me to hear Dad's little silver BMW cruise up the drive about four minutes before he marched into my studio, armed and ready to make my ears bleed.

"What the hell is wrong with you?" Dad growled before the door to my studio had even slammed shut. "I didn't raise you to act like this."

I stared at the half-painted canvas in front of me and pressed my bare feet against the cold, concrete floor to wake me up. He was either pissed about me skipping again, or he found the half-empty bottle of bourbon I had taken from his desk. "You didn't raise me to act any way. You would have actually had to be around to do that."

I picked up a brush, dipped it into bloodred paint, and slashed a wound across the white canvas. Dad's well-polished oxfords clicked across the concrete floor until he was standing next to my canvas, blocking my light. He hadn't changed yet, which meant he was still in lawyer mode. *Damn it.*

Out of habit, my gaze wandered to the window where Emma's house once stood. It was just a clean foundation now, waiting for some stranger to build a new house and move in. The fire hadn't left anything more than memories and a crap-ton of hospital bills. Escape wasn't as simple as walking across the yard anymore.

Who was I kidding? Escape didn't exist anymore. It used to be so easy to find. In the bottom of a bottle. In the backseat of my Bronco with a girl who was just as needy and fucked-up as me. Or my favorite way, curled up in Em's bed, letting the soft sounds she made as she slept drag me under with her. But none of those things could help me escape from the hell I was living in now.

I sighed, dropped my brush back into the bucket, and retrieved a clean one.

"Look…I'm sorry, okay? Whatever you're pissed about, I'm sorry. But I can't do this right now, Dad. Can you just yell at me tomorrow?" I pinched the bridge of my nose to fend off the throbbing inside my skull, dipped the clean brush into a dark, unforgiving black, and swiped it down the canvas, blotting two thick smudges for eyes. It still wasn't dark enough.

Dad leaned around the canvas to see what I was working on. "What's this one supposed to be?"

I narrowed my gaze on the canvas, at the shadow eating up the fiery sunset behind it. Its hungry, hollow eyes watched me. Its gaping mouth, a cavern of bloody darkness, drooled. A chill ran down my spine.

"I haven't figured that part out yet," I said. God, I wish I knew. If I knew, maybe I could find a way to make them stop.

"Have you eaten dinner yet?"

I shook my head.

"How long have you been out here?"

I dropped my brush into a bucket and stared at the ceiling. "Do you need something?"

He took a step back and frowned. "Your principal called."

I slid my gaze his way, careful not to make eye contact.

"He said you've been skipping school again."

"I told you, I haven't been feeling good."

He crossed his arms over his burly chest. "You never feel good anymore. Haven't you been using the inhaler they gave you? Taking the breathing treatments?"

I'd been cramming my body full of meds for a little more than a week since the fire. None of it worked. Whatever was wrong with me, whatever it was that was stripping my insides away a little each day, wasn't anything modern medicine could cure. I needed a freaking witch doctor. A priest. Or better yet, a miracle.

I picked up a clean brush and started again. The eyes still weren't right. Could you even call them eyes? They looked more like black holes when they watched me at night from the corners of my room. The edge of my bed. I squeezed my eyes shut and shuddered.

"Cash?"

"Hmm?" I opened my eyes and flicked my wrist. Another violent stroke of black. Another shadow driving ice through my veins.

"Are you doing drugs?"

I laughed. "Not lately."

Dad made a sound in the back of his throat like he did when a case didn't go his way. "It's not funny. I'm being serious."

"So am I." I spun around on my stool to face him. His blue button-down had a coffee stain under the breast pocket. His salt-and-pepper hair wasn't quite as neat as usual, and the lines bracketing the corners of his mouth were a little deeper than they'd been this morning. He'd had a bad day and I wasn't in the mood for one of his stress-induced lectures. If only he'd get laid. Maybe then I'd get some peace.

"I think you should talk to someone about what's going on with you," he said. "If you don't want to talk to me, then there are people we could pay—"

"You think I need a shrink?" I laughed.

Dad pulled a business card from his front pocket and chose to look at the fancy font on the front instead of me. "Dan's nephew saw this therapist. He's supposed to be good."

"You talked to your snob coworkers about me?" I was about to explode. I could feel the anger boiling under my skin. If anybody in this house needed a shrink, it was him. The guy was married to his work and hadn't been on a date in like eight years.

He threw his hands up. "What do you expect me to do, Cash? Pretend this isn't happening? Pretend everything is fine?"

"Look, I don't need a father-son talk right now," I said. "And I sure as hell don't need your shrink."

"Then what do you need?"

I tensed as a dark-as-death shadow slithered across the ceiling.

Not now. Not now. Not now.

Tearing my eyes away from the shadow, I took a deep breath. The smell of death and decay tainted the air. It felt like a cold rattle in my lungs. I coughed into my fist, trying to get the cold out, and something electric buzzed under my skin. I flexed my fingers as the tingling sensation raced throughout my hand until it felt like it might explode out of my fingertips. What the hell? I shook my hand until the feeling dulled.

"I need to finish this." I nodded toward the half-painted canvas, still flexing my hand. "That's what I need."

Dad's gray eyes watched me. Waiting. For what, I didn't know. Just like those damned shadows. He finally nodded and turned on his heel to leave, but stopped in the open doorway.

"You left your phone inside," he said. "Emma called. Five times. And she left that for you on the front porch."

He nodded to the container he'd tossed on the table when he'd walked in. A bright-pink label with "zucchini bread" scribbled in familiar bubbly writing was stuck to the lid. *Emma.* My best friend. At least the girl I thought was my best friend. The fact that she thought she could buy me off with food just twisted the knife in my gut even further.

"You two have a fight?"

Fight? As in she'd been living a double life, blowing me off so she could date some dead guy, and then letting said shiny new boyfriend be the one to tell me about it? Not to mention somehow getting me caught in the middle. Why else would these…these…whatever the hell they were, be following me around, looking at me like I was lunch? It was the only explanation. Her dead boyfriend gets a brand-new life and mine goes to shit.

I wouldn't call it a fight.

More like a total betrayal.

"Her mom told me she had a new boyfriend," he said, almost hesitantly. "Got anything to do with that?"

"No." *Yes.* "We're fine, Dad. Leave it alone."

"All right…" He rapped his fingers on the doorframe. "You better be in school tomorrow. Got it?"

I nodded.

"I mean it, Cash," he said. "This crap you're pulling reflects badly on both of us. It's your ass if I get a call like that again."

"I said I'd be there, didn't I?"

"No. You nodded."

I shrugged. "Same thing."

Dad muttered something under his breath and pushed through the door. Cool air rushed into the room as it slammed shut and I flinched. I never knew what kind of cold was creeping over my skin. A breeze? A shadow? A hiss sounded from the other side of the studio and I spun around on my stool, holding my paintbrush like it was a machete. A shadow curled into the corner, opened its wide, dripping mouth, then seeped through a crack in the windowsill, where it dissolved into the night. What did I think I was going to do with it, paint them to death? I knew it was ridiculous, but I couldn't seem to make myself let go. And, hey. It disappeared, didn't it?

A breath of warmth swept over me. It started at the base of my neck and rolled over my shoulders, down to my fingertips, like raindrops, warming my skin as it went. The brush fell from my limp fingers and clattered to the ground. Black paint spattered across the concrete like a web of darkness.

This wasn't the shadows. Whatever *she* was always chased them away. Maybe it was her warmth. The way she smelled like thunderstorms and dreams instead of nightmares and decay. Maybe I didn't know what the hell she was, but I knew she was female. I'd been on the merry-go-round of chicks and one-night stands enough times to know that soft, lingering presence wasn't a dude.

I snatched my brush up off the floor and threw it into the bucket.

"I know you're here," I said, wiping my hands on a rag. It looked like it needed to be in an evidence bag by the time I was done with it. "And I know you're not like them. They wouldn't scatter like rats every time you showed up if you were."

She didn't answer but I could still feel her warmth. Smell the scent of rain all over me.

"Why won't you let me see you?" I asked. "The others don't seem so shy."

Only silence answered me. I balled my fingers into useless fists that were still tingling with something so electric it made me twitch.

"What, are you ugly or something? Three heads? Medusa snakes? Cankles? You can't look any worse than the rest of them. Trust me."

My voice broke off into a fit of coughs that left me doubled over, spouting off words that probably made my little stalker blush. I couldn't care less. Since the night of the fire, nothing had been right. It was like something was staining my insides with death. Every cough, every nightmare, every time I saw one of those damned shadows, I got a little blacker inside. A little weaker. And I hated feeling weak.

As soon as I could breathe again, I picked up the canvas and studied the shadow, then tossed it across the room. The still-wet paint left swirls of color smeared across the gray concrete floor.

A shock of cold sliced through the room and I shut my eyes. It's what I felt every time she left. Her warmth being sucked away to somewhere I couldn't find. The windows crackled as frost crept up the insides of the glass despite the balmy spring temperature outside. I froze, paralyzed by fear, listening to the shadows hiss and growl as they crept back in. I wanted to scream for it all to stop. I wanted to scream for them to tell me what the hell they wanted.

I bit the inside of my cheek until I tasted blood. I didn't have to ask what they wanted. Deep down…I think part of me already knew.

Chapter 2

Anaya

I should have been thankful for the warmth. I wasn't. How could I be when I'd left Cash in such a cold, dark place alone with those…those…God, there wasn't even a word for how vile they were. There should have been a name worse than "shadow demon" to describe them.

I couldn't stand this anymore. How much longer was Balthazar going to drag this out? The woman walking beside me gasped and gripped my hand a little tighter. I squeezed back as we watched the gates pull apart and the light explode from between them.

"It's—it's…" she stammered, smoothing her free hand over her purple nightgown before combing her thin white hair with fragile fingers. I reached up and tucked a curl behind her ear.

"I know."

A gust of warm wind swept over us. Dandelion cotton swirled around us like a song. Stars glinted and glowed not just from the sky above, but from every space in between. I took a deep breath and filled my lungs with peace and the scent of the sea. It reminded me of home.

"Is it…Heaven?" she asked.

I laughed. "What do you think?"

Her pale wrinkled fingers slipped from mine as seamlessly as her soul had slipped from her body while she slept. I loved my job when it was like this. No blood. No tears. Just peace. Joy. She'd lived a full, happy life and she'd been ready. That always made it easier. She stepped forward into a whirlwind of light. Amber and gold wisps of color engulfed her, smoothing the wrinkles from her face. Placing the shine back in her naturally blond hair. The aged gray color dripped away and dissolved into the clouds beneath our feet. The innocent light of youth caught fire and blazed back into her eyes. When she faced me again, she didn't look a day over seventeen.

"I'm…" She stared at her smooth, flawless hands.

"You're home," I said.

Don't be jealous, Anaya. I stepped back and smiled, wondering if the day would ever come that I wouldn't have to remind myself. Wouldn't have to wonder if the soul I was ushering to the other side would shake my father's hand. See my mother's smile. Look into Tarik's soft brown eyes. I turned and sprinted through the gates, away from the warmth, the memories. If I didn't get away now, I'd remember. I'd remember what Tarik's hands felt like in my hair, his lips on my mouth, his laughter against my neck. I barreled through the mist, into the Inbetween, and collided with a black blur.

"Hey! Slow down," Easton said, spinning around to look at

me. I looked at his leather pants, T-shirt, and combat boots, all black, and shook my head. The violet eyes that lit up his face were the only splash of color in the shadow that was Easton.

"Why do you always look like you're going to a funeral?" I brushed the ash from my arm where he'd grabbed me. As a reaper for Hell, ash seemed to follow him everywhere.

"Already with the compliments, Anaya?" Easton grinned. "You know people are going to get the wrong idea about us if you keep flirting with me like this."

I rolled my eyes. "Only in your sickest dreams."

"I don't have dreams," he said. "When you live in my world, the best you can hope for is nightmares." He looked me up and down with cold eyes. "And, sweetheart, you wouldn't last five minutes in one of mine."

I sighed and pretended to pick at a nonexistent thread on my dress so I wouldn't have to look at him. "Charming, as always."

Easton laughed and waved to a reaper carrying a soul over. The boy's soul looked over at us, blue eyes wide, afraid. He reminded me of the way Finn had looked when Easton had brought him to us. A little younger, sure, but the look in his eyes was right. I hated that look. The guys always said I was the lucky one, only having to deal with the Heaven-bound. I suppose they were right. None of my charges ever had that look on their face when I offered them eternal peace and happiness.

What they didn't understand was the torture. Knowing your family, the ones you loved, were so close and still so untouchable. My eyes may have been stained gold by the utter perfectness of that place, but it didn't take the sting away knowing how unwelcome I was there. But not for long. Once this was done, Balthazar would give me what I'd been working a thousand years for.

Redemption.

"What are you doing here?" I hooked a braid behind my ear.

"A better question is when am I *not* here?" Easton growled. "I swear to God, if they don't get a replacement for Finn in here soon, I'm going on strike. I can't handle his workload *plus* mine anymore."

"Hey, I've been helping."

"Not enough." He frowned. "Maybe you'd have more time if you weren't spending all your time stalking the human kid."

A thread of guilt sewed a knot in my gut. I looked down at Easton's dusty boots. A gray glittery mist circled them like fog.

"I'm doing my job," I said. "If you have a problem with it, take it up with Balthazar. Trust me, babysitting a human isn't exactly my idea of fun." I didn't mention the invisible thread that kept me tethered to Cash. Balthazar's orders or not, when I wasn't reaping it's like it wasn't even a choice. It was like… gravity.

"What's Balthazar doing, having you keep him hanging on like that, anyway?" Easton said. "Kind of cruel, isn't it? He can't last much longer in that body. It's got to be shutting down by now."

I flinched. "It's not my business to know. I'm just doing what I was told."

"Which is?"

"I'm just supposed to look after him, and when his time comes around again, collect him. End of story." I left out the part where I was supposed to completely swindle the poor boy out of his destined afterlife and deliver him into Balthazar's scheming hands. "I'm sure Balthazar has a good reason for doing this." He better. I may have been a slave to death, but cruel I was not. It didn't bring me any joy to see a boy as vibrant and alive as Cash withering mentally and physically before my very eyes. And Balthazar's secrets made me uneasy.

"Why do I feel like you're keeping something from me?"

I forced a laugh and tossed my braids over my shoulder. "I think spending your days with liars and crooks is making you paranoid."

"Right." Easton rolled his eyes. "Keep your little secret, then. Just don't come running to me when this blows up in your face. This isn't going to end well. Not for that kid anyway. I can feel it."

"I'll make sure he's okay." I looked away. "Don't worry about it."

Easton made a growling sound deep in his throat when his scythe burned at his hip. I cringed away from the smoke that twirled up from the scorching blade. It smelled like death. "Just promise me you'll stay out of trouble. I don't need your workload, too."

I closed my eyes, drowning in guilt. Why couldn't Balthazar just let me take the boy? He could have been happy right now. At peace. Instead he was sick and afraid and confused every minute of the day and night. I shouldn't have done it. Shouldn't have followed orders, knowing nothing good could come of them. I'd never been that weak before. And being around Cash, close enough to memorize the tilt of his lips while he painted, the rhythm of his breathing while he slept, see every fleck of color behind his rich, dark eyes…it wasn't safe. Something about those eyes…he made me feel like I was unraveling. I hadn't felt that way in a thousand years. He made me feel things I had no right to feel.

"Anaya!"

"I've got it, okay?"

Easton looked me over and nodded once, seeming satisfied. "Good. I'll catch up with you later."

I watched a black puddle of screams bubble up through the mist and swallow Easton whole. Suddenly I was alone in my head again. Cornered with the memories. I ran for the gates to the Inbetween, needing to get back to Cash for reasons I didn't really understand. Reasons I didn't want to understand. Part of me wanted to pummel Balthazar for getting me involved in this. If he hadn't put this on me, forced me to spend every free moment with him, then I wouldn't feel so…so…

I gritted my teeth and shook the thought right out of my head. I did not feel *anything* for this boy. I couldn't. In fact, I was about to prove it. Once I was clear, I closed my eyes and gasped, allowing the wispy white ground to fall out from under me. Warm midnight wind whipped through me. A golden light bloomed across the black of night as I split the sky. For a few perfect moments I was weightless. I landed light as a feather on the soft green Bermuda grass outside Cash's bedroom window, leaving stars smeared across the sky behind me. They were already here. The shadow demons. I could smell them. Death and decay and rot.

You want to be here with him. Lie to yourself all you want, but Balthazar has nothing to do with what you're feeling inside.

I scowled at the thoughts taunting me and slipped through the brick wall. It was cold and uncomfortably solid for a second, and then I was engulfed in the warm smell of Cash. The clean lemony scent of his shampoo, and the leftover bite of paint. I walked across the room toward the curled-up lump under the covers. Pale moonlight barely illuminated his outline. His chest was rising and falling beneath the navy-blue comforter; steady, like waves pushing up from the bottom of the sea.

The only part of him I could see were a few disorderly black spikes of hair sticking out of the top of the blanket. A hiss sounded from the corner of the room and Cash's entire body went rigid. I spun around on my heel and jerked the scythe from my holster.

A shadow demon shrank back from me into the dark corner of the room, curling up behind a big oak dresser. I'd expect to see one of them at a reap. The slime of the underworld were always looking for scraps, a soul we'd left behind, but not here. Not near a boy as alive as Cash. It didn't make sense.

"I suggest you leave." I waved my blade at it. "I'm not in a very forgiving mood today."

The black puddle of scum opened its gaping hole of a mouth to bare its bloody throat before slipping through the drywall and out of the room. I sighed and turned back to Cash. He'd pulled the blankets off his face and was staring vacantly at the poster of a half-naked girl on his ceiling. I didn't think he was seeing her, though. He swallowed and something fluttered like a hummingbird's wings in my chest as I watched his Adam's apple bob up and down.

"Thanks for coming back," he whispered into the dark. I could tell it cost him to give me that much. To him, I was just something else he didn't understand—or want.

I sank down to my knees next to Cash's bed and folded my arms over the edge of his mattress. I propped my chin up on my arms and breathed him in. Watched his eyelids get heavy. Studied the way his lips opened just enough to blow a slow breath out between them. From here the moon glinted off the silver ring in his eyebrow. He shifted out of the blankets and his bare shoulder came to a rest against my lips. If I'd gone corporeal in that moment, we would have been touching. My lips on his skin. I hadn't thought about another person's taste in a thousand years. Not since Tarik. A heavy, achy feeling tugged at the empty space in my chest and I caught myself chewing on my bottom lip. I had to stop thinking like this. Every thought, every image, every pang of want was a betrayal to Tarik.

I moved away from the bed.

"Please don't leave," Cash muttered sleepily. "I just need a little sleep. I can't sleep when they're here."

I hesitated, torn between my duty and what was right. "I won't leave," I finally said, knowing he couldn't hear, but wanting to say it anyway.

He blinked at the ceiling, waiting for just a moment. When he realized I was still there, he turned over on his side.

I laid my palm over the place in my chest where the familiar ache had started to form. It hurt. It hurt in the kind of way that made you crave it. I felt like I had when I was free-falling through a black summer sky. I felt like I had the first time Tarik held my hand. I felt…alive. I glanced down at Cash, at the half frown pulling his lips down. I didn't know why, but I would have done anything to keep him from hurting. From being afraid.

I sat back on my heels, wrapped my arms around my knees, and stared at the ceiling. Listened to Cash breathing, trying to understand why I liked the sound of it so much. I may have forgotten what having a home felt like. I may have been stripped of the right to have one. But here in the dark, in this room, with this boy, I'd never felt closer to it.

Chapter 3

Cash

I pushed through the swinging metal doors with my shoulder, and noise exploded around me. A hundred voices fought for space in the cramped fluorescent-lit cafeteria. I pressed my earbuds in a little deeper and cranked the volume up on my iPod a few notches. A girl named Jennifer nudged my arm and winked as she strolled by with her lunch tray. Bottle-blond curls dangled just above her waist, swaying with her hips, as she walked away with a silent invitation to follow. I waited for that familiar part of me to kick in. The part of me that usually would have had me turning around to get one more look at her painted-on skinny jeans. The same part of me that would've had her in the back of my Bronco by Friday. When it didn't come, I shrugged my bag up over my shoulder and walked on past. Jennifer was background noise with the rest of it. Nothing meant what it used to. Especially girls. I was starting to think whatever part of me that allowed me to live a normal life had died in that fire.

I spotted Emma and Finn across the room and stopped cold. They looked like two puzzle pieces that fit together. The way they moved around each other, always touching, never allowing more than a breath of air to separate them. I wasn't ready for this. To face her. To face *them*. But I couldn't do this by myself, and he was the only one who could help me.

I wasn't a rocket scientist, but I could connect the dots. And they were leading me to Finn. He had to have answers. And he was damn well going to give them to me. He'd stolen the most important person in my life. Deluded her into thinking she was in love with him. Filling in the blanks for me was the least this bastard could do.

Breaking this fucked-up voodoo love spell he had on her would have to come later.

Fueled by determination, I started toward the table and noticed that Emma was upset. She had on that blue sweater I gave her for Christmas last year. I always liked how it brought out the almost sapphire hue in her eyes. And now, those eyes looked tired, her lashes dark and wet. Had she been crying? Emma looked up, catching sight of me across the room, and her face lit up. I sort of hated myself for missing her in that moment. If I really meant what her eyes said I meant, she wouldn't have kept all of this from me. Left me in the dark. Because now that dark was eating me alive from the inside out.

When I got to the table I tossed my bag down on the bench, and as much as I hated to, sat down next to Finn so I could face Emma. He had her hand wrapped up in his like a present. I noticed his fingers squeeze hers as I sat down, and I ground my teeth.

"Hey," Emma said, brokenly. She *had* been crying. Shit. And I'd really had my heart set on being mad for at least a month.

"Hey," I said.

"You're back."

"Yeah, well, it's go to school or see a shrink." I fiddled with my earbuds. I hated small talk. Especially when there was something this big between us. "I'm trying the school thing."

"I tried calling you."

I looked up, and she brushed the curtain of blond hair out of her face. "Yeah, I know."

Finn shot me a killing look and sat back in his seat, letting Emma's fingers fall out of his. "Stop punishing her." He pinned me with that freaky-ass green gaze of his. He didn't look like his perky self. He had dark circles under his eyes and his T-shirt looked like he'd slept in the thing. He looked like crap. I would've told him so myself, but I was pretty sure I didn't have room to talk.

"She lied to me." I folded my arms across my chest and shuddered when a ghostly shadow slithered down the white brick wall and under the table. I could feel it curling around my ankles. Filling my lungs with ice. I coughed into my fist, needing the ice out.

Stay cool. It won't hurt you. It won't hurt you.

"I didn't lie!" Emma looked up at me, eyes glistening with hurt.

"You kept it from me," I whispered across the table. "Same difference."

Emma folded her arms onto the table and leaned closer, her blue sweater balled up in her fists. "Would you have believed me?"

"I—" I stopped. I wouldn't have. Before all this…no way would I have believed her if she'd told me she was dating a freaking reaper. A dead guy. And that he'd magically come back to life to be with her. Hell, I probably would have driven her back to Brookhaven Psychiatric Hospital myself. I took a deep breath and said, "No. I wouldn't have believed you."

"Then why are you avoiding me?" she asked. "I know there's something wrong. Why won't you tell me? Why won't you let me help you?"

I kicked at the thing crawling around my feet and gritted my teeth. My pulse raced. I tried to swallow the lump of fear that was lodged in my throat, but it wouldn't budge.

"You can't help me, Em." I sucked in a painfully deep breath that stretched my lungs and turned to Finn. "You, on the other hand…"

Finn sat up and his brows furrowed together. "What do you mean?"

Stealing a quick glance around the crowded cafeteria to make sure no one was close enough to hear, I leaned across the table and lowered my voice.

"You need to tell me what the fuck is going on," I whispered. "I've got these…*things* following me. I know I'm not crazy. This shit is real. And it all started the night of that fire, so in my eyes, it all comes back to you, dead boy."

Finn sat back, shaking his head as his gaze darted back and forth between Emma and me. "What exactly do you mean by *things*?"

"How the hell am I supposed to know what they are?" I pushed my fingers through my hair and blew out a breath. He was going to make me explain it. Say it out loud so we all could hear just how batshit crazy I sounded. "They look like shadows. At least that's the best way I can describe them. But they're not shadows. It's like they're alive or something. They never leave me alone. Day, night, sleeping, awake, they *never* fucking leave me alone."

"Shadow demons," Finn breathed, sitting back and lacing his fingers over the back of his neck. "Shit."

"Excuse me?" I raised a brow at the word demons. He had to be kidding. Please let this guy be kidding.

Finn clenched his jaw and his eyes drifted to Emma.

"W-why would shadow demons be following Cash?" Emma's face turned white. "I though they only came around when someone dies?"

"Someone want to tell me what exactly a shadow demon is?" I asked. "You can leave out the visuals. I think I've got that at least."

"When I was a reaper," Finn lowered his voice, "I took souls to the Inbetween where they got the chance to be reborn or earn their way into Heaven. The problem is, the life span of a soul is only about ten years. As time passes, they decay. Lose themselves and the humanity that lives inside. They can't exist in limbo like that forever. If they're not reborn, or don't manage to earn their way upstairs within those ten years, they turn into what you're seeing. Shadow demons. They're souls that are damned to roam the Earth, hungry and wanting for eternity. They feed off of souls, usually ones fresh from the body. You see them at reaps a lot, hunting for scraps."

"Why would they be following me?" I asked. "I'm not dead."

"I don't know why they're here. I don't know what they're waiting for. And I sure as hell don't know how to get rid of them." Finn rubbed his temples like he was getting a headache. "I need to talk to Easton. He'd know more about this."

"So, talk to him," I shouted, slamming my fist down onto the table. "Today. Hell, right now."

"It's not that easy," Finn whispered. "I can't just call him up. It's not like they gave me a cell phone to the afterlife. I'm alive now. I'm not connected anymore."

I stared at the table. "So, what? I'm just supposed to go on with these things following me around? I can't do that. I can't live like this!"

"He visits me sometimes," Finn said, hesitantly. "But it's been a while."

"Great," I muttered. "I'll just clear my calendar then."

I leaned over and pressed my forehead against the cool tabletop, trying to calm my breathing and the sharp pain developing in my chest. Emma's fingers slipped over my folded arms and as much as I wanted to push her away I didn't. After a week of nothing but fear and pain, it felt too good. I missed her.

"You did almost die at the fire," Emma offered. "Maybe it has something to do with that. Maybe they're just curious and they'll go away once they realize they can't get anything from you."

I listened to Emma's glossed-over, hopeful theory, but lifted my head to keep my eyes on Finn. He twisted the cap to his water, keeping suspiciously silent on the subject.

"Finn?" she asked. "What do you think?"

"I don't know," he said. "Like I said, I need to talk to Easton or Anaya. They'd know more about this."

"No theories, huh?" I arched a brow, studying his pinched, guilty expression. "Nothing to add?"

He pushed away from the table, his features shifting from guilty to pissed. "Look, I said I'd try to find out. I don't know what else you want me to say."

He knew. He knew more than what he was saying and he had the nerve to sit there and lie. Not just to me, but to Emma.

"Screw you, Finn," I said, refusing to acknowledge the way Emma's mouth dropped open at my words. Finn's didn't. He looked like he was expecting it. The shadow under the table hissed and that was the last straw.

I grabbed my bag and pulled my legs out from under the table. I had to get away from that…thing. I had to get away from the look in Finn's eyes. Maybe he wasn't saying the words but that look said everything I needed to know. I wasn't going to be okay. There was no end to my nightmare in sight.

I didn't look back as I let my legs carry me out of the cafeteria as fast as they could without running.

"Cash, wait!" Emma called out from behind me.

I stopped and exhaled, listening to her footsteps echo down the empty hall. She touched my shoulder and I spun around.

"What?"

She pulled her hand back, looking hurt. "You've been out of the hospital a week. You don't answer my calls or texts. You don't answer the door when I come over. Are you going to be mad at me forever?"

I looked her over, this girl who was as close to me as anyone was ever going to get. I wanted to stay mad at her. I didn't want to hug and make up yet. I didn't want to say everything was fine, because it wasn't. I wasn't sure if it ever would be again. "I don't know. Are you going to keep screwing the corpse?"

Emma took a wide step back and her breath caught in her throat. Most of the time that sound, that little intake of air, was as close as she'd let herself get to crying in public. That little sound was all I needed to hear to know that I'd hurt her.

"H-he's not a corpse. He's a-a—"

Shit. Without thinking I grabbed her wrist and pulled her into me, pressing her face into my chest. Breathing in the warm, familiar scent of her hair. Her bag fell off her shoulder into the floor. She felt stiff, but didn't pull away. I didn't want to miss her. I just wanted to be pissed off and say mean things that I didn't really mean. Couldn't she give me that? After all of this, wasn't I allowed to be mad? When Emma relaxed into my hold, I squeezed her tighter against me and sighed. As much as I hated it, this was so much easier than staying mad.

"I'm sorry," I said into her hair. "I'm just pissed, Em. I don't want any of this. You might have chosen it, but I didn't."

Emma wiped her eyes on my favorite *Blink if you want me* T-shirt and pulled away. "You think I chose all this?"

"Yeah. I think you did. You chose to love a dead guy, didn't you?"

She glared at me. "You can't help who you love, just like *you* apparently can't help being a jerk."

I stared at my reflection in her watery blue eyes. Let my gaze trace the same path that my brush would've on a canvas. The soft curve of her cheek, the smooth white column of her neck. She was wrong. You could choose. I could've loved this girl if I'd let myself. Anybody who got as close to Emma as I had would know it's harder *not* to love her than to just give in. But I always knew she could do better than me. Better than somebody who was even more broken inside than her. Instead, she found *him*. A freaking corpse. She gave her heart to someone who didn't even have one.

"What?" She looked like she wanted to crawl out from under the way I was looking at her.

"Nothing," I said. "Look, I have somewhere I need to be."

I messed with the strap of my backpack so I wouldn't have to look her in the eyes when I lied to her. I may have lied to a lot of people in my life, but Em was never one of them. It made me feel like shit having to do it now.

"So this is it?" she asked. "You're just going to throw away our friendship over something I can't control?"

I rolled my eyes, hating every second of this. I didn't want to fight with her. I just wanted to get away from her, the way she was looking at me, like I was some broken thing she needed to fix.

"I don't know," I finally said. "Maybe I just need some space to deal with this. Besides, you've got Finn now. It's not like you need me hanging around all the time anymore."

Her eyes narrowed as if she couldn't quite believe what I was saying. "Are you pissed at me because you think this is my fault, or because I'm with Finn?"

I didn't even flinch. I just said it. "Both."

Emma shook her head and took a few more steps back, palms raised. "You...you're unbelievable. You of all people I thought would be happy for me."

"Happy for you?" I narrowed my gaze on her and closed the space between us. "I'll be happy when you wake the hell up. You're not supposed to be with him, Em!"

"Then who am I supposed to be with?" Emma shouted.

Me. We stared each other down, chests heaving, and everything in me was screaming to say it. I couldn't. I didn't want to say it, because saying it meant acknowledging I'd pissed away something that could have been everything. I didn't want to say it because I felt like someone was putting my heart in a vise grip and I didn't know why. Was I jealous? Did I want her? Or did I just want my best friend back? There were too many lines blurring for me here. Finally I grabbed control of the emotions ripping me apart inside and exhaled.

"Not him," I whispered. "Just…not him."

Emma pressed her lips together, wrapping her arms around her chest, and started to back away from me.

"Em, wait…"

"No, you don't get to say sorry," she said. "And if you're more interested in being pissed at me than finding a way out of all of this, then be my guest. I'm done."

She grabbed her bag from the floor and dug out a Tupperware container. Her fingers shook as she shoved it into my hands and backed away.

"You look like you haven't been eating," she whispered. "Just…you need to eat something."

I stood still as stone, watching her disappear through the swinging metal cafeteria doors. I probably could have stopped her if I wanted. It wouldn't have taken much with Emma. She was too good. Too forgiving and kind and…well, she was all of the things that I wasn't. I glanced down at the container in my hands filled with some kind of homemade granola bars. The note attached to the top said, "Don't worry, there's chocolate in them, too!" I stared at Em's trademark smiley face that she'd been leaving on her notes to me since the sixth grade, and my heart thudded almost painfully in my chest. I…was an asshole.

Damn it! Why did I have to run my mouth like that and make her cry?

I shoved the container in my bag, hiked it up over my shoulder, and shut my eyes against the fluorescent school lights. Against the regret swirling around in my head. When I opened them again, I spun around and slammed my fist into the set of blue lockers that lined the wall. I expected pain to explode in my hand, but…it didn't. I didn't feel anything. Blood began to trickle down my split knuckles and I turned my hand over to inspect it. What the hell? Finally, I gave up trying to figure it out. I wiped the blood on my jeans and headed for the only place I could think of to find some kind of answers.

I hadn't been in a library since like ninth grade when I got detention for drawing big-boobed cartoon women in the backs of the entire R.L. Stine *Goosebumps* collection.

Desperate times called for desperate measures.

Chapter 9

Anaya

"I know you're there." Finn tied the laces on his tennis shoes, and a half grin carved a dimple into his cheek. "No use in hiding."

He stood up as I stepped into sight, allowing him to see me. I hesitated a moment, not really knowing what to think of this new Finn. Gone were the plain jeans and gray T-shirt I'd seen him wear for at least the last ten years. Now he wore a pair of black running shorts and a sleeveless blue shirt. He looked ridiculously human. Placing my hands on my hips, I surveyed the sparse living room that Finn now called home. There weren't any pictures hanging from the walls like I'd seen in most humans' homes, just a picture of Emma on his nightstand. Then again, Finn hadn't really been around long enough yet to capture any memories in frames. What he did have was life, pure and fragile, coursing through his veins, fueling his heart. It was evident in the golden glow of his skin and his flushed cheeks. The vibrant light in his eyes that I'd never seen in over seventy years of knowing him. I couldn't help but feel a little jealous. "How did you know? Aren't you supposed to be human now?"

Finn chuckled and raked a hand through his hair. It was lighter now, a little longer. He linked his fingers and stretched his arms behind his back. "Guess I got to keep a few tricks. I must be lucky."

"That or I'm losing my touch," I grumbled, following him as he made his way out the front door and into the early morning sunlight. Dew coated the grass and the light breeze smelled fresh, like rain. I'd always loved mornings. How quiet and at peace the world the seemed. Finn took off at a jog and I picked up speed to stay in step with him.

"Wow," I breathed. "You really have gone all human on me. You even jog now."

Finn snorted and cut down a wooded path. The soles of his shoes pounded out a rhythm on the dirt trail, but I didn't leave a single print. "I'm not trying to fit some kind of mold here, Anaya. It just helps."

"With what?"

"He gave me a new body," he said. A bead of sweat glistened on his forehead and his brows pinched together. "He didn't give me a new mind. You don't forget. Everything I've done. Everything I've seen…"

Finn pressed his lips together and his feet pounded against the trail a little harder, picking up speed. "I don't want to remember. This helps."

"Are you happy?"

Finn skidded to a stop in the middle of the trail and bent

over, bracing his palms on his knees to catch his breath. My hand absently clutched my chest, wanting the burn that he was feeling. "Why did you do it, Anaya? Why didn't you take him? I've tried again and again to wrap my mind around it…and I can't. I can't come up with one good reason why you'd deny him an afterlife."

I lifted my chin, not knowing what else to do. I couldn't show weakness when I was guarding Balthazar's secret. Not to him. Not to anyone. There was too much at stake for me here, whether I agreed with what I was doing or not. Balthazar would turn my dreams to vapor in the space of one of Finn's fragile heartbeats if things didn't go his way. If I'd learned anything in my thousand years in the service of the second in command to the Almighty, it was this. "You did it to Emma."

Finn's head snapped up and his eyes flared with anger. "That was different. You don't even know Cash. What you did goes against everything we've ever learned. How the hell did you even get away with it?"

I hesitated, not knowing how much to reveal. Finn was a human now. Would Balthazar care if he knew? A gust of wind rustled the budding canopy of branches above us, bringing with it a burst of resolve.

"I did as I was told," I said, feigning more confidence than I felt. "Maybe you've already forgotten, but that's what we do, Finn. They command. We deliver."

Finn leaned forward, curling his fingers around his knees, and narrowed his gaze on me. "That's just it, though. You didn't deliver this time."

I raised a brow and ran my fingers over my blade out of habit. "Who said I'm finished with him?"

"He's expired, isn't he? That's why the shadow demons are

making his life hell," Finn said, realization lighting his emerald eyes. "He's so close they can smell it on him. It's the only explanation that makes any sense."

Hating the way Finn's accusing glare made me feel, I turned away, listening to the world wake up around us. Birds chirped. In the distance the steady hum of the highway leaked through the trees. Shadows pooled in the corners of the forest, but a glow of sunshine lit the space where I stood. "This really isn't your business anymore, you know."

"He's hurting. Hell, he's more than hurting. The kid is losing it. He's deteriorating, slowly and painfully, a little more every day." He sighed and came to stand beside me. "The Anaya I knew never would have aided in something like this, let alone sit back and watch it happen. Do you have any idea what will happen to him when that body gives out? What those shadows will do to him after all of the pointless suffering?"

"Nothing!" Something inside of me snapped at the image of Cash ending up in the bellies of those creatures. "Nothing will happen to him, because I will be there. I'm going to take care of him. I have orders from Balthazar, Finn. Don't question matters you know nothing about."

His jaw tensed. "You know what I think? I think *you* don't even know what Balthazar is up to. I think he's got his claws in you so deep, you're not even bothering to try to get away."

I shook my head and my braids scattered over my shoulder blades, hopefully hiding how violently I was shaking. With guilt. And fear. And a thousand other emotions I had no right to feel. "He wouldn't be doing this unless he had a good reason." I had to believe that. I had to because this human was starting to make me feel things no human should. I closed my eyes, trying to find peace in the warmth that ran through me, but all I found was guilt.

Finn folded his arms over his chest, and something about his silence drew my gaze to his.

"Fix this, Anaya," he pleaded. "I know what I'm asking of you. I know it seems impossible to give, but I have to try. I have to try because I put my happiness before so many others, and he's on that list. It's too late to make it up to the rest of them, but I have to believe I can make it up to him. He didn't deserve what I did to him. Taking his body, using him to be with Emma…it was inexcusable, and I regret it every day. If I hadn't crossed the line, maybe none of this would've happened."

"Finn—"

"Let me finish." He held his hand up. "I don't know what Balthazar has on you, what he's promising you, but you need to ask yourself something. Is it worth it? Is it worth losing the very things that make you worthy of that light you carry around inside of you?"

I slipped my arms around my waist and tried to calm the hollow throb of shame staining my insides. Finn was right. Balthazar may be pulling the strings here, but I made a choice. I made a choice to put my happiness before this human's.

"He's confused," Finn continued. "If nothing else, he deserves some honesty. He deserves to know what's going to happen at the end of this."

I nodded and Finn's hand ghosted through my fingers. "I kept so many things from Emma. I did so many things the wrong way. Don't make my mistakes, Anaya. Trust me when I say they will haunt you for an eternity."

With that, Finn turned and jogged away. I didn't follow.

Instead, I closed my eyes and searched for that pull to Cash. Maybe I couldn't stop Balthazar or the things he'd already put into motion, but Finn was right. Cash deserved answers. What he didn't deserve was blind fear, eating away the last of his moments on this earth. Maybe Balthazar would have had a problem with me spilling what I knew to an ordinary human, but Cash was something else. If he were ordinary, Balthazar wouldn't want him. I thought about his expired body, his soul inside, pulsing to be set free. No human should have survived more than a couple of days like that, yet Cash was still alive.

No. He was no ordinary human. If he were, he'd be dead.

Chapter 5

Cash

The library was too quiet. I needed noise. Distraction. I felt like a walking target without either. Not that I was naive enough to think I could hide from the little bastards, but I didn't want to make it easy for them, either. Me being in the same place twice in a matter of two days made me feel way too obvious. I kept my head down, ducking from book stack to book stack. The musty smell of pages that hadn't been turned in a decade made my throat itch.

I stopped in the art section, just for a minute, and ran my fingers over the spines of a few of the colorful books collecting dust. What I really wanted to do was curl up in a stack of Jackson Pollock prints and pretend my world wasn't falling to pieces around me. In the end, my need for answers won out. I didn't even pluck one from the shelf. Instead I slipped down a slim, dark aisle that contained big, dusty, underused books on mythology, religion, and the supernatural. The people of Lone Pine obviously didn't get much use out of this section. I could have grilled Finn some more, but honestly that idea sounded about as appealing as putting out a lit cigarette on my arm.

I grabbed a few books, leaving behind the ones I'd read the day before, let my backpack slip off of my shoulder, and sat in the floor. I didn't know what I was looking for yesterday, and still didn't. A handbook for how to deal with cheating death? A spell to ward off demons? It sounded so freaking stupid when I put the thoughts together like that, but I couldn't sit around doing nothing, waiting for some dead guy to show up who *might* have answers.

I zipped my coat up to fight off the chill consuming me, despite the fact that it was at least eighty degrees in this sweatbox of books, flipped through the two mythology books, and found nothing. Nothing real that applied to me, anyway. Then again, who was I to say what was real? Nothing *felt* real anymore. For all I knew, Zeus himself could have been laughing down at me right now, a vampire at his side as they plotted the zombie apocalypse.

I squinted into the last book and found a section on demons. A few sketches. A couple of eyewitness experiences. I froze and ran my finger over one of the drawings. It was one of them. A shadow demon.

Shadow demons are often associated with poltergeists. Not considered to be ghosts, these demons are generally described as black, shapeless, shadowlike entities that appear quickly out of the corner of your eye. Some people have reported the appearances of shadows like these hovering next to their bed while they sleep. These particular demons tend to feed off of emotions. Fear. Depression. Anger. They—

I rubbed my eyes and blinked when the letters started to melt together. They what? I looked down at the page again and the words blurred out of focus.

"Damn it." I pinched the bridge of my nose, fighting off the headache creeping up on me. A cold prickling pain spread across the inside of my chest, my skull, the walls of my throat. What was wrong with me? I leaned my head against the stack of books behind me and stared up through the towering shelves. One of the skylights was just an aisle over, so you could see the dust motes twirling through some of the stray rays of sunshine that made it over into my section. If only those rays would bring a little warmth my way. I was starting to wonder what it was going to take for me to shake this chill.

My phone started to buzz in my pocket and I flinched. I looked at the screen and sighed. Shit.

"Hey, Dad," I said.

"Hey, Dad?" he seethed. "Where the hell are you? I know you're not in class. Your principal just called me. Again."

I let the back of my head thump against the shelf of books behind me. "I'm…at the library."

"Don't lie to me, Cash."

"I'm not lying," I said. "I really am at the library."

"I don't care if you're in church talking to the pope. You are supposed to be in class." Something slammed down against his desk on the other end and I flinched. "Richard's son got accepted to Harvard today. *Harvard.* And what is my son doing? Acting like a lunatic. Skipping school. Pissing away *every* opportunity to have a successful life that I give him."

My jaw clenched until my teeth hurt. "Maybe you should adopt Richard's son, then. You guys could swap since I'm so disappointing."

Dad's chair squeaked and he sighed. I could picture him leaned back in his leather chair, pinching the bridge of his nose as if he couldn't endure another second of listening to me. "Trust me, Richard wouldn't put up with your shit like I do. You'd be in a military academy by Monday. Hell, maybe that's what I should have done a long time ago. Maybe I'm the failure here."

"Look, Dad—"

"No, you look," he said. "We had a deal. You broke it. I'm calling Dr. Farber."

I sat up. "The shrink?"

"Don't start with me. You're going."

"But Dad—"

"Get to class."

I opened my mouth, but he hung up on me before I could get the words out. I stared at my phone for a minute, boiling, anger turning all of those cold prickles of pain into flames. I did not need this shit right now. I didn't need him telling me what a disappointment I was. He didn't care if I had a good life—he wanted a trophy, another damn accomplishment to hang on his wall. But if I did happen to make anything out of my life, I'd be damned if he got credit for it. I didn't need his approval any more than I needed him. What I needed was someone who could actually help me get my life back.

"Damn it!" I threw my phone across the aisle. I wanted to hit something. I wanted something to hurt as badly as I did. Where was the numbness when I needed it? I balled up all of the anger and hurt inside and tried to force it out of my body on an exhale. It didn't work. Why did I think it would? Nothing worked out anymore.

I shivered under my coat as goose bumps rose along the

back of my neck, unable to shake the feeling that someone was here. Watching me. An almost painful current spread through my fingers, the strange buzz throbbing in each fingertip, and I flexed my hand trying to get it out.

I sat up, heart pounding, searching for shadows and not finding any. My eyes caught the flicker of a gray coat disappearing around the end of the book stack and I jumped up, clutching the book in my hand.

"Hello?" I made my way down the aisle, listening. It was him. The kid I'd seen in the hall that day. It had to be. He'd seen the shadows. Hell, he hadn't just seen them, he'd seemed...*amused* by them. These books didn't have the answers I wanted. He did. "Come on man, I just want to talk."

No answer. When I got to the end of the aisle, I stopped and looked around, completely alone. Was I seeing things? Was this even real? I knew my insides were broken, failing a little more each and every day. I could feel it, the echo of death, tainting every breath of oxygen I took. What I didn't want to accept was that my mind might be going, too. I pressed the cool cover of the book in my hand against my forehead and cursed.

"You're not going to find any answers in those," a girl's voice split the silence. "And last time I checked, you had to open them to read the words inside."

"Maybe I'm trying to read by osmosis," I replied, dropping the book to my side. I turned around, expecting to see a fellow student giving me crap, but froze when my gaze fell on the unfamiliar girl in front of me.

"Hi," she said. She leaned with her back against the stacks, holding my cell phone, just a few feet away. Her gold eyes glinted as they looked at me. She looked like a shined-up pearl next to the dusty old books.

Finally, she tossed my cell phone to me and I dropped the book to catch it with both hands. I had to let the words roam around in my mouth for a minute before I could get them out.

"Do I know you?"

"Sort of." She shrugged. "I know you."

I squinted at the pretty, unfamiliar girl in front of me. Long brown braids tumbled over her shoulders, and her skin looked like honey against the bright-white straps of her dress. The laces of her gold sandals wrapped around her calves. Though I wasn't sure if you could call her sandals gold. Not next to those eyes. Those eyes were a color all their own. They didn't even look real. Neither did the faint glow that bathed her from head to toe.

A warm sensation swept over me and a shiver exploded across my skin. I looked around, but there weren't any shadows. Hadn't been for a while.

My heart stuttered in my chest before seeming to stop all together. It was…her. Her eyes. Those were the same eyes I'd seen at the fire. And that same warmth that settled over me like a blanket of safety any time *she* came around. It had to be her. Normal girls didn't look like that.

"It's you." It was stupid, but I didn't really know what else to say. Seriously, how often do you meet a dead girl?

"'You' works," she said. "But you could also call me Anaya if you want to." She sat down against the stack, motioning for me to do the same, and wrapped her arms around her legs. She rested her chin on her knees and looked me over.

"Anaya?" The memory came flooding back. Finn had mentioned an Anaya. Hesitantly, I crossed over to where my bag sat on the floor and sank down across from her.

"What…what are you?" I stopped and inhaled as big a breath as my lungs could hold. They ached and protested before forcing me to cough it all back up.

She cocked her head to the side, studying me, as if she were trying to decide what to say. "I'm a reaper," she finally admitted. "You should be familiar with that term by now."

I swallowed, pressing back until the shelf dug into my back. "Like Finn."

She simply nodded, so eerily calm, it made my skin crawl. How could she be so calm? I felt like my brain was about to explode, questions filling up my head so fast they pressed against my skull. "Are you here to take me?"

Anaya stood up, but she wouldn't look at me. Instead she focused those amazing starlit eyes on the floor. "No. Not yet."

"Yet? What the hell is that supposed to mean?" She said it like there would be a later.

"I'm here to watch over you, Cash," she said, exasperated. "No need to look at me like I'm some kind of villain. I think we both know there are things much worse than me out there to fear."

"You mean them." I pushed myself up to stand, nodding to the book. "The shadow demons?"

Anaya raised a brow and walked a circle around the books I'd discarded on the floor. "Maybe those books had some answers after all."

"I had to look somewhere. It's not like anybody else will give me answers." I tried to concentrate on breathing. It was hard not to feel dizzy in the presence of her warmth. It made part of me long for her to come closer. The other, more sane, part of me screamed for her to stay the hell away. "Why are these things following me? What do they want?"

"I'm not exactly sure, but I imagine it has something to do with the fact that you're in an expired body," she said.

"Expired?"

"You're not dead, but you're not exactly alive right now, either. You're balancing on this tightrope between life and death, a side effect of putting you back in your body at the fire. These shadows are attracted to the scent of death and the emotions that accompany it. The closer you get to death, the more appealing you seem. It's the only reason I can come up with. I've never seen them go after one of the living this way."

Thoughts spun around in my head fast enough to make me dizzy, or maybe that was just the fact that I was breathing too fast. I grabbed the shelf beside me for support and felt my brows pull together. "Wait a second…what do you mean *the closer I get to death?*"

At that moment the pain in my chest spread and burned through me. I pushed against the spot with my fingers. No. That was from the fire. Right? I just needed my inhaler.

A sad look passed over Anaya's face as she watched me collapse on the inside. "You're dying, Cash. Can't you feel it?"

My fingers hovered over my heart, feeling it pound against my ribs with fear. She was lying. She had to be. I mean, yeah, I knew I was fucked up, but *dying?* I wasn't even eighteen yet. I hadn't even graduated. I couldn't be dying. I retreated until my back slammed into the stacks, knocking a few books onto the floor.

"You're lying," I whispered, wishing it were true.

"I'm not." She took a step closer. "I wouldn't be here if you weren't."

I forced my gaze to meet hers and swallowed. God, she was pretty. I should have realized that somebody that pretty was dangerous. She was like a freaking walking Venus flytrap. "Why? Why am I dying now? They released me from the hospital. I could go back—"

"It won't matter." She cut me off. "You were meant to die in that fire," she admitted. "You were on my list. I was supposed to take you and I didn't. I let you stay."

"What do you mean you let me stay?" I asked. "Like you saved me?"

Anaya laughed, bitterly, and pushed herself away from the book stack. "Saving you would have been taking you to Heaven where you belonged. No, Cash. I didn't save you. I think we both know that."

I barked out a laugh. "Heaven? Me? Now I know you're full of shit."

Anaya tossed a tired expression my way and stepped into a dusty stripe of sunlight. If it was possible, she looked even more beautiful. Wait…beautiful? I shook my head, hoping the thought would bounce right out of my ears. She was Death. A walking nightmare. No way did that word belong anywhere near this girl.

"The second I pushed you back into that body, it began to expire," she said. "It won't last. It *will* deteriorate. This is just a waiting game now."

Deteriorating? As much as I wanted to deny it, I knew it was true, because it's exactly how I felt inside. I was dying. Fuck. I didn't want to die. Not yet. I wanted to go to art school. I wanted to get away from my dad and prove him wrong. And Em… Damn it, I couldn't leave Em.

Her molten eyes slipped over me, filled with something dark. Guilt, maybe? Pity? Whatever it was, I didn't like it. She finally straightened her back and looked away. "I'm sorry."

"You're sorry?" I balked. "You tell me I'm dying and that's all you can say?"

"Look, I know this isn't fair to you," she said. "And I'm not cruel. I'm just doing my job, following orders. If I'd had any idea that this would happen…" She shut her eyes and shook her head, causing a few silky braids to tumble over her shoulder. "I'm going to try to make this whole thing as easy as possible on you. I'll tell you whatever you want to know. You deserve that much."

At a loss, I just stared at her. Words. I still knew how to form words, right? It was like this chick sucked every ounce of sense right out of my brain.

"Why didn't you just take me at the fire?" I whispered, knowing that if I could have this one question answered, maybe I could deal with the rest. But the not knowing was killing me. "Why put me through this?"

Anaya's light dimmed and she frowned. "It wasn't my choice."

"Then whose choice was it?"

"Someone much more powerful than you and I combined."

"Stop being so fucking vague, Anaya," I growled. "Who? Your boss? God?"

She flinched at my tone, but I didn't care. I was so sick and tired of all of this.

"Not God, but yes. I work for him," she admitted.

"And why the hell would he want me to stay like this?"

"I don't know. I'd tell you if I did. All I know is there must be something terribly special about your soul for you to attract his attention."

She didn't know? How the hell could she not know? If she didn't, did anybody? Was I going to live the rest of my short life like this? Stalked. Terrified. Never knowing why. Or was the rug about to ripped out from under me? From now on, I'd wonder every second if the breath passing through my lips would be my last. My fingers started to shake along with the rest of me and I curled them into fists that I ground into the floor. My throat was closing up. I couldn't seem to remember how to breathe.

"You need to calm down," Anaya whispered, her warmth suddenly right there, forcing my throat open to let the air pass through. The prickling pain had flared back to life, but Anaya's warmth seemed to keep it tolerable. She didn't touch me, though she was close enough that her words cascaded like honey over my skin. "These shadows are drawn in by emotions that accompany death. Fear, anxiety, even anger. You need to learn some control. I can't be here all the time to ward them off. Breathe, Cash. Just breathe."

I took a couple of deep, calming breaths, and Anaya looked down at my trembling hands.

She gave me a sad smile and her fingers brushed my arm. "Much better."

I shook off the overwhelming urge to touch her back. To close the space between us. No way should I want that. What the hell was wrong with me? I glanced over her shoulder at a lone shadow demon weaving its way in and out of the books, its cold battling with her warmth. "You said the closer I get the more appealing I seem," I said, brokenly. "Why? What do they want?"

She ran a fingertip along one of the books and left a trail of gold sparks in its wake. "They feed off of souls. Usually ones fresh from the body. If they think you're close…"

I stared at her incredulously, tying to comprehend what

she was telling me. They wanted to eat my soul? This wasn't as bad as I thought. This was worse. Much, much worse. It was like someone had suddenly turned over an hourglass of invisible sand to count down to my inevitable death. And those things were waiting for the last bit of sand to run out. "So they're hanging around, waiting on my ass to die so they can have a freaking dinner party. Please tell me you're joking."

"You're not going to go through this alone," she whispered. "I won't let anything like that happen to you."

I grabbed my bag off the floor and slung it across my shoulder. "No. You're just going to wait for me to die."

She pressed her soft pink lips together and the light in her eyes dimmed. We stared at each other, my lungs eating up the air between us.

"You know what?" I pointed a shaky finger at the girl, all five foot four of otherworldly perfection, standing in front of me. "Stay the hell away from me."

The way she made me feel was too confusing. No good could come from wanting to have my hands on a chick who wasn't even alive. I took off down the aisle but I could still hear her voice as I walked away.

"That's not an option, Cash," she shouted. "I'm sorry."

What wasn't an option? Her staying away, or me not dying? As I pushed out of the glass doors and stepped into the sun, I couldn't help but think she meant both.

Chapter 6

Anaya

Cash gripped the steering wheel so tightly his knuckles looked as white as paper. His jaw was clenched, anger radiating from him like steam. I sat in the passenger seat of his Bronco and stared at the road stretching between the towering mountains as daylight turned to dusk. When I let myself look at him, my eyes insisted on focusing on ridiculous things. Like the way his paint-splattered red T-shirt clung to his biceps. Or the flicker of silver that appeared on his tongue every time he licked his lips. Yes. The road was definitely a safer view. Cash slammed his fist into the radio to shut it off and I flinched.

"You realize this is seriously creepy," he finally said. "Stalking me like this."

I shut my eyes, letting gravity take hold of me. When I opened them again, Cash was staring at me.

"You should watch the road." I pointed to the windshield,

anything to keep his eyes off of me. I had completely underestimated this boy. Even in a fit of rage, the way he looked at me made me feel stripped down to my insides. No one looked at me like that anymore.

Cash shook his head and returned his attention to the highway.

"Death is giving me safe driving tips," he muttered. "You've got to be fucking kidding me."

"How do you do that?"

"What?"

"How do you know when I'm here? You shouldn't be able to do that."

Cash shrugged and kept his intense gaze focused on the road. "I don't know. I...feel you, I guess. Everything gets warm and smells like it does right after a thunderstorm," he said. "You've never met anyone else who can do that? Sense you?"

I crossed my arms over my chest watching him. "Not in a thousand years." Unless you counted Finn, but Finn wasn't exactly normal.

"Guess I'm just special then."

I'd never seen Balthazar care about the fate of a human. Especially one like Cash. Yes, he was definitely special. I just didn't know why yet.

"Where are you going?" I asked, watching all signs of civilization zip past us, only to be replaced by open highway and hills. Most humans were predictable, but I still couldn't figure this one out.

"I don't know," he said. "Anywhere away from you would have been good. But I can see that's not going to happen."

"You don't have to be so rude," I said. "I'm just doing my job."

"Bullshit." Cash flipped on his headlights and passed a sign that said he was leaving Lone Pine city limits. "Your job is taking souls and I'm still here."

"Are you forgetting you *asked* me for this?" I reined in the anger that simmered beneath my voice. "How many times did you beg me to show myself? And now I'm here with answers, and all you can do is yell at me."

Cash glanced at me from the corner of his eye and made a huffing sound.

"Don't you have questions?"

He tapped on the steering wheel with his thumb as an oncoming car's headlights splashed light over his features. "Can they hurt me? The shadows?"

"No." Some of the tension melted away from his frame and the needle on the speedometer dropped a few numbers. I bit my lip to keep the guilt inside where it belonged. The truth was, I didn't know. I didn't know *what* Cash was and that meant I didn't know what dangers our world held for him. I had never in a thousand years seen these shadows go after someone so aggressively, but he didn't need to know that. "They feed off of souls. You're still alive, so for the time being they should be nothing more than an annoyance. It's when you die that you have to worry about them."

"When you said if you had taken me I'd have gone to Heaven…" His gazed darted to me and back to the road. "Is that the only place you take souls?"

I touched my blade and thought of how many souls it had brought peace to over the years. Too many to count. I wished I could tell him yes, but it wouldn't have been true. There was far more bad than good out there. It's one of the reasons Easton stayed so busy.

"No," I finally said. "There are other places. Each reaper has a territory. I am assigned to the Heaven-bound."

Cash smirked. "Let me guess. Finn was assigned to Hell. He had to be."

The venom in his voice took me by surprise. I couldn't understand where it was coming from. Finn may have made a lot of mistakes in his afterlife, but to his core he was good. "No, actually he collected for the Inbetween." When he raised a brow I went on. "You might think of it as a sort of purgatory. A type of limbo for souls who don't quite belong in Heaven or Hell yet."

Headlights passed us, splashing light over Cash's confused expression. "How did he get to be alive again? Did he just quit? Cash in his human card?"

I pulled my bottom lip between my teeth and stared out the windshield. "It's not that easy. What happened with Finn… it's unheard of. He had to have struck quite a bargain with Balthazar to get this."

I was afraid to find out what he'd sacrificed. Knowing Finn, he would have given anything to be with Emma.

"Balthazar?" Cash said. "Is that your boss? Is he the one stringing me along?"

"Yes."

Cash nodded and pulled off the road onto a scenic overlook. Outside the windshield, daylight was dying. The sun dipped low in the sky, setting the mountains on fire with color. The valley below was a sea of black, seemingly bottomless in the night. Cash leaned his head back against the headrest and closed his eyes. "This is so screwed up."

I focused on his chest. The rise and fall of his lungs, something so foreign to me it was almost too painful to watch.

"I know it is."

"Do you really?" His head rolled to the side and his eyes looked like caves staring back at me in the dim cab of the Bronco. "This is the kind of shit you deal with every day. It must be normal for you."

I thought of the eyes of the souls I carried over every day. Full of wonder and light and hope. Even the memory of them dimmed in the darkness that surrounded Cash and his uncertain future. And I thought about the warm, unsteady feeling Cash left blooming in my chest every time I looked at him. The way, even now, my fingers ached to close the small space between our hands.

"No," I said. "This isn't normal for me."

We stared at each other for an immeasurable moment. It felt like we'd been here before. Looking at each other from inches away. The phone in the cup holder between us vibrated and Cash broke eye contact to grab it. He looked at the message on the display and tossed it back without answering it.

"Emma?"

He stared at the phone in the cup holder. "Yeah."

"Why are you blaming her for this?"

Cash opened his mouth, and then closed it again. He finally shook his head, staring at the steering wheel. "Because I don't know what else to do."

I pulled my legs up underneath me and the golden light from my eyes spilled across the vinyl seat between us. "You know this isn't her fault. Even if you hadn't decided to go into that fire, fate would have found another way. I still would have been sent to stop it."

When he didn't say anything, I went on. "She would have

chosen to burn in that house rather than get you involved if she'd been given the choice. You know that, right?"

Cash looked out his window and drew lazy circles on the glass with his fingertip. "I know that."

I watched him carve shapes in the foggy window until he rested his forehead against the glass and exhaled.

"You love her." It wasn't a question. It was clear. And for reasons I couldn't place, my chest twisted in discomfort as I admitted it out loud for both of us.

"Of course I love her. But…" He paused and sat back in his seat. "She's my best friend."

"It's more than that."

He sighed and ran his palms in circles over the steering wheel. "You don't get it. Nobody does."

"Then help me understand."

"She saves me," he said, quietly.

I cocked my head to the side, trying to figure out what the look on his face meant. "From what?"

He laughed, bitterly. "Myself. Half the time, I feel like I'm drowning. Even before this. Like I'm in a room full of people screaming my lungs out and none of them can hear me. But Emma…she always hears me. She never lets me sink. She never lets me go, even when I know damn good and well it would be easier for her if she did." His hands dropped into his lap and he finally gave in and met my gaze again. "But she can't save me from this."

Outside the window, behind him, a shadow slipped like sludge down the glass. Another slid across the hood before disappearing into the night. The desperation seeping out of him was drawing them in like cattle called to feed. He knew they were there. I could tell. But he didn't let his fear show.

"No," I said, softly. "She can't."

Cash pressed his lips together and nodded as if he'd hoped for a different answer but hadn't expected it. After a silent moment he asked, "What's it like?"

"What?"

His gaze met mine. "Dying."

I thought back to the day I left my flesh behind. I'd been so foolish thinking death could give me escape. That it would lead me home. I turned toward the window and blinked away the memories. "It's different for everyone."

"For you," he said. "I want to know what it was like for you."

I bit my lip, fighting the ache swelling in my chest. "It was like being lost. Being lost and thinking I'd finally made it home, only to realize I'd taken a wrong turn, and was still a world away from where I wanted to be."

My voice broke and Cash moved across the seat in one swift motion. "Hey...I didn't mean to—"

I placed my palm on the seat to scoot away and his fingers accidentally slid over mine. We both froze. If I wouldn't have known any better, I would've said the world stopped spinning in that moment. Everything was so still. So unbearably still and quiet. I stopped breathing, watching Cash's chest rise with a sharp intake of breath. His eyes focused on his fingers pressing into my flesh, then traveled up until his gaze collided with mine.

Connection sparked, heating the air between us, making every square inch of my body aware of just how close he was. Cash tilted his head and let his fingers trace a slow, maddening line from my knuckles to my wrist, the look in his eyes so intense my insides fluttered with anticipation. Slowly, his fingers turned my hand over and his thumb rubbed a slow circle against my palm that felt so tight and warm I thought I might explode if he stopped.

This…this was wrong. *Tarik. Think of Tarik.* Just hearing his name echo inside my head was enough for me to feel sick with regret. No man should be touching me this way when Tarik couldn't. I tried to let go of the corporeality, but…I couldn't. Under his fingers I was solid. Blue smoke twined around my arm, as if it were securing me to him.

Cash exhaled a shaky breath and I came to my senses, jerking out from under his fingers, snapping the luminescent blue connection binding us together. I rubbed my wrist, where I could still feel his touch like a brand. Power surged uninhibited though my body, allowing me to relinquish my flesh for something less substantial. Something safer. How had he done that? He'd touched me. He'd forced me into corporeality. My eyes widened and the soft glow from them spilled across Cash's face. What was he?

"I'm sorry," he said, brows pulled together as he watched me squirm. "I just…I didn't know I could touch you. I didn't know you'd feel so…real."

I smoothed my hands over my dress and dropped my gaze to my lap. "Neither did I."

When I met his unwavering gaze, the heat there caused the invisible strings between us to pull tighter. He'd touched me. And he looked like he wanted to do it again. He shouldn't want that, and neither should I.

A slow heat started to burn at my hip, rivaling the heat throbbing in my chest, under every inch of my skin. The way he was looking at me made me feel like I was on fire with no way to extinguish the flames. I rubbed my thumb over the pearl handle of my scythe, thankful for the interruption. Not the dead. This was Balthazar.

"I have to go, but I'll be back."

Cash blinked as if he were coming out of a daze. His gaze cut away from mine and he slid back across the seat, putting safe distance between us. He gripped the steering wheel and stared at his hands. After what felt like forever, he leaned over to flip on the music and cranked it up until my ears throbbed. I'm not even sure if he heard it when I said, "Stay safe."

Chapter 7

Cash

They were out there. Shadows. I hadn't left the porch light on, so it was too dark to see them, but they were there. I could feel them, cold and consuming, waiting for me. Knowing they couldn't hurt me as long as I was alive should have made a difference, but it didn't. Instead, it left me wondering—if they wanted me dead so badly, how long would it take before they took some kind of action that gave them what they wanted?

I exhaled and squeezed the steering wheel, wishing I hadn't touched her. That was such a stupid thing to do. But it had been the first time in weeks I'd actually wanted to touch a girl, and I *never* went that long without touching a girl, let alone wanting to. I told myself it was just curiosity. A sick fascination. But even I knew I was lying to myself. I hadn't been able to stop myself. Even now, I wanted to do it again. She'd felt warm and deceptively real, her skin so unbelievably right under mine compared to the cheap, empty feeling that went hand in hand with my usual hookups. I'd felt so completely connected to her. Like we'd been there before. It had been enough to put me completely off-balance.

For a moment, I'd let myself forget what she was. I couldn't let that happen again. She wasn't some girl who was going to end up in the back of my Bronco or my heart. She wasn't even a girl as far as I was concerned. She was the reason I was here, living in the ninth circle of Hell on Earth. Right? I shook my head trying to sort out the emotions running through me. Shadows dripped down the windshield, changing shape as they pooled along the wiper blades. A reaper would have come in handy right about now.

Screw it. I had to get in this house. I couldn't sleep in my truck all night. I flipped on the headlights just to make sure my path from the driveway to the front door was clear, and stopped cold. Two beams of light spilled across the concrete drive and landed on...a guy. He stood, arms folded across his chest, caught between the two beams of light. He wore a gray wool coat with the collar turned up and had ash-blond hair that brushed the space just below his eyebrows. His eyes were gray, a shade lighter than his coat, and what looked like a spiderweb of black tattooed lines crept up his neck. Shadows curled around his ankles, giving him the illusion of floating on smoke.

It was *him*. The guy from school and the library. I pushed open the door to my Bronco and hopped out onto the driveway, heart racing.

His gaze shifted from me to a car rolling past the driveway, the neighbors' noses all but pressed up against the glass. He frowned, watching them until they were over the hill, and muttered, "God, I hate small towns."

"You," I said, approaching him cautiously. "I saw you at the school."

The guy looked me up and down with cold, calculating eyes and nodded. "I'm Noah."

Thrown by his introduction, I tried to get my bearings. I don't know what I expected from him, but it sure as hell wasn't his name. "And I'm Cash, but something tells me you knew that."

Noah chuckled and flicked his fingers, shooing the shadows away. To my amazement, they obeyed, scattering to the edges of the driveway, creating a tight circle of darkness around us. "Well, now that the introductions are out of the way, I believe you wanted to talk."

"Are you a reaper, too?"

"No." A grin curled Noah's lips. "I'm better. They get an afterlife of slavery with no reward. Do you want to know what I get, Cash?"

I took a step closer, knowing I shouldn't, watching Noah pull an apple out of his pocket. He took a bite and tossed it into the yard as he swallowed. He swiped the back of his wrist across his mouth and smiled. "I get to live."

"Slavery?" I asked. "Who are they slaves to? Balthazar?"

Noah sneered the second the name passed through my lips. "Yeah. That's him. He's got them all on strings. Like freaking puppets."

"And what about you?" I shoved my hands in my pockets, trying to snuff out the sparks going off beneath my skin, setting my veins on fire. "What are you?"

Noah walked a slow circle around me and the shadows mimicked his movement, creating what looked like a cyclone of black oil around us. They slipped through and over each other so quickly, they started to look like a single slithering entity instead of a horde.

"I'm like you," he said, effectively stopping my train of thought. "We're two of a kind, Cash. And believe me when I say we're a rare kind. You, my friend, are in high demand."

I swallowed, watching a shadow slip away from the circling mass and mold itself around one of my boots. Noah's eyes narrowed into slits and he knelt down in front of me, eyeing the demon. He wrapped his fingers around the shadow's neck, watching it writhe and hiss under his grip, then tossed it back into the group, where it faded into blackness.

My breathing calmed as I counted backward from ten under my breath. Anaya said to keep my emotions under control, but that was easier said than done. Noah stood up and looked me over.

"How…how did you do that?" I asked, feeling something like adrenaline surge through my insides. I flexed my fingers, the skin around them feeling tight and electric. "Why do they listen to you?"

"You feel it, don't you?" Excitement lit up his dim features. The black lines stretching up his neck like burned branches pulsed with something dark. "The power. It's dying to get free from that shell you keep it in."

I went stone-still as Noah approached me and turned my hand over. We both stared down at my wrist where the veins had darkened to a deep purple, throbbing as if the liquid inside wanted to burst through the skin. The shadows around us went into a frenzy, hissing, closing the space between us an inch at a time.

"You're closer than I thought," he said. "I would have

come sooner, but your reaper girlfriend is always around."

I would have corrected him about her being my girlfriend, but it felt ridiculous to clarify it. She was dead, for Christ's sake. Which left me wondering…

"You said you're like me." I crossed my arms over my chest and Noah's gaze flicked down to the paint splattered across my arms. "What did you mean by that? Are you dead?"

Noah groaned and shoved his hands in his pockets. "Labels are only going to confuse you right now. Dead. Alive. None of it applies to you and me. What I *can* tell you is, there is no one out there that's going to understand what you're going through like I do."

"Oh yeah?" I said, hearing how skeptical I sounded. "How's that?"

"Because I've gone through it, too," he said. "I've stood where you're standing. I've been hunted, coerced, manipulated, and now I'm on the other side." He took a deep breath and raked his fingers through his hair, laughing. "I have to say, they've really upped their game, bringing in that hot piece of reaper ass to win you over. They never tried that tactic on me." He flashed me a knowing grin. "But I guess we all have our weaknesses, don't we?"

Distracted, Noah looked around at the shadows that were close enough to blot out every inch of concrete surrounding us. "I've got to go. They're getting restless." His Adam's apple bobbed as he swallowed thickly and took a step back, drawing the shadows with him.

"Look." His eyes darted around the dark yard. "I want to help you. There's a lot more to say, but you've got to promise me something."

I nodded, thinking I might agree to anything to get more

answers. To get a sliver of hope. I didn't know what to think about Noah, but one thing was clear to me. He was offering me some kind of lifeline. Maybe it wasn't the kind I should be grabbing for, but when it was the only kind being offered, I didn't want to let it go.

"You can't tell anyone about me," he said. "I mean it, Cash. I know that reaper girl might be pretty. She might be sweet. But there is a side you're not seeing. If they ever got their hands on me…" His gray eyes darkened and his entire body tensed. "They would destroy me. And don't think for a minute that they won't do the same to you. Trust Balthazar and his minions and you're as good as dust. Vapor. Do you understand what I'm telling you?"

"Yeah." I nodded again and shoved my hands in my pockets to warm them. "Okay. I won't say anything."

"Good." Noah smiled. "I'll see you soon, then." He gave me a two-finger salute, then disappeared into thin air.

I stopped cold and spun in a circle. He was…gone. In the sudden absence of him, the shadows slipped and slithered across the ground around me, staining the white concrete black. I swallowed, tripping over my feet as I backed up. I stumbled up onto the porch, knocking a potted plant over, and pushed through the front door. When I got inside, the house was sleepy and dark. Dad's car was gone. At least I wouldn't have to hear it from him. After him catching me ditch class today, I'd kind of expected him to come home just to torture me. But that was something a good parent would have done. I grabbed the yellow note off the fridge and read Dad's chicken scratch.

PULLING AN ALL-NIGHTER TONIGHT.
BIG CASE NEXT WEEK. YOU HAVE AN
APPOINTMENT WITH DR. FARBER AT
9:00 A.M. BE HOME IN THE MORNING TO
PICK YOU UP. DON'T EVEN THINK ABOUT
SKIPPING OUT.

DAD

I crumbled the paper and tossed it into the trash. He was really doing this. Making me see a shrink. After what I'd seen tonight, I wondered if maybe that's exactly what I needed. I felt dizzy from the thoughts racing around my skull like a speedway. What was Noah? Could I trust him? He said I was like him, yet he was obviously scared of Anaya and anyone like her. What did that say about me?

I turned my hand over and touched the veins pulsing under the skin of wrist. There was a better question that I needed answered. What the hell was I? Remembering the darkness that lived under Noah's skin, I wasn't sure I wanted to know. My T-shirt was damp with sweat so I tore it off and headed for Dad's office. It's where he kept his good bourbon. Dad said it tasted like a little slice of heaven. I thought it tasted like lighter fluid, but hey, at least it made me numb and sleepy. At this moment in my life, that's all that really mattered. I filled one of Dad's fancy glass tumblers and downed it all in one drink, then poured another and did the same. My throat burned, but by the time I made it to my bedroom and kicked off my shoes, everything felt warm and tingly. Nice. I left my jeans on and fell back onto my bed, watching the ceiling spin.

I couldn't sleep. How was I ever supposed to sleep again

after all of this? Especially when part of me was terrified that it would be that scary-ass blade of Anaya's waking me up, or shadow demons waiting to suck the soul out of my eye sockets. I turned over on my side and watched shadows move across the wall. Sometimes, when my brain was fried from paint fumes and booze like this, I couldn't tell the difference. The easiest thing to do was close my eyes and pretend they weren't there.

I was inches away from the escape that sleep would provide when something pinged off my window. I flinched and sat up, rubbing my eyes, wondering if it was Anaya. Hoping it was Anaya and hating myself for it. I wasn't even sure if I should trust her at this point. Another tap. This time from a set of fingers. I climbed out of bed and pushed open the window. Emma stared back at me, her hair orange from the glow of the security light outside. I sighed and moved out of the way so she could climb in.

"What are you doing here?"

Emma pulled herself through the window and pushed the hair out of her face.

"I need to talk to you." She clutched a bag to her chest and looked around the room as if she was expecting to see someone there. Then it dawned on me that she was looking for a girl. She had no idea how much things had changed. When she realized we were alone, she pulled out a thermos and a paper bag that smelled like cookies. It would have been a hell of a lot easier to let her go if she'd stop trying to take care of me, reminding me why I loved her so damn much.

I fell back onto the bed and sighed. "About what? I thought we covered everything. You're dating Death and I'm being stalked by shadow demons." I peeked at her under my arm. "Does that cover it? Oh yeah, and now a reaper for Heaven is babysitting me like there's a freaking countdown clock to death stamped on my forehead. But hey, at least she's hot. Could be worse, right?" I carefully made sure to leave Noah out of it. Maybe I didn't know everything about him, but he was the one offering me actual answers. I wasn't about to jeopardize that.

"Wait." Emma's brows furrowed and she narrowed her blue gaze on me. "A reaper showed herself to you?"

I nodded and she sank down onto the bed beside me, looking so much like the worried little girl who used touch the space between my eyebrows and tell me everything would be okay when I was missing my mom the most.

"Who is she?" she asked. "What does she want with you?"

I pressed my lips together, trying to keep it in. She couldn't help me. Why did she even want to know? In the end, my need to tell her everything inside me won out. "Her name is Anaya. She's been following me since the fire. She just showed herself to me today."

"Anaya?" Emma shook her head, staring down at her lap. "And what does she want? Tell me exactly what she said."

I probably shouldn't mention that I'd practically tried to feel the girl up. That I couldn't get her out of my head. That even now, there was something in my chest aching over the fact that she'd been hurting and she wasn't here now. God, how far would I have let it go if she hadn't stopped me from touching her? Yeah, she was hot, and sort of sweet, but she was also *dead*. Maybe Dad was right. Maybe I really did need to get my head checked.

I brushed the curtain of blond hair away from Em's face so I could see the emotions playing there. "She said she's waiting for me. That it's only a matter of time before…"

Her head snapped up and her eyes glossed over with moisture. "Before what?"

"I die." I combed my fingers through my hair and tugged. "What else would a reaper want with me?"

When I gave in and looked over at her, she was shaking her head, a glossy gaze fixed on her fingers, twisting my bedsheets into knots. "No. No…you're not. It has to be a mistake. You must have misunderstood her."

"Em…" I sighed, wishing I had a different answer to give her. One that included me living out a long happy life with her by my side. It made my chest ache to think of how much I was going to miss. She'd go to college. Go after her dreams and make mistakes. I wanted more with this new Emma who wasn't scared of the world. I wanted more and I wasn't going to get it.

"Stop looking at me like that," she whispered in a broken voice. A tear slipped down her cheek and I reached out to wipe it away.

"Like what?"

"Like you've accepted this."

I ran my tongue ring back and forth against the backs of my teeth and shook my head. "I was supposed to die in that fire. I'm not even supposed to be here now. And she's not lying. It's not a mistake. I feel it, Em. I feel it every damn day. I'm dying."

Emma caught a sob in her throat and slid her hand over mine, lacing our fingers. I let her. It felt too good not to.

"You are not going to die. I won't let that happen." She ran the back of her hand over her cheeks to wipe away the wetness.

I sat up and faced her. "Are you God? Yoda? Gandalf the Grey?"

Emma just stared back at me, clearly not amused.

"Then you don't have any control over this," I said. "So stop trying to fix it. Stop trying to fix *me*."

Emma pressed her lips together, probably holding in an ocean of words she wanted to drown me with. She finally folded her hands in her lap and started messing with my pillowcase. That was one perk of being someone's sidekick for this many years. She knew when to quit. She knew when to stop pushing.

I studied the outline of her profile in the moonlight and realized I couldn't do it. I couldn't stay mad at her. I didn't want to. "Is Finn waiting for you?"

She shook her head. "No. He had to work late. He got a night job at that auto body shop in town."

"Where is he staying now?" *Please don't say in your bed. Please, in a world of shittiness, just give me this.*

"He got a little garage apartment," she said. "The guy that owns the body shop is renting it to him until he can afford something better."

As much as I hated it, I felt a little bad for the guy. It couldn't be easy being thrown into a life where you had to start over from scratch. No family left alive. No money or friends. I stopped myself there. I wasn't ready to go there yet. I didn't want to like him. I scooted to the far edge of the bed and left enough space for Em. We didn't have to say anything. It was understood. I didn't want her to go. I couldn't stand the thought of being alone right then. She kicked off her shoes and lay down beside me, pulling the cover up over us both.

"Do you love him?"

Emma blinked up at the ceiling. "Yes."

"How much trouble will you be in for staying with me?"

She laughed a little. "My mom's dating a cop now, remember? They'll probably send a search party."

"I meant with your boyfriend."

"You can't hate him forever," she said. "He's a part of my life now. He's not going anywhere."

I sighed. "I know that. But I'm not ready to like him, Em. Don't ask me to."

Emma lay silent beside me, her breaths causing her back to press against my side. She finally wiggled like she was uncomfortable and said, "What about me? Are you going to hate me forever?"

"I don't hate you." I turned over onto my side and tugged on a piece of her hair that was splayed across my pillow. It looked pale and shiny in the splash of moonlight coming through my window. So different from Anaya's dark, silky braids. Wait…why was I thinking about Anaya again? I shut my eyes and sighed. "I love you too much to hate you."

"I love you, too."

"Enough to show me your boobs?" I grinned into the pillow when she elbowed me in the gut. The bed shook with our laughter. "Come on. Consider it my dying wish."

"No!" Her smiled dimmed and I knew I'd screwed up by mentioning me dying again. "And you don't get a dying wish, because I'm not letting you die. I'll take care of you."

"You're always taking care of me," I said. "Why?"

"Because you're too stubborn to take care of yourself." She smiled across the pillow at me and pulled the blanket up around her neck. "Now go to sleep, perv."

"You going to stay?"

She patted my leg. "I'll stay till you fall asleep."

I stared at her fingers on my leg, and questions that had no place in my head bubbled to the surface. Questions I couldn't ignore anymore. If I didn't get them out, I was going to do something really stupid. Like kiss her. Words were going to work much better here.

"Can I ask you something without you getting pissed?" I asked, unable to stop myself from breathing in the scent of her hair all over my pillow. Asking her this could very well screw everything up between us beyond repair, but I had to know. If I didn't I'd never be able to walk away from her. From the *what might have been*s. "Do you think you ever could have loved me if Finn hadn't come along?"

She broke eye contact with me immediately, running her index finger over the pillow between us. "I already love you."

I tugged her chin up. "You know what I mean, Em. Did any part of you ever wonder if we might end up together?"

Emma watched me silently for a moment, chewing on her bottom lip before finally saying, "Of course I could have loved you. But I'm with Finn now…I'm always going to be with Finn."

I gritted my teeth and nodded. I didn't really know what to say. Mostly because I didn't know what I really wanted. I was so fucking confused my head hurt. All I knew for certain was that I wanted my best friend back. I didn't feel like *me* without her. The other shit was just petty jealousy and noise. I needed to get the hell over it.

"Cash, you're my best friend," she pleaded. "Please don't—"

"I know." I closed my eyes. "I was just trying to… Never mind. Forget I said anything."

I exhaled an achy breath, wondering if knowing was going to give me the closure I needed or just screw with my head even further. Instead of dwelling on it, I just said, "Good night, Em."

I turned my face to the pillow and tensed, trying to ignore the shadow slithering up to perch at the foot of the bed. With Emma here and my eyes shut, things felt halfway normal again. They felt right. I didn't want it to end.

"What's wrong?" Emma turned over to look at me, afraid. "Are they here?"

Her arm curled around me protectively, as if she'd actually be able to do something if they decided to make a move. A flurry of darkness swept past the open window. I shut my eyes and grabbed her hand, forgetting about the awkwardness I'd created between us, and pulled her against my chest. "They're always here."

Chapter 8

Anaya

The Inbetween.

The place where souls came to be reborn. Or die.

I shivered as I approached the gates. It felt strange not having a soul in tow. I usually tried to avoid this place at all costs. And that usually wasn't a problem, but since Finn had left, I found myself having to visit at least once a day. Only this time it was different. This time it wasn't a soul that had brought me here.

I stepped up to the big iron gates and raised my chin at the hooded guard.

"No soul?" he pushed his hood off, revealing a head full of dark curly hair, then pulled open the gates.

"No," I said, breezing through. "Balthazar wishes to see me."

His brows furrowed together and he nodded, as if he

were sending me to my second funeral. Under normal circumstances, Balthazar would call a reaper in for a one-on-one meeting only if something had gone awry. Usually these meetings ended in punishment. These weren't normal circumstances, though. No, if this turned out the way it was supposed to, I was getting a *reward* at the end of this journey. I could only hope that he was calling me in to tell me we were at the end.

I skirted past each hollow soul with ease, ducking under the shelter of shadow shapes to go unseen. As long as I didn't make eye contact with any of them, I wouldn't have to feel guilty for sending some of them here. There were too many children. Some souls were already approaching their ten-year mark. You could see the decay setting in. The madness was driving their transition into shadows. I couldn't stand it.

Someone grabbed me and I flinched. Thin white fingers dug into my arm with a desperation I couldn't fathom. A young girl emerged from the hemlock-shaped shadow and gazed up at me with dark eyes and feathery blond curls that she kept tucked behind her ears. The blackness had already eaten away the whites of her eyes, and whatever color they used to have.

"Y-you're a Heaven's reaper?" Her voice was all static.

I nodded, slowly.

"Help me," she whispered. Her eyes darted around. "Please. You could take me across. I don't belong here."

Pain blossomed inside my chest. I wanted to. I would have given anything to take her hand and lead her home. But her chances of getting through those gates weren't any better than mine. I looked down at the black spidery veins creating a road map up her arms and down her neck. No. Her chances were even worse. The darkness had already taken hold. She was beyond help.

"I'm so sorry," I whispered, squeezing her hand.

Her eyes widened. "No! Please!"

"Anaya, dear." A voice boomed from ahead. I jerked my hand away from the girl and turned around. The mist parted and revealed Balthazar, a light among the dreary darkness. He motioned for me to follow him. I fell into step behind him, my chest constricting with fear as he led me up the marble steps to the Great Hall. I'd never been inside. Few had, and the few that had never emerged. Balthazar lifted his hand and two mirrored doors swung open to allow us entrance.

Inside, the walls and floors were glass. Thousands of images flashed across their surface. Humans. Each in their last moments of life, in the cold grip of death. One by one the life left their eyes, and they were replaced by a new face. A new death. Balthazar cleared his throat, snatching my attention away from the images. He nodded and I followed him into an office. It was glass in there as well, with stars glowing behind every surface. Balthazar sank down in an oversize iron chair and settled his palms on a clear, shimmering table.

"How is the boy?" he asked.

"Fine," I said, standing ramrod straight, trying to calm my nerves. It wasn't easy to turn away from Cash's soul. Which is why I hated this place so much. It was much easier to pretend that it all didn't exist. "I've done as you've asked. He hasn't been touched. The shadow demons are contained, but I need to know something. Can they hurt him in the state he's in? I need to know what the dangers are here. I need to know what I'm dealing with."

Balthazar's gaze swept over me, scrutinizing, as if he

were searching me for something. He finally leaned forward, clasping his hands together against the glass. "He's rare, Anaya. The closer he gets to death, the more they are going to want him, for more reasons than one. If his soul gets close enough to the surface I suppose they could do some damage, but I doubt they will. He's too valuable."

"Why?" I asked. "What is he?"

Balthazar sighed, exasperated. "I don't have time to answer questions that don't concern you. Do you or do you not have this under control, Anaya?"

A droplet of fear trickled down my spine. A warning. "Yes."

"I can always count on you to do as you're told." Balthazar smiled, but it didn't reach his eyes. "It's a great comfort to me."

I almost laughed. Almost. He said it like it was a choice. None of us were fooled. This was no democracy he was running.

"Can you tell me how much longer?"

"In a hurry?" He raised a brow.

"No, I mean how much longer until I can bring the boy in," I said. "I'm eager to see Tarik."

I was also eager to end this poor boy's torture and give him the everlasting peace he deserved, but I didn't say that. I was ready for this sick experiment of Balthazar's to end.

"I know it seems cruel to you, but it is a process that is necessary for him to become what he has always been meant to be. And we can't rush that process now that it's started. What I wanted to know has been proven. But I can't end a life and neither can you. This is a waiting game now. A game you are going to have to win. His body is expired. He *will* perish. In the meantime, you need to gain his trust. I need this situation to stay free of complications. Can I count on you for that?"

I nodded and twisted the hem of my dress in my hands. "Of course. But wouldn't it be easier if you just told me what you wanted him for?"

Balthazar looked off into the horizon outside the one enormous window that dominated one wall. The clouds parted at his command, and the frozen sunset set the fog on fire with an orange burst of color.

"Do you know what I don't need, Anaya?" He raised an expectant brow. "I don't need one of my most valued reapers in possession of knowledge that could very well get her dragged to the underworld for interrogation, then tossed aside as a chew toy for the demons of Hell. As your keeper, your commander, I am telling you to trust me. All will be revealed when the dangers have passed, but as of now, you are better off being kept in the dark. Do you understand?"

I simply nodded as I clutched my scythe. Fear washed through me, dousing my heat.

"Good." He looked up and rubbed his chin. "Also, I thought I should warn you."

"About what?" I stepped forward. The fog swam circles around my calves, leaving an icy imprint on my skin where my ankles were submerged. "There's not a problem with my transition, is there? You promised when I was finished, that my debt would be paid. That I could cross." I forced my lips to close around the rest of my words when he narrowed his gaze on me.

"A complication has arisen," he said calmly. "Nothing to do with your...*transition*. It's just something that's going to make your job a little more difficult."

I stepped back. How could this possibly get any more

difficult?

"What is it?"

Balthazar sighed. "Another death, of course."

He slid a gold tablet across the table toward me. His ledger. No one ever saw this ledger. And he was offering it to me like it was a boon. My eyes flitted up to meet his for assurance and he nodded for me to read. Letting my fingers rest a breath away from the tablet I began to drink in the words. Name after name. Death after death. I was just about to pull away when the familiar name made me stop. My fingers shook as I pulled them away and looked at Balthazar.

"No," I said.

"Do I need to remind you how much I dislike that word?"

"But it's not fair. It's—"

Balthazar shot up from his chair and leaned across the table. His palms pressed into the glass. Frost began to crackle across the surface.

"Are you questioning me?" he growled.

I stuttered and took a step back, shaking my head. "N-no. Of course not."

"Then I can trust you to handle this?"

I closed my eyes and images flashed behind my lids. This wasn't right. On any level. But did I really have a choice? I opened my eyes and let them focus on Balthazar. The power rippled out around him like an electrical current.

"Anaya?" he said. "Do I need to have someone else deal with this?"

I rested my palm over my scythe when its heat began to wage a war with the cold surrounding me.

"No," I said. "I can handle it."

It wasn't often that I found myself searching for Easton. That probably explained the look on his face when he melted up from the black cloud base beneath him to find me calling his name. He twirled his scythe between his fingers like it was a six-shooter and shoved it back into the black holster at his side as he walked over, grinning.

"You rang?"

"Yes," I said. "I need your help." Easton's violet eyes widened when I gripped his duster and pulled him under the shelter of a shadow.

"Oh, God," he groaned. "What did you do now?"

"Why do you automatically jump to the conclusion that I *did* something?"

"Because you either dragged me in here to make out, or you screwed up again and you need me to get you out of it." He raised a brow at me and folded his arms across his chest. "Something tells me it's the latter."

I opened my mouth but nothing came out, so I closed it again, trying to come up with a way to make this sound less bad than it actually was. When I realized there wasn't a way to explain it like that, I sighed. I tucked a braid behind my ear and averted my gaze. "Well, it certainly isn't the first one."

"That's what I was afraid of," Easton said. "So what is it this time?"

"He touched me, Easton. *Touched* me."

"The human?" I nodded and Easton cursed under his breath and stalked away before coming back, eyes blazing. "I told you this would happen. Did you not learn anything from

Finn's mistakes?"

"I didn't do it on purpose! He touched me when I was in *soul* form, like it didn't mean anything for him. He just laid his fingers on me and…forced me into corporeality. Do you have any idea how this is even possible?"

"Maybe." Easton grabbed the back of his neck and looked around. "I've heard of something like this."

"I'm not in the mood for a guessing game, Easton."

"Well, I'm not in the mood to get caught in the middle of the shitstorm you've just created, *Anaya*," he hissed.

Easton started to pace and I bit my lip to keep from snapping back. The serpent tattoo that covered the right side of his neck flashed, seeming angrier every second that he ignored his call. Black smoke rolled up from his scythe into the air around us. He was vibrating with the need to go. But he didn't.

"You don't have to…" I started, but he held his hand up.

"A shadow walker," he said, his violet eyes cutting through the curtain of smoke between us. "It's the only way he could've forced you into corporeality like that. That's one of the reasons the guys upstairs and down go nuts if they get a whiff of one coming into existence."

I blinked at him, watching the golden glow from my eyes clash with the black smoke dueling for dominance in the small space between us. Dark and light. There didn't seem to be an in-between anymore since Finn was gone.

"A shadow walker?" I blinked at him, confused. Shadow walkers were rare. So rare, in fact, that I'd never seen one.

"A soul caught between life and death. Straddling the line," he said. "Think about it, Anaya. It makes sense. He was dead and you brought him back. This…" He stopped pacing and shook his head. "This is a real possibility."

"But Finn...he brought Emma back. She's fine. I see her practically every day and she's not dodging shadow demons at every turn. How could Cash be one?"

Easton looked me over thoughtfully. "A shadow walker is born from a very old soul. One that's been around a whole hell of a lot longer than Emma. Any idea how many times the Cash kid's soul has been cycled through?"

I rolled my eyes. "How would I know that?"

"Can't you tell?" Easton smoothed his palm over his blade as if to soothe it. "I can practically taste it. Stale. Bitter. You know?"

"No, I don't know," I said. "Besides, I didn't have much time with him. I didn't even let him exit the body."

I pressed my lips together to hold the secrets in when a group of reapers walked by. One stopped and peered into the shadows, his golden eyes amused. Darius. Almighty, if there was one person I didn't want to run into, it was him. There had been many who had tried to win my heart in the last thousand years, but Darius was the one who didn't know when to quit. Easton must have sensed my body tensing from head to toe. He wrapped a heated arm around my waist and pulled me against him.

"Gotta problem?" He narrowed his gaze at Darius.

Darius's jealous stare burned into me for a few seconds, his jaw clenched, setting his face into angry angles. He finally relaxed and shook his head, raking his fingers through his white-blond hair. "Come find me when you're done slumming it, Anaya. I have a feeling you'll be left wanting a little more when you're done with that one." He walked away laughing and I squeezed Easton's arm to keep him in place.

I let Easton's arm singe me a minute more until I was sure we were alone, then pushed him away. "He's not worth it."

Easton's face twisted into a scowl. "I should shove my scythe up his ass."

I waved him off, and then curled my fingers back into a fist when bright sparks flew from them and landed on Easton's black coat. "What should I do? Do you think this is why Balthazar has an interest in him?"

"It would definitely make sense," Easton said. "They are the only beings in existence that have the power to track down and capture the souls that are quick enough to escape their bodies before we can get to them. Both sides have been using them for years to poach the souls lost between worlds. The shadows could use him for anything from a food source to a recruiter. And as for Balthazar, he could have him bringing in lost souls in spades. *Before* they have a chance to transition into shadow or cause the kind of damage Maeve did when she tried to steal Emma's body. If not for that, I could see him wanting him just to keep him out of the underworld's hands. It still doesn't explain why he's having you keep him alive, though. Unless…"

"Unless what?"

"He could be testing him," he said. "You and I both know there is no way a normal soul would have lasted this long in an expired body. They would have succumbed in hours. But this kid…"

He wasn't just lasting. He was setting some kind of record. I looked away to avoid Easton's gaze. Balthazar wasn't having me keep him alive as some kind of reward. He just wanted me to keep him out of the competition's hands while he tested his little theory. After his needless torture was over, he wanted him for himself.

Easton brushed off the sparks that were burrowing little holes into the arm of his duster. The threads burned black and red, like a bed of coals that had been raked over, before weaving together and repairing themselves before my eyes. "Just keep an eye on him for now. I'll see what I can find out on my end. But if that's what this is…" Easton's gazed latched onto mine, pulling my fears out like a siphon and dumping them on the floor between us for the world to see. "If that's what *he* is, this is only going to get worse."

I didn't even want to think about what would happen if what Easton said was true. If my selfishness had changed this boy's world forever. Made him a pawn in some game between the dark and light. I nodded and watched Easton melt into the swirling black abyss below him and whispered, "I know."

Chapter 9

Cash

Courage: Fear is only as deep as the mind allows.

I folded my arms across my chest and glared at the framed motivational poster hanging on the waiting room wall. Only as deep as the mind allows, huh? Try telling that to someone who's being stalked by bloodthirsty shadow demons. Dad elbowed me in the ribs.

"Cash."

"What?" I jerked away and rubbed my side where he'd jabbed me. He used the *People* magazine he'd been flipping through to point at the man standing in front of us. "He called your name. You're up."

Dr. Farber looked about Dad's age, only Dad still had a full head of hair. This guy had scraps at best. He shoved his hands into the pockets of his pressed black slacks and plastered on a warm, fake smile for me. This was real. I was really here. In a freaking shrink's office about to be analyzed by a dork wearing an argyle sweater vest.

I groaned and stood up. I did not want to be here. He couldn't help me with my problems, because my problems were real. They weren't in my head. They were nightmares brought to life. Unless he had a voodoo priest back there who could negotiate with the dead, I didn't see the point in this.

"Nice to meet you, Cash." Dr. Farber held his hand out. When I just looked at it, he dropped it to his side.

"Are we going to do this or what?" I asked.

I heard Dad stand behind me. "Cash!"

Dr. Farber held his hands up. "No. No. I get it, Cash. This is the last place you want to be." He stepped aside and held his arm out to lead the way into his office. "What do you say we get this over with?"

I looked back at Dad. At the familiar *you're grounded* look on his face, and sighed. "Okay."

Everything was wood in Dr. Farber's office. Even the walls were wood paneling. Books, diplomas, and pictures of family broke up the darkness. I sank down into the burgundy leather couch and linked my fingers together in front of me.

"I'm not lying down," I said.

Dr. Farber laughed and sat down in the chair across from me. "I wasn't going to ask you to."

I nodded and bounced my fists in my knees.

"Are you nervous?"

"No." Actually, yes. The thought of cracking myself open and letting some stranger see what was inside of me made me want to vomit. I couldn't help but wonder if this was how Em had felt every time they'd put her through this bullshit. I leaned back into the plush sofa cushions and let my eyes scan the room for shadows. The only one I could find was the one the green floor lamp made when its light poured over me and splashed my outline across the big Oriental rug between us.

"Funny T-shirt," he said with a smile. "Did you wear that especially for me?"

I glanced down at my shirt. I couldn't even remember which one I'd pulled out of the hamper and thrown on. I almost laughed when I saw it. It was the white one with a gruesome-looking fake bloodstain in the side. On the front it said in big block letters, *I'm fine.*

I looked up and sighed. "Pretty sure you're not charging my dad a fortune to talk about my T-shirt collection."

"Fair enough. So, tell me about you, Cash." He leaned back in his chair and clicked his pen.

"I'm sure my dad's already filled you in, so I don't really know what you want me to say here."

"I want to hear it from you."

"I'm fine. There's nothing to talk about."

Dr. Farber cleared his throat and set the pen down. "Okay. Why don't we start with the fire."

"What about it?" I averted my eyes to the big, glossy, cherrywood desk behind him and tried to hold my eyes open. When I let them close there were flames. Smoke. Chaos.

"Your father seems to think that's when most of your problems started."

"So?" I asked. "Wouldn't you be a little screwed up if you'd almost died in a fire? Does that make me crazy?" Not crazy. Just haunted. Though *hunted* would be a more appropriate term.

"Let me ask you something." He leaned forward and pushed his glasses up his nose. "Why did you go into the house that day? It was clearly dangerous. You could've waited for the fire department to show up."

I finally let him snag my gaze. "And what? Just let her die?"

"Her?" Dr. Farber looked down at his notebook. "I assume you mean your neighbor."

I swallowed and looked out the window. "Her name's Emma."

"Girlfriend?"

"No."

"Do you want her to be?" he asked.

I shook my head, feeling uncomfortable in my own skin. "No. No, of course not. Emma's my best friend."

"Then why are the two of you estranged?"

I laughed and slapped my hands over my knees. "How much did my dad tell you?"

"Answer the question."

"We're just going through a rough patch. That's all," I said. "Friends disagree sometimes. It's not a big deal."

He scribbled something on his pad. "And it has nothing to do with the fact that she has a boyfriend now?"

"No," I said, my mind reeling with memories and feelings I didn't want to deal with. He was fishing. And I could feel his hook in me, bringing it all up my throat. Hell, maybe it was just because she finally found a boyfriend and I was a jealous ass. Or maybe it was because I was dying and I couldn't stop myself from thinking I'd pissed away the past eleven years with her and now I wasn't going to get any more. "Okay. Maybe I used to think that someday…"

I closed my eyes and groaned.

"It's okay, Cash," he said softly. "Keep going."

"I used to think that later, maybe when I was done being stupid, and she was done being scared of everything... I thought that maybe we might end up there. Together."

He nodded and waited for me to go on. When I didn't, he shifted gears.

"What about other girls?" He cocked his head to the side to watch me. "Any other relationships?"

I rubbed my palm over the back of my neck. There were too many discarded girls to count. What did Emma always call them? My "disposable girlfriends." I felt so detached from that guy it was almost as if the old Cash didn't exist anymore.

"I've dated a lot of girls." If you could call an evening in the back of my Bronco or on the sofa in my studio "dating."

"Anything serious?"

I stared at my sneakers, feeling a little guilty. What I felt for her was beyond my control. Like it had always been there, just waiting for her to bring it out. "No."

Dr. Farber wrote something else on his pad. "Let's talk about your mom."

I clenched my jaw and sat back. "There's nothing to talk about. She's not a part of my life."

"How old were you when she left?"

"Six," I said.

"That must have been hard."

"Of course it was hard." It would have been a lot harder if it hadn't been for Em and her mom. They'd fed me when Dad forgot. Let me sleep over when he was still at work past dark and I was too scared to be alone. Em even insisted they take me on vacation with them every year. God...it was no wonder I clung to her like a freaking security blanket all these years. I didn't really know how to survive without her.

"Do you think that's why you push people away?" he asked. "Are you afraid they'll leave like your mom?"

I leaned forward and met his gaze head on. "She left us. Left us to have a life with her yoga instructor. She left a six-year-old son without a letter or a phone call and never looked back. If that taught me anything, it's that anybody is capable of anything. I'm careful with who I let in. There is nothing wrong with that."

"There's nothing wrong with being cautious," he said. "But from what I can tell, you are more than cautious. If the things your father tells me are true, you have alienated yourself. Pushed everyone you love away. The question is why? What has its claws into you so deep that you can't let anyone else see what it is to help you?"

As if his words had pulled it into the room, a shadow slithered through the air-conditioning vent in the ceiling. It looked like an oil slick sliding down the wall, before it took shape and hopped up onto the desk behind him.

"Talk to me, Cash," Dr. Farber said. "This is a safe place. I promise."

The shadow demon opened its mouth and hissed over his shoulder, sliding down to the arm of Dr. Farber's chair. Fear pulsed in my stomach, my chest, my temples. I shook my head and stood up, ready to bolt.

"No," I said, retreating out of the room. "It's really not."

Nowhere was safe anymore.

Chapter 10

Anaya

I stared at Cash's house, feeling so twisted inside I wanted to be sick. I'd never seen a place covered up in so much death. The brick looked bloodstained under the dying sunset. Shadows dripped from the awnings and splashed through the gutters in a mad dash to join the cloak of nightfall. The windows, shaded with toffee-colored curtains, glowed with light. That glow signified life. Life I was about to take away.

I closed my fingers around the pretty pearl handle of my scythe. Its warmth melted through my fingertips and raced through my body like lava. It was almost time. I closed my eyes, unable to believe I was about to do this to him after everything I'd *already* done. After I'd looked him in the eyes and said I wouldn't let anything hurt him.

What a lie.

I opened my eyes when I heard Finn's familiar voice and

realized he was standing on Cash's walkway, headed for the front door with a cell phone in his hand. I allowed the sun's warm rays to soak through me, fusing me together cell by cell until I knew I was visible to him.

"Finn?"

He stopped, a shocked look playing across his face before he shoved the phone in his back pocket and made his way toward me. His skin looked sun-kissed and his green eyes were warm and alive. Easton may have always looked like he was born from the night, but Finn always looked like he'd been dipped in summer. Especially now.

"Being human agrees with you." I smiled at him and looked back at the house.

"You're human too," he said as he stood beside me, squinting at the sunset. "Dead. But still human."

I sighed and chewed on my bottom lip. My scythe was so warm it would've burned me if I'd been alive like Finn. I was stalling, and if I didn't stop it was going to get me into trouble. "I wish I could be as optimistic as you."

"You could be if you wanted."

"No." I shook my head, feeling my braids snake across my shoulders. "I can't. Not anymore. The afterlife may have turned out to be some sort of fairy tale for you, but it's not like that for the rest of us. I'm still here. Taking life. Never giving it back."

"What's wrong with you?" Finn narrowed his gaze at me. "You love your job. And what are you doing here anyway…"

Finn's gaze darted down to my hand, wrapped tightly around the scythe there. It burned between my fingers, making them glitter and glow. He frowned as he slowly made the connection. His eyes swung from the house to my hand and back again like a pendulum, until I could practically hear the pieces click into place inside his mind.

"No." It was only one word, but it spoke thousands. Finn stepped in front of me, blocking my view. "Not him, Anaya. Not after everything he's already been through. It'll kill Emma. Just give us some time to figure it out. Help us."

"For once, this doesn't have anything to do with Emma," I said, taking a deep breath. I didn't need it, but the pressure in my lungs felt good. "I got a call. I'm doing my job."

Balthazar had made it very clear what would happen if I didn't. It wasn't worth the risk.

"You don't have to."

I turned my golden glare on him, letting his words swim around in my mind. If only they were the truth. I would have given anything. "Yes. I do."

I pushed past Finn and seeped through the brick, leaving the suffocating warmth of the oncoming summer behind me. The second I stepped into the empty hall, the scent of everything Cash hit me like a slap in the face. But this wasn't just Cash. This was his father's cologne. The scent of their dinner simmering on the stove. The smell of leather and cigars and the leftover scent of paint that followed Cash wherever he went. This was everything that made up his family. His life. There was so much more to him than that cold studio filled with portraits of the dead. I wondered if he'd ever see it. I doubted it after today.

I drifted down the hall and stopped at Cash's bedroom. Finn was banging on the front door. I just wanted to see him one more time before I broke everything all over again. I needed it. I let my fingertips linger on his white doorframe, waiting for him to emerge. Cash breezed through the doorway, pulling a T-shirt over his head. Reaching out, I let my fingers brush over his bare ribs just before the shirt covered them, then cursed myself for doing it. I knew I shouldn't, but I couldn't help it. I had to make him stop. Had to prolong this moment. Delay the inevitable. I just wanted him to have a few more seconds of peace. Cash stumbled to a stop, looking confused, and ran his hand over the very spot I'd grazed. He closed his eyes like he was trying to compose himself and then darted down the hall.

I sank down onto the carpet and pulled my knees up to my chest. I couldn't do this. I couldn't take this away from him. Not this. I glanced down at my scythe, burning, throbbing, wanting the soul it came to take.

"Whoa! What the hell are you talking about, man?" Cash backed into the hall and Finn followed. He caught sight of me hunkered down like a coward in the hall and pressed his lips into a tight line.

"She's going to take you," Finn said looking at me. "She's here. Now."

"N-n-n-no, she's not." The color drained from Cash's face, leaving it ash white as he combed his fingers through his damp hair. "She's always here." He spun around, searching. "Tell him, Anaya. Tell him what you told me. You said it wasn't time yet."

I swallowed and closed my eyes, feeling like another piece of the puzzle that was me and Cash had snapped into place.

"Damn it, Anaya, tell him! You promised me." His chest started a steady rise and fall as he tried to catch his breath.

Finn narrowed his gaze at me. "You talked to him? You let him see you? What were you thinking?" Finn groaned. "Balthazar will have your head for this."

If only he knew the sick game Balthazar was playing. I was just another pawn. I nodded and smoothed my white dress over my knees as I stood. I couldn't help but think it shouldn't be so white, so pure. With all of the death I'd touched, I should have been cloaked in bloodred or, better yet, Easton's darkness.

"Why won't she let me see her?" Cash shouted. "Come on, Anaya. I thought we were past the hiding."

"I'm not here to take him," I said carefully, looking at Finn as I slid the blade from its holster at my side. Finn took a slow step back and turned his attention to the kitchen, where Cash's father was scraping something that smelled burned off a frying pan.

I moved between them and stopped at the end of the hall. But I didn't look at Cash. I didn't look at Finn. I couldn't. Instead I spoke to the ceiling, hoping Finn would hear.

"Tell him…I'm sorry." I squeezed my eyes shut. "I'm so, so sorry."

I heard the frying pan clatter to the floor and my eyes opened. I didn't listen to Cash shouting behind me. Didn't even flinch when he rushed right through me like I was nothing more than a wisp of wind. I followed him into the kitchen where he knelt over his unconscious father and beat on his chest. He scrambled for his cell phone and uselessly called 911. All I could think about was the heat burning me from the inside out. Needing. Wanting. Clawing.

I closed my eyes and let the weight of the blade slice though the smoky kitchen air and sink into his father's chest.

Chapter 11

Cash

"Stop looking at me like that," I snapped at Finn and his sad eyes. I couldn't take this. The waiting. The not knowing. He may have been an absentee asshole most of my life, but that didn't change the fact that he was my dad. And he was somewhere in this hospital, alive, dead, dying, afraid. I didn't know. I shoved my fingers into my hair and pulled at the long spikes until my scalp throbbed. I tapped my foot to keep from kicking something. Destroying something.

"I just…" Finn averted his gaze to the scuffed linoleum floor and watched a nurse's shoes scurry by. I didn't really see the nurse. I was too busy watching the rotten little shadow demon that had followed me here. It crawled in creepy little circles around me, filling up my nostrils with its disgusting scent. I finally managed to break my attention away from it to realize Finn hadn't finished.

"You just what?"

"I don't want you to get your hopes up." Hesitantly, he met my gaze. "She was there for—"

"For *me*. She was there for me," I said. "You said it yourself."

Finn watched an old man on a stretcher roll by. Eerily silent. Dead white. A shadow hovered at the foot of his bed, waiting. So…they didn't spend all their time harassing just me, then.

Finn kept staring even after he'd been pushed out of sight. "I was wrong."

"Stop saying that!"

Emma and her mom rushed down the hall toward us and I jerked my hands out of my hair and bit my tongue. My dad was not dead. He wasn't. He couldn't be. I'd seen the man win impossible cases. Survive the hell my mom had left him in for eleven years. Dad was built from steel. It was going to take more than a freaking heart attack to bring him down. And he wouldn't leave me alone. Not like this.

"Cash?" Emma touched my shoulder and I shook my head, realizing from everyone's worried expressions that they'd probably said my name more than once.

"He's gonna be fine, Em," I said, feeling my voice catch around the uncertain *fine* that fell out of my mouth.

Emma looked at Finn then back to me, nodding. "Right. He's going to be fine."

My gaze drifted down to the shadow circling Emma's ankles. Flicking its dripping tongue out to get a taste of the denim that covered her calf. Without even thinking, I shoved her away and knelt down in front of it. Noah had grabbed one. If we were so much alike, wouldn't I be able to do the same? And right now, choking one of these little bastards sounded too damn good to pass up. I flexed my fingers, watching it rise up within an inch of my hand, then reached out to grab it. Pain exploded across my hand like I'd dipped it into a flame and the shadow demon passed through my hand like smoke.

"Mother fu—" I stood up, wiping my burning hand on my jeans, and stomped on the thing. I stomped until I couldn't breathe. Until I was sure I'd smashed it to bits tiny enough to be blown away by the sickly sweet smell coming through the hospital vents. I stomped until two hands wrapped around my shoulders and jerked me back.

I looked up at Emma, breathing hard, and realized Finn had two fistfuls of my T-shirt. Everyone was silent, looking at me like I was that crazy guy who stood on the corner of Fifth and Elm and threw sticks at people's cars.

"There was…" I stared down at the floor where the shadow should have been. Nothing. Just some off-white waiting room tile with a questionable stain.

"Mr. Cooper?" a hesitant voice said from behind me. Finn squeezed my shoulders once and let me go. I turned, not ready to hear what Finn already knew.

"That's me."

The doctor's dark brown hair was plastered to his head with sweat. His glasses kept slipping down his nose. I stared at the blue scrub cap that was protruding between his clenched fingers. I couldn't look at his eyes when he told me this. It was too much. If I saw the truth in his eyes, I wouldn't be able to pretend this wasn't real.

"Is he…?"

"Your father had a massive heart attack. I don't think we could have helped him even if he'd been here on a gurney when it happened. We did everything we could. I'm so sorry."

I nodded. I felt…empty. Hollow. Where was the pain? My

dad was dead. Gone. There should have been pain, right?

"We have grief counselors you could speak with," the doctor said. I held up my hand, shaking my head mechanically, and he stopped.

"Cash?" Emma's voice. It sounded muffled. Off.

Nothing. How was it possible to feel this much nothing?

"Cash, answer me." Emma again.

"Stop it. Just give him some room. Let him breathe," Finn said. Breathe? Was that even possible? I felt like I was suffocating.

"Cash!"

Something inside me snapped at the sound of Emma's voice. It was *the* sound. That same rawness I'd heard in her voice the day her dad had died. I'd never understood what that sound meant. But hearing it now, in this place, forced me to.

Everything came rushing into me all at once. The wall I'd built up around myself after Mom left, decimated. The wound that would forever replace my father, ripped wide open. And it…hurt. Oh, *God* did it hurt. Just a stinging at first. But before too long it was throbbing. Burning with things I should have said. Things I should have done. I shouldn't have shut him out. I shouldn't have been such a moody little prick to him all the time. I couldn't even remember what the last thing I said to him was. Shit! What did I say? What was it?

"It's gonna be okay," Emma whispered against my neck. "I promise."

I closed my eyes and shook my head against her shoulder. I couldn't catch my breath. Couldn't stop shaking. "I said… we're out of bread."

"What?" Emma pulled back, her blue eyes full of questions.

I stared over her shoulder at the wall and swallowed the lump in my throat.

"That was the last thing I said to him," I said. "We're out of bread."

Emma opened her mouth but stopped when Finn crouched down beside us and stared at the blank spot on the wall with me.

"He won't remember that," he said. "He'll remember the good parts. Where he went…the good parts are all that exist."

I nodded and closed my eyes. He was someplace better. That should count for something, right?

"Um…Cash, sweetheart," Emma's mom, Rachel, stepped up behind me and touched my shoulder. "Is there anyone we can call? Any family? Someone you could stay with?"

I shook my head. The only living family who still talked to us was Aunt Sara, and she lived in Germany on a military base. No way was she making it back. No way was I moving there.

"What about your mom?" she asked, hesitantly. I shot her a look that could've cut through steel, and she winced. The mom I hadn't spoken to since I was six? The mom who hadn't even bothered to send a birthday card in *eleven* years? The mom who had made damn sure I'd never find her? Hell, I didn't even have her phone number.

"He's staying with us," Emma spoke up. "He can stay in the guest room."

"Emma, honey, I'd have to talk to Parker—"

Emma stood up and pinned her mom with the stare that had shut me up more than once. "He's staying."

Rachel looked at me like I was a dog in the pound about to be euthanized. "You're right. Emma, take him home to grab some of his things. I'll get the guest room set up for him."

Funny how she talked to Emma like I wasn't even there. I wondered if that's how I looked. Vacant. It's how I felt. Like part of me had checked out. Gone south for the winter. Emma grabbed one of my arms, Finn grabbed the other, and they pulled me to my feet. But I didn't want to be on my feet. I wanted to be on the floor with the shadows. In that empty moment…I wanted to let them have me. I watched one of them, a black silhouette of death, slither from one side of the hall to the other. Never stopping. Never taking the hollow holes that were its eyes off of me. Its shape changed as it moved. Sprouting wings, tentacles, arms and legs. It melted into the dark shape of a man, reached its dripping hand out to me, and I felt my grip start to slip from Emma's.

"*Come*," it hissed. That hiss melted through me, burrowing deep. Somewhere in the back of my mind, someone was saying, *It would be so much easier just to go…*

Emma jerked on my arm and forced me to look at her. "What is it?" she asked.

"They're here for me." I swallowed the broken sound down my throat and took a shaky step forward.

"Don't even think about it," she whispered, tightening her grip on me. "I'm not letting you go."

Chapter 12

Anaya

Every moment of my existence revolved around death, but I hadn't been to a funeral in a thousand years. Now I remembered why I hated them so much. I closed my eyes and fought off the memory threatening to claim me. Tarik. My father. My mother clutching my hand as the sea blew wind and salt and hair into our eyes. The awful, hopeless feeling flowing through me, knowing they were never coming back. Knowing the two most important men in my life now belonged to the sea.

Each of the cold graves surrounding me represented a soul gone from this earth. A lifetime of kisses, laughter, and love now just dust and bones and memories. That's what Cash's father was now. To this earth, he was just another memory.

I lingered on the outskirts of the crowd of quivering

bodies all cloaked in black. I kept my eyes on the stone fixture that was Cash, praying with everything in me that I didn't get called away now. The only parts of him that moved were his hair and the ends of his burgundy scarf, tossed around by the wind. His steady brown gaze was focused with a desperate intensity on the closed casket being lowered into the ground. A slightly off-key woman in the corner of the bright blue tent sang a haunting hymn that echoed across the cemetery. The hollow sound moved through the headstones like smoke, leaving an imprint of sadness wherever it went. Cash's dark brows drew together as if he thought he could force the tears to stay inside. He didn't look right like this. All buttoned and ironed without one of those ridiculous T-shirts. He looked… broken.

A memory sparked. I tried to fight it off, but it rushed back anyway. Something about seeing Cash like this, drowning in loss, dredged up memories of my own. Suddenly, I saw Tarik standing on the dock that day. His dark hair whipping in the wind. Hiding his eyes. I still remembered the warmth of his palm as he cupped my face and rubbed a stray tear from my cheek. The salty taste of the sea, dry on my lips. The way his hair sifted through my fingers like silk when I reached up to push it out of his eyes.

"Anaya…there is no need for tears," he whispered into my hair. Every part of me lit up. Burned out of control knowing he was touching me like this where everyone could see. "I'll return. It's only three days, love."

I gripped his shirt in my fist and breathed him in. He smelled like fish, but I didn't care. It almost smelled nice next to the basket of warm bread I was balancing on my hip.

"It always feels like a lifetime," I said.

He laughed and kissed my forehead despite the disapproving look my father gave him as he hauled a basket full of supplies onto the boat.

"My Anaya…" He smiled. Warm. Beautiful. The way I'd always remember him after that. "We should be happy your father gave me this job."

"You hate this job."

Tarik sighed and tugged on one of my braids. "No. I only hate smelling of fish guts when you always smell of dreams."

"I love you," I whispered. "Even when you smell like fish guts."

Tarik's lips tipped up into that cocky grin that left my knees weak and wobbly every time. He gripped my chin and brought his lips to mine. Kissed me once. Soft. Reassuring.

"And I love you." He kissed me once more and then he was waving to me from the ship deck. Sending me kisses to be carried by the wind. Then he was just a dot on the bright-orange horizon. And then he was gone. Forever.

I blinked away the memory and looked down at my empty arms, half expecting to see a basket of bread there. The crowds began to thin as people retreated back to their vehicles. All that remained was Cash, with Emma and Finn acting as beams of support at his sides. Emma wiped away a tear and Cash pulled away from the iron grip she had on his arm.

"I want to be alone," he said.

Emma and Finn exchanged a glance and Emma touched the sleeve of Cash's jacket, unsure. "Are you sure? I can stay—"

"I'm sure, Em." His voice cracked and pain began to chip away at the protective layer around my heart. "Please. Just let me be alone with him. I'll come straight to your house after."

Emma placed a soft kiss on his cheek and then reached

for Finn's hand before disappearing over the hill. A few excruciating moments later, Cash looked in my direction.

"Are you planning on talking to me or are you here on a haunting gig?" He shoved his hands in his pockets and stepped out from under the blue tent. "Wouldn't want to interrupt a side job you've got going."

I stepped into the light, allowing him to see me, my hands linked behind my back to mask the way they trembled. Would he hate me for this? He should. I'd caused this unbearable pain he was feeling. I wanted so badly to take it away.

"I'm so sorry," I said, hating how inadequate it felt.

"Was it your call or Balthazar's?"

I bit my lip and looked away. "Balthazar's. I didn't have a choice."

He nodded almost mechanically, but I could see a flare of heat in his gaze.

"You reap for Heaven, right?" He came to stand beside me, staring off into the distance, his gaze avoiding the big blue tent and what was buried beneath it.

"Yes."

He nodded and shut his eyes. "And that's where you took him?"

"Yes," I said. "I took him home. He's happy there. I promise you that."

A muscle in his jaw ticked and he shook his head. "See, that's the problem. I'm kind of having a hard time knowing whose promises to believe these days."

Without thinking, I reached out and grabbed his hand, not expecting it when he laced his fingers through mine to keep it in place. "You can believe mine. Always."

Cash squeezed my hand as if he were testing something,

and blue sparks twined around our wrists. This time I didn't pull away and neither did he. Right or wrong, I needed this contact as much as he did.

"God, you feel warm," he whispered, letting his arm fall against mine so that our skin was fused together along our shoulders, fingertips, and everywhere in between. The heat beneath my skin blazed, reaching out to warm the boy beside me.

"I don't know anything about you," he said, breaking the fragile silence between us. "Besides the fact that you're dead."

"Do you want to?"

Cash shrugged and tilted his chin down to look at me. "Only seems fair. You know all of my secrets."

I bit my bottom lip, thinking. I didn't want to tell him stories about death, but that's all my existence had consisted of for the past thousand years. For some reason I didn't want him to see me that way. I wanted him to see something else when he looked at me. Something I didn't get to be anymore. Alive.

"I lost my father, too," I said, softly. "Just before I died. At the time I'd been so angry. I thought he'd been taken before his time."

"And now?"

I shook my head, purposely hiding behind my braids. "Now that I'm on the other side, I see how foolish it is that people try to fight it. Like it's a choice. Like it hasn't already been written."

"Did it ever stop hurting?" he asked.

I thought about the ache that I had carried with me all these years. The one for Tarik, so deep and cutting that the most fleeting memory of him tore it wide open all over again.

"Some wounds never heal," I admitted. "They simply become a part of us."

Cash stared down at me, his gaze lingering on my lips. He squeezed my hand and swallowed. "Have you ever wanted something, even knowing you shouldn't?"

Nervous energy washed through me. I should have walked away. From the way he was looking at me. Touching me. But I didn't. Instead I nodded, unable to look away, and said, "Yes."

I wanted him.

The instant I thought it, I wanted to take it back. Needed to take it back. Not because it wasn't true, but because it was wrong. Cash studied my face for a moment and his eyes flashed with a decision. He started walking, tugging me behind him toward the parking lot. Only a few empty cars littered the pavement, the gathering from the funeral already having moved on to the next destination.

"Where are we going?"

He pulled me in by my wrist and backed me against the door of his Bronco. In an instant, he was right there, so close to my lips. "It hurts so fucking bad, Anaya." His voice shattered in a broken whisper. "Maybe you're right. Maybe we have to live with the hurt forever, but that doesn't mean we can't numb it. Help me forget. Please. I just want to forget for a little while."

His brown eyes swept over me like he was committing every inch of me to memory. If I were still full of blood, I imagine that look would have had me warm all over. I couldn't help but wonder how many girls he'd looked at like that. He wouldn't have been looking at me like that if he weren't decimated and begging for escape.

"Cash, I can't," I said. *Stay calm, Anaya. You don't care.*

He's just a human and you can leave. He has no power over you. I scooted back, trapping myself against the door. Trying to inch away from Cash's heat. His smell. The way his eyes were looking right through me. The way the tilt of his lips said he didn't want me to go even as the anger behind his clenched fists said he didn't want me to stay.

"Don't go," he said.

He took a step closer, effectively erasing the space between us, and pressed his palm against the door behind me to steady himself. His black hair lay in damp spikes against his forehead. His eyes looked dark and tortured. He was so beautiful and sad that it hurt to look at him. God...he deserved so much more than this.

"You don't want me."

"You have no idea what I want," he said.

"You don't need me," I whispered. "You need something any other girl in this town could give you."

His thumb brushed the side of my face and he swallowed. "I don't want them."

Something inside my chest began to pound. Or maybe it was just the memory of what my body was supposed to do with a boy this close.

He leaned in closer and I closed my eyes. *This is wrong. This is wrong.* I kept repeating the thought, but my body wasn't listening. Instead it was burning up. Leaning into this boy who was drawing me in with every breath. Cash's cheek grazed mine, solid and warm, and my knees wobbled. Oh my God. How could he make me feel like this? How could he ignite sensations that had been dead for a thousand years? I couldn't lose myself to this, no matter how good it felt. Not now. Not ever.

I exhaled, letting go of the corporeality, to step through him, but he stopped me just like he had in the car. Panic flared to life in my chest as my gaze traveled down to his fingers wrapped around my waist. I focused, trying again, but under his fingers, I was solid. Flesh. Every brush of his skin on mine was pushing the death out of me and filling me with artificial life.

"I want *you*, Anaya." I tilted my face up and he took it as an invitation. I gasped as his lips grazed mine, asking for something.

"I want your taste in my mouth. I want your heat in my veins." One of his hands came up to cradle my jaw as he gently kissed my top lip, them my bottom, lingering there the longest. I whimpered into his mouth and every part of him shook with what I could only guess was restraint. He pressed his forehead to mine and closed his eyes. "I want it to erase everything that's inside of me right now. Say it's okay, Anaya. Tell me you want me, too."

His thumb traced my bottom lip where his mouth had just been and I swayed into him. Some part of me wanted to give in, but I knew he didn't really want me. He was too good at this. No matter what he said, he just wanted what every other girl he sought out gave him. Escape. A way to forget. I let the taste of him linger there for an instant, then broke away and gently shoved him back. I couldn't do this. Tarik. Tarik was so close. I'd waited a thousand years for him! I couldn't let myself ruin everything now.

"I can't," I whispered. "I'm sorry."

Cash pulled back and stared at me, his jaw set into a hard line. He raked his fingers through his hair and backed away.

"Why'd you have to save me? Why couldn't you have just

done your damn job at that fire and taken me!"

"That wasn't my decision. I just did as I was told."

It sounded so cheap. So awful on the heels of the intimate moment we'd just shared.

"I hate this, Anaya!" He backed away shaking, pulling at the tie around his neck as if it were choking him, fighting the tears glistening in his eyes. "I want my life back!"

Cash's eyes searched my face, pleading. The desperate look in them sent a shiver of fear down my spine.

"Take me," he said.

"What?"

"Take me," he repeated. "If I need to die first, just tell me what I have to do. Then you can take me to be with my dad and all of this will be over. Right?"

"I…I can't do that."

"Why the hell not?" His hands slammed against the door, caging me in.

"Because I care about you," I said, trying to catch the breath I didn't need. It wasn't a lie. I did care about him. But it wasn't the truth, either, and the words tasted awful coming out of my mouth. I should have told him the truth. I was trading his misery for my redemption. His torture for my chance to get through the gates that had taunted me every day for the last thousand years. I took away his chance at eternal happiness so that I could get back to Tarik. But I couldn't say that. Not after he'd just kissed me.

"There's more." He stood frozen in place, refusing to let me free. "What aren't you telling me?"

I slipped out from under him and stilled. The dead were calling. So warm and sweet. The scythe in my holster wasn't as patient. It burned my hip through the leather and the thin white barrier of my dress.

"I have to go," I said, my voice barely a whisper. "I'm sorry if they come back. Really, I am...but I can't stay here. Just remember what I told you. Keep calm. Keep control."

Cash sagged against the Bronco, watching me. "This isn't over, Anaya. Not even close."

Chapter 13

Cash

I was done. Huddled in the corner of Emma's bathroom surrounded by shadows, so thick I felt like I was sitting in a cloud of ink, I'd never been more sure of anything. I pressed my head between my legs, trying to block out the stench and the sound of them. It didn't work. They were too close, all around me, all over me. A hiss sounded next to my ear and I reached out to bat it away.

"Fuck!" Pain flared across my arm and I jerked it back against my chest. As if it sensed the weakness, another shadow pounced, wrapping around my other forearm, and a matching pain blazed across my skin. The burn was so at odds with the chill running through me that I bolted to my feet. Two long red burns marred both of my arms, the skin blistered and stinging. *Son of a bitch*. My gaze traveled down to the puddle of writhing darkness below me and I blew out a pent-up breath.

Anaya said they couldn't hurt me. She lied to me. Why the hell would she lie to me about this?

"Break it up!" a voice boomed across the bathroom. Shadows scattered and escaped through the cracked window. They slipped and slithered across the cream-colored tile until they found refuge in the dark bathtub drain. Noah grabbed one by the neck as it reared up to take a bite out of his throat. His eyes were glassed over and cold as he squeezed it until it wiggled and screamed, tore and twisted under his fingers. A black, glittery ooze melted across his wrist and he cursed before dropping it onto the tile, allowing it to scurry away.

Noah watched it spiral down the drain and rubbed his wrist. "Well…that was fun."

"You're back," I said numbly, not really caring. It didn't matter if he was back. I was done here. So, so done. I pushed away from the bathroom wall and Noah backed up a few feet to give me space as I rummaged through the medicine cabinet.

"I'm a man of my word," he said, his voice trailing off as I popped open a few pill bottles.

There wasn't much to choose from, mainly just leftover antidepressants and pain pills from Emma, but it would have to do. I just hoped Anaya was ready, because it was time to fix this black hole of an existence that had become my life, whether she was ready for it or not. If ending it was the only way, so be it. Anything had to be better than this. Who knows, maybe I'd see Dad again. Maybe I'd get a chance to make things right with him.

Noah stepped up beside me and examined one of the pill bottles. "Mind if I ask what you're doing?"

I shrugged my jacket off and rolled the sleeves of my

white shirt up to my elbows. I braced my palms on the counter and stared at my pathetic reflection in the mirror. Black hair that usually stuck up in disorderly spikes lay damp and limp across my forehead. My skin looked ashen against my white shirt and red tie. Dad's red tie. I didn't own one, so I'd had to raid his closet. Even now, hours after I'd watched them lower him into the ground, it felt heavy and wrong around my neck. And those eyes, dark and dull, full of pain, who the hell did those belong to? I didn't know who this kid was staring back at me. I just knew that I didn't want to be him. Not anymore.

"Sorry, Em," I whispered, then brought one of the opened bottles of pills to my mouth.

"Whoa!" Noah slapped the bottle out of my hand, only allowing me to get a couple down before he raked the spilled pills and the rest of the bottles off the counter. "What the hell are you doing, man?"

Triggered by anger, I shoved Noah against the bathroom door. I hadn't been in many fights, but I was ready to knock someone flat on their ass if they tried to stop me. Dead or alive. "This isn't any of your business. Stay out of it. You don't want to watch? Then fucking leave."

Noah's gray eyes opened wide as they flicked down to my finger jabbed in his chest. He held up his hands in surrender. "And what are you going to do if the shadows come back before she does?"

All that waited for me on the other side with Anaya was a big question mark. Unanswered questions. At least I knew where I stood with the shadows. I was nothing more than a meal to them. At least I'd be gone. There would be nothing if they got me first. I stepped away from Noah and my arms fell to my sides, the pain a dull throb now.

"Maybe that's what I'm counting on," I said. My body didn't seem to agree with this plan. Fear filled up my chest and my heart started to pump with life behind my ribs, as if it was trying to prove to me that we could still beat this.

"I get it." Noah stared down at me, looking a little panicked. "I promise I get it. I've been there, and I'm telling you this isn't the answer. There is another way through this, Cash. A better way."

I lifted my chin to face him, feeling the lump in my throat swell to an unbearable size as I tried to wrap my mind around what I was doing. The pill bottles scattered across the floor caught my attention. What if Emma had been the one to find me, just a few feet from where she slept? What would that have done to her? A choked sound seeped past the lump and I pressed the heels of my hands into my eyes.

"You've got a better way than this?" *Please say yes. Please show me, because I'm ready to do anything.*

Noah's hand rested against my shoulder and it felt as cold as I did. "Better than letting that bastard upstairs and his reapers make a slave out of you? Yeah, man. I've got a better way."

"Show me," I said.

Noah grinned and his hold tightened around my shoulder. "I thought you'd never ask."

A tingling sensation started in my veins, buzzing under my skin, and light exploded around us. I felt like I was going to burst out of my skin, leaving tiny pieces of Cash strewn all over Emma's bathroom, but then…we weren't in the bathroom. My vision swam in darkness and a dripping sound echoed somewhere behind me. I blinked, searching my surroundings. Brick walls surrounded us and wet pavement settled under my feet. The sound of a car alarm sounded somewhere in the distance. We were in an alley. Cold, damp air ruffled my hair and I shivered, feeling a wave of nausea roll through me. Noah's hand fell from my shoulder and he took a step away.

"You all right?"

I nodded, bending over to brace my hands on my knees, and stared at the oily puddle I was standing in. "I feel sick."

He chuckled. "That's normal. You'll get used to it."

I stood up, swallowing excess saliva, and glared at him. "Get used to what? Tell me what the hell is going on or I'm not taking another step. Tell me what you are."

He nodded and a breeze blew a slash of his blond hair into his face so it covered one eye. "I'm a shadow walker." He paused and folded his arms across his chest. "And so are you."

I studied the hard angles of his face, the tense set to his shoulders. He was serious. "Am I supposed to know what that is?"

"You think your reaper girl has power?" He raised a brow. "She is doomed, Cash. Doomed to be a slave for all of eternity. Doomed to walk the Earth and afterlife as nothing more than an echo of the corpse she used to be."

My chest twisted uncomfortably. I didn't like him talking about Anaya like that. She might have been dead, but she wasn't a corpse. She was so much more than that.

"And what makes us different?"

Noah smiled. "We can walk among the living," he said. "And we can cross over as the dead. We're hovering somewhere in between. You have more power in one fingertip than a reaper has in their entire body. Enough power to force a soul into flesh. Enough power to scare the shit out of them. Why do you think Balthazar wants you under his thumb so badly?"

I stared at my fingers, flexing them open and closed, feeling the energy buzzing under the surface. He was telling the truth. I could feel it.

"You've got a choice in what and who you use that power for," he said. "I'm just trying to help you make the right choice."

I thought about Anaya and her light, the goodness that poured out of her like sunshine. She couldn't possibly be batting for the wrong team. She was too good. I watched the darkness pulsing in Noah's veins, buzzing beneath his pale skin. In answer the blood in my veins pulsed back. Maybe Anaya wasn't the bad one here. Maybe it was me. Maybe it was Noah.

"They'll destroy you," Noah said as if he could read my thoughts. "You are too much of a danger. They'll destroy you just like they would destroy me if they ever got their hands on me. They'll stop at nothing to keep you out of the underworld's hands, even if that means baiting your human hormones with a girl who looks like Anaya."

"And who are you using your power for?" I stepped forward, my boots creating a mini tidal wave in the puddle beneath me. "Because from where I'm standing, it seems like you're in pretty deep with the same things that want to suck the soul right out of my skin."

Noah frowned, no doubt hearing the distrust in my voice. "You want to know what I use my power for? What I'm asking you to use yours for as well?"

I nodded and Noah spun around, his gray coat flying out behind him. "Follow me."

Maybe Noah was batting for the dark side, maybe I was walking into a gigantic trap, but I had to know. No way could I walk away from all of this, not knowing what I was, where I ·

was going to end up at the end. I took off at a jog after Noah and we emerged onto a busy city street. Shock stole my breath as I looked up at the high-rises in the distance and the people crowding the sidewalks. Two girls with beads dangling from around their necks walked past us, laughing. The blond one with purple streaks and a leather miniskirt spun around and grinned, giving us a little wave before her friend dragged her off, giggling.

"Wait…they can see us?" I asked. "They can see *you*?"

Noah grinned at me over his shoulder. "Like I said, you walk with me, you get some perks. Women, food, booze… There is nothing off-limits for us, Cash. Not on my team."

"Where are we?" I spun a quick circle as I walked. "Why did we leave Lone Pine?"

"First rule. Avoid small towns," he said. "I do my best to avoid your reaper friends, and trust me when I say there are a whole hell of a lot of them out there. It's easier to find souls that slip through the cracks in the bigger cities. Stick around Podunk towns like yours, and you're asking for trouble."

"And why are we trying to find souls?"

He grinned at me over his shoulder. "You're about to find out."

We walked a few more blocks, the city air so humid I felt like I was suffocating. Despite my skin feeling like ice, sweat caused my dress shirt to stick to my frame. Noah stopped in front of an old abandoned warehouse. Windows were shattered and spiderwebs clung to the dusty brick.

"What are we doing here?"

Noah turned to face me, the look on his face deadly serious. "Do you know what happens to the souls that reapers take?"

I shrugged. From what Anaya had explained, there were several ways a soul could go.

"Some go to Heaven. Some go to Hell." He glanced back at the rotting building behind him and pressed his lips together. "But these kinds of souls. The escaped. The banished. They don't even get those options."

"Wait…" A streak of blue light zipped past one of the broken windows. "There are souls in there?"

Noah nodded solemnly. "Yes. And do you know what happens to them after the decay sets in? After they have wandered this place long enough for the darkness to take hold?"

A hiss drew our attention to the crumbling brick wall at the top of the steps. A shadow, dark as oil, slithered into a corner where it was met with three more just like it.

"Them," Noah said, motioning to the shadow. "That's what they turn into. I can save them from that. Take them to a place where they will never have to watch the darkness eat away at everything they once were. A place where they will never have to live in fear of becoming just another eternally hungry monster. Where I take them, they will never wander lost or alone. They will *never* become a shadow demon. I can give them peace."

Shadows had begun to gather around the base of the building. Drawn in by Noah and me or the buffet of souls inside, I wasn't sure. I did know that whatever Noah's intentions were with me, he needed to get those souls out of there unless they wanted to become dinner for some sick shadow demon.

"There are your choices, Cash," he went on. "You can help me give souls the peace they deserve, or you can aid in delivering them into an eternity of torment. That is *if* they even decide to keep you around for that. For all I know, your other option may very well be eternal death."

I nodded, feeling numb and confused. I didn't know what to think. Who to trust. I just knew in that moment, I wanted whatever option got those souls out of here before it was too late.

"Just think of how many we could help if we worked together," he said.

"What do we do?" I stumbled back a few steps as the shadows closed in tighter. Knowing they could hurt me was enough to kick my fear up a notch. Noah didn't budge, allowing them to surround him like a second skin. He glanced up to one of the windows where a set of luminescent eyes peered out at us before disappearing back into the dark.

"I'm going to take care of them," he said. "And you're going back home. You're not ready for this yet."

"But—"

Noah clamped his hand over my shoulder again and the words got caught like peanut butter stuck to the insides of my mouth. The ground vibrated under my feet and the world around me began to blur. Noah smiled at me and winked.

"No worries, friend," he said, sounding distorted and muffled. "I'll see you soon."

Darkness engulfed me in an instant and then the slap of cold tile exploded against my cheek. I opened my eyes, feeling like I'd gone ten rounds with a heavyweight and the heavyweight had won. Bile rose up my throat and I scrambled for the toilet to choke up the pills I'd swallowed earlier. When I collapsed back onto the floor, unable to move, my thoughts slowly came back in pieces. A few blue pills lay the in the coffee-colored grooves of the bathroom tile near the toilet. The bathroom. I was back in Emma's bathroom. I didn't have much time to contemplate what any of it meant, because by the time I took my next breath, a thick hazy darkness was pulling me back under again.

Chapter 14

Anaya

I couldn't believe I was about to do this—cross over to the one place I'd vowed never to go. Hell was only a fall away, and fear swam inside my chest at the thought that I might not make it back. But I had to go. I needed answers. I had to do this for Cash.

"Are you sure you want to do this?"

I let my gaze drop to the puddle of swirling screams that opened up in front of us, then looked back up to Easton. He looked worried. Like I should have been. The underworld wasn't a place for someone like me. To them I'd be a shiny new toy. Or even worse, dessert. I pushed the thoughts away.

"Yes," I said. "I need to see what I'm dealing with."

Easton hesitated, as if he were waiting for me to change my mind. I shut my eyes, still able to feel Cash's face buried in the hollow of my neck. His breath against my lips. If Balthazar wasn't going to give me answers, I'd go after them myself. I refused to deliver Cash into his hands not knowing what he would be used for.

I grabbed Easton by the hand and stepped up to the gateway to the underworld. He squeezed my fingers in his. They felt impossibly hot.

"You don't have to do this," he whispered one last time. "It's not too late to let him go."

"Just don't let me go," I said. Easton linked his arm through mine to get a better hold.

"I won't." Easton stepped forward, pulling me with him, and the world fell out from underneath us.

I was swallowed by screams. Awful, gut-wrenching screams that rattled my insides. The blackness was so dark it ate up my light, so I squeezed my eyes shut. Easton's arm remained twined with mine. He tightened his hold a little when he realized I was trembling, and suddenly heat exploded beneath me.

"Anaya," he said, shaking me. "We're here."

I opened my eyes and realized there was solid ground beneath my feet. Letting my arm fall away from his, I tested the rocks. They weren't very sturdy, toppling and tumbling around under the soles of my sandals. I tried to focus and change back into elemental form but nothing happened. I was solid. Easton must have seen the terror in my eyes.

"You can't do that here," he said. "Once you cross into this place, you're flesh."

"Why?"

Easton raised a brow. "Do you really have to ask?"

No, I didn't. This was a place fueled by torture. It would be a little hard to torture a soul in elemental form. I shuddered at the thought.

Easton strode forward and I followed, overwhelmed by the smell of ash and sulfur and Almighty only knows what else. Dark gray clouds that looked more like smoke than part of the sky rumbled with thunder overhead, but no rain fell. Easton stopped at the edge of a stony cliff. Rocks crumbled where the toes of his boots pressed against the ledge.

"That's it," he said and pointed ahead. "Umbria. Shadow demon central."

I placed my hand over my mouth to hold in the sound. It was unlike anything I'd ever seen. Unlike anything I'd ever wanted to see. Black frothy waves battered the cliff side. Enormous, hollow stones carved into skulls lined the places where the cliffs met the sea. And then there were the shadow demons. Everywhere. Scouring the cliffs. Diving into the sea only to emerge searing in flames. Screaming and writhing in agony as they scrambled up onto the thick ice around the base of each skull. I flinched when a swarm of crimson-colored butterflies fluttered between Easton and me before disappearing into one of the skull-eye caverns. I touched my shoulder where one of their wings had brushed my skin. Blood.

"Blooderflies." Easton grinned.

I gaped. "You find this funny?"

He shrugged. "You become numb to it all after a while."

I shook my head and wrapped my arms around myself. A bitter-tasting wind that burned my skin whipped my braids into my face.

"This must be Hell," I whispered.

Easton laughed. "This?" He folded his arms across his chest and looked out over the sea. "No. This is paradise compared to what's past those gates."

"Gates?"

Easton clasped his hand over my shoulder and turned me around. A mountain towered over the barren land of stone and ash. At the base were two blazing gates of fire. They stood open as a steady stream of souls marched in between them, each disappearing into the black billowing smoke inside. There were so many. My heart ached for each of them. They'd never know peace. All that awaited them was pain. I wrapped my arms around my waist. The wind carried screams and moans that swirled around me, tugging me toward the flames.

Easton's attention was elsewhere. He pointed to a boy standing at the edge of the cliff a few yards down from us.

"I've been doing some digging," Easton said. "There are only a few in existence. Balthazar has one of them. Your human will be another. And him."

"A shadow walker?" I breathed, staring at the boy on the cliff, whose blond hair blew in the heated breeze.

He pressed his lips into a tight line and nodded. "Balthazar never got his hands on that one. He never even had a chance. I'm not sure how, but the shadow demons caught him early."

I looked at the shadow walker. The turned-up collar of his gray coat framed a face made of angry angles and a furrowed brow. A group of at least ten screaming souls trailed behind him. He gripped the wrist of a girl, shimmering and brilliant against the darkness, and pulled her away from the rest. Her red hair looked like a flame waiting to be snuffed out. She wailed and tried to jerk away, but he held on to her as if it were as easy as breathing. He stared down into the waves where shadow demons crawled up the cliff. Across the water they began to melt out of the gaping eyes and nostrils of the skull caverns, moaning, screaming, hissing with the need to feed.

I stepped forward and reached for my scythe. Easton squeezed my shoulder to stop me.

"Don't," he said. "We're not here for that."

"We're just supposed to stand by and watch while that innocent soul is fed to the scum of the underworld?"

"Yes." Easton slid me a sideways glance. "That's exactly what we're going to do. Do you honestly think we could take on all of them?"

My gaze drifted beyond Easton to the shadow demons clambering up the cliff. There were thousands. They looked like a single entity, moving as one, all with the same goal in mind. Feed. I flinched when the blond boy shoved the girl over the cliff edge and released her wrist. She flailed for a heart-stopping moment, her pretty blue dress plastered against her like a second skin as the wind enveloped her. The shimmer around her exploded with panic as she disappeared into a sea of writhing black shadows, her screams blotted out by the hungry hisses and growls. The boy jumped out of the way as shadows clawed their way over the edge and pulled the wailing souls in one by one. The shadow walker watched for a moment, as if to make sure the deed was done, then turned to walk away. He stopped and met my gaze, his eyes cold and gray. Deluded by madness. He grimaced and looked to the sky.

"Stop!" I shouted taking a step forward, reaching out. Pleading. "You don't have to do this."

He hesitated, only for a moment, then whirled, his long gray coat spinning out around him, and disappeared.

My hands were shaking. My legs felt weak. I stumbled

back and Easton's warm chest stopped me. His hands settled on my shoulders.

"Why?" I whispered. "Why would anyone agree to do that?"

"They got their claws in him before he knew any better. Now it's him or them. Feed or be eaten," he said. "What do you think Cash will choose?"

I shook my head, feeling sick inside. Sick and helpless and cornered.

"Balthazar will be using him, too, you know?" Easton offered. "Maybe not to this extent, but that kid is never going to have the peace you want him to have."

Peace didn't seem to matter in that moment. I couldn't let this be an option. Yes, Balthazar would use him. But it had to be better than this. Anything had to be better than this.

I shook off Easton's hold on me and stared up into the sky. Drops of fire began to fall like rain from the billowing gray clouds above. Somewhere in the distance screams created a staccato rhythm that rang of pain and death. I closed my eyes, unable to look at this place another second.

"I'm going to make sure he doesn't have that choice."

Chapter 15

Cash

The guest bedroom of Emma's house was suffocating. Unfamiliar. The shadow demon perched on the end of the bed wasn't helping matters. At least it wasn't touching me. As long as it was just the one and it wasn't making a move, I could think. The only problem was, I wasn't sure I wanted to think.

I glanced out the window, at the starlight and steady glow of the moon filtering through the parted blinds. Vertical lines of twilight painted stripes across the green comforter. I couldn't help but wonder where Anaya was. Heaven? Hell? I sort of felt like I was both places when I was with her. Maybe she didn't know what I was. What happened when she found out? I let my gaze drift to the shadow demon sitting in the dark, a twisted gargoyle with holes for eyes. Its black mouth opened into what I could only guess was its version of a grin. It made me sick.

"Who did you used to be?" I said, searching for something, anything human left inside of the thing. I twisted the comforter in my fist and glanced around the otherwise empty room. "Your friends call in sick?"

It just stared at me, unmoving.

"What do you want?" I groaned, letting my head plop back onto the pillow.

"Youuuuu," it hissed into the dark.

I sat up on my elbows and watched it twitch and jerk beneath its oil-black skin. Hell to the no. Sleep was not happening tonight. I climbed out of bed and a breathed a sigh of relief when the thing didn't follow. It just watched me as I closed the door and padded silently down the hall to Em's room.

I stood outside her door for a minute. It wasn't her old room—the one I'd grown up in that always smelled like cinnamon and flowers—but it was her. And Emma was home, despite everything else happening. And I was so homesick, I could barely breathe. I twisted the knob and slipped into the dark, shutting the door behind me. Her mom waking up and finding me in here was the last thing I needed.

"Em," I whispered and stopped when a deeper voice cursed under his breath and the bedside lamp switched on. The room exploded with muted light. Emma sat up and pushed a mop of tousled blond hair out of her face and rubbed the sleep from her eyes.

"Cash?"

"Finn?" I said, feeling my brows hike up an inch or two.

Finn stood next to the bed in his navy-blue boxers. I followed his gaze down to my black boxers. When I looked back up, he was shoving his legs into a pair of worn-out jeans.

At least *I* was wearing a shirt. The lack of sleep must have been getting to me because it took me a minute to react. I finally held up my hands and laughed.

"Hey, I can leave," I said, placing my hand on the doorknob.

Emma rolled her eyes and sat back against her headboard. "It's not like that. We weren't—"

Finn raised a brow at her that kept the rest of the words in her mouth.

She turned eight shades of red and looked away. "We weren't doing anything. Finn can't sleep at—"

"Emma," Finn cut her off. She looked up at him, surprised, and he just shook his head. Now that I looked at him, I could see the damage that lack of sleep had left behind. The bruised look under his green eyes. The lines worn into his face. So Finn wasn't sleeping, either. I wondered what could possibly keep Death himself up at night.

Emma sighed and looked back to me, her sleepy blue eyes softening in a way I didn't deserve. Not after the way I'd been to her lately.

"Is something wrong?" she asked.

Yes. Everything. Instead of telling her the truth I just said, "I couldn't sleep."

"Join the club," Finn grumbled. He leaned over pressed a soft kiss to Emma's mouth. I couldn't watch it. It felt...wrong. I guess I always wanted her to find someone, but I never really thought it would happen. Emma was always so hell-bent on being alone. I still didn't know how to feel about this. How to accept it. How to share her with someone else.

"Think I can use the bathroom without waking the warden up?" I had a feeling he didn't really have to go, but I nodded.

"Use the one by my room so they think it's me," I offered.

"Just don't get caught." Em waved him off with a grin. "I'll be grounded for eternity if mom finds out about our slumber parties."

I nodded my thanks and Finn slipped out of the room.

Emma flung the right side of the covers open. "If you're gonna wake me up and chase my boyfriend off, then you're at least going to come talk to me," she mumbled into her pillow. I crawled in beside her and bunched the spare pillow up under my head so I could look at her. Dr. Farber was wrong about a lot of things, but he was right about this. I had alienated one of the most important people in my life. And I didn't want to lose Emma. Not before I had to.

"So?" she said through a yawn.

"I'm sorry."

Emma grinned and flipped a lock of hair off of my forehead. "I know. You couldn't have told me that tomorrow?"

"There's…" I swallowed. "One of those things in my room." I closed my eyes and breathed in a scent that didn't belong to Emma. That scent belonged to Finn. One more thing telling me that this wasn't where I belonged anymore. But I knew that before I came in here, didn't I? No matter what Noah said, the only place I felt like I belonged anymore was with Anaya. She could push me away all she wanted, but when she looked in my eyes, I could see it. She felt it, too.

"Did it follow you?" Her gaze flicked to the edge of the room and I shook my head. She relaxed into her pillow. "Good. You can sleep in here if you want to."

"No way. Your bed smells like a dude," I said.

She laughed that sleepy laugh that reminded me of when we were kids camping out in the backyard, hopped up on marshmallows and chocolate.

"How many times have I had to endure the various god-awful perfumes left behind in your room? Payback's hell, isn't it?"

She was right. She'd put up with my sleeping around for the past two years. Payback was exactly what I deserved. I didn't have a right to be jealous of Finn, or any other guy she decided to date. Not when I'd been throwing girls in her face for as long as I could remember.

She touched the spot between my brows and frowned. "Did you drink the green shake I made for you earlier?"

"You mean the sewage you put in a glass and gave to me?" I arched a brow. She slapped my arm and I grinned. "I drank it. I won't tell you it was delicious, because it wasn't. It kind of tasted like ass. But it did make me feel better," I lied.

"It's good for you," she said. "And you look pale. Do you want some juice? I looked up this recipe earlier that had carrots and apples, so it might taste a little bett—"

I grabbed her hand, cutting her off, and sighed. "Em, *stop*. You don't have to keep doing this. You don't have to take care of me."

Her bottom lip trembled and she squeezed my hand. "I don't know what else to do. I can't lose you, Cash."

I hated that this was happening to us. It took her so long to get over losing her dad. She still wasn't all the way there. What was going to happen when she lost me?

"You know what? I think I could go for some of that juice you were talking about." I was getting too good at lying to her. "I bet it will help." Anything to erase the hurt, helpless look in her eyes.

"Really?" Her face lit up.

"Yeah, really." I smiled and sat up, rubbing my hand around on her head to muss her hair even more than it already was.

"Hey!" She batted my hand away and ran her fingers through the tangles, cringing. "I've got knots now, jerk."

"That was the point." I sat on the edge of the bed and stared at the door. I didn't want to go back into that room. I couldn't. I didn't really want to stay here either, though, pretending that things were the way they used to be. Emma's hand settled on my shoulder.

"This is going to get better," she whispered. "I promise."

"I don't believe you," I whispered back through the ache in my throat. "I want to. But I can't."

"Then I'll believe enough for both of us."

The door creaked open and Finn crept in, settling on the end of the bed, looking uncomfortable. Thinking about what Noah said, I didn't know how to feel about him. I knew better than to mention Noah, but he didn't say I couldn't ask questions.

"Did you work for Balthazar?" I asked him. "Before all… *this*?"

He looked surprised, but answered. "Yes."

"Is he bad?

"What do you mean?" His brows pulled together.

"I mean, what is he capable of?" I asked. "Do you trust him?"

"He has the power of God at his fingertips, Cash," he said, a hard edge to his voice. "He's capable of anything. Do I think he's evil? No. Do I think he'd go unimaginable lengths to get something he wants? Yes."

I studied Finn's expression, trying to determine if he was telling the truth. As much as I wanted to trust him, Noah's warnings kept coming back to me, telling me not to trust anyone on this side. I knew I trusted Emma. But this guy who had swept in and stolen her out of my life…no. I wasn't ready to trust him yet. Not when he was hiding things from me. And even now, I felt like there was more to the story than he was telling. Maybe even more than he wanted Emma to know. The fact was, Noah was the only one being honest with me in this. He was the only one giving me enough information to make any kind of choice.

"And what do you think he'd do to get me?" I finally asked.

Finn frowned, something dark and secret flashing behind his eyes. "Why do you think he wants you?"

I stared out the window and shook my head, not really knowing how much to say. Em was sitting right here and that pretty much made my decision for me. "Just what if he did?"

"If he really wanted you?" Finn sighed. "He'd do anything."

The nighttime air felt good in my lungs. The rest of me didn't seem to like it so much. I pulled the scarf a little tighter around my neck and looked up and down the quiet street before stepping out onto the road. A chill pulsed through me, all the way through to my bones. My teeth chattered as I walked under the green glow of the streetlamp. My jaw felt sore. Everything did. My stomach clenched and ached from puking up the radioactive-looking shake and two glasses of carrot juice Em had forced down my throat. But I couldn't go back in that room. Not when I wasn't sure if I'd wake up. A warm glow spread out around me and a set of soft footsteps approached me from behind. Anaya.

"Hey," I said brokenly, then stopped to clear my throat.

"Wow," she said. "A real greeting. Don't you want to yell at me some more?"

I sighed and turned around to face her. She looked like her own little sun standing there in the night. So out of place in the dark around her.

"Don't you ever get tired of fighting with me?" I shoved my hands in my pockets and looked up at the moon so I wouldn't look at her. I wanted to look at her more than I should. And that scared me more than the rest of it combined.

"Yes," she said so soft I almost didn't hear her.

I gave in and let my eyes gravitate back to her. "So what are you doing out here, lighting up the whole neighborhood like a firefly?"

Anaya smiled. Just a small one, but it was enough make warmth bloom inside my chest.

"I've been out here for a while," she said, staring at the ground. "I figured out I don't have to be in the room with you. Most of them will stay away even if I'm just outside. I thought this might be…better."

She bit her bottom lip and looked away. She looked… hurt. She was Death, for Christ's sake. Was that even possible? Besides, I was the one who got rejected the last time we'd been together. I frowned at the uncomfortable twist in my gut seeing her this way and walked over to one of the big maple trees that lined the street. I pressed my back against the bark and slid down until I felt the cool grass beneath me.

I patted the ground beside me. "Sit down."

"Why?"

I closed my eyes. "Because I want to talk to you and I can't stand up anymore."

Anaya hesitated for a second, then crossed over and sat down beside me. So close our thighs almost touched. So close her warmth reached out and latched onto me, making me shiver.

"What happens to me after all of this, Anaya?" I asked. "After all of this is over, what are the chances that I get the kind of peace you give to all those souls you carry over? What are the chances that I'll get to be with my dad?"

She tensed beside me. I leaned my head back, letting the bark dig into my scalp, not wanting to acknowledge how much I wanted to touch her in that moment. Just how much I wanted the things she told me to be true. When Anaya didn't answer me, I cracked an eye open to look at her. Her golden eyes were closed but her lids still glowed. Her skin looked like bronzed silk under the moonlight.

"Anaya?"

Anaya averted her gaze so that I couldn't see her face and whispered, "Can't we talk about something else?"

My heart thudded painfully in my chest. Noah was right. This wasn't going to end well for me. I looked down the street to the dark windows of Emma's house where the shadows waited. I should have demanded answers from her, the kind Noah was willing to give, but I didn't. I didn't think I could stomach it if she lied to me.

"Does it hurt?" she whispered.

"A little," I said. "It's hard to breathe. And I'm so freaking cold. I'm tired of being cold all the damn time."

Anaya rested her hand on my wrist and I opened my eyes.

"Maybe I can help," she said. "If you'll let me."

I swallowed and nodded. Anything. I was starting to think I'd do anything this girl asked me to. Even with Noah's words ringing in my ears, I was helpless when it came to wanting her. I couldn't deny it anymore. I looked down at her hand. Hell, what did I have to lose? I was on my way out anyway.

Anaya sat on her knees and leaned in close to me. I couldn't help but notice her white dress bunched up around her thighs. I probably shouldn't have been looking. Probably.

"Cash?"

I tore my eyes away and Anaya was grinning. "Huh?"

She laughed and her whole face softened, taking the serious edge away, leaving just a pretty girl with gold eyes staring back at me, making my heart work a little faster. She reached up to cup my cheek with her palm and I flinched. Her fingers spread out, consuming the right side of my face.

"Just breathe," she whispered. I took a deep breath. Exhaled. Took another breath, focusing on the feel of her open palm against my cheek. That last breath stayed stuck in my lungs when the warmth began to flow. Slow. Steady. It poured from Anaya's palm and fingertips. Straight sunshine, seeping into my pores, setting my skull on fire. I closed my eyes and placed my hand over hers to hold it in place. God… *Oh my God*, she was so warm. So right. The heat spread down the left side of my neck. My heart pounded like it had been frozen for so long, it'd forgotten it could pump this fast. I needed more. Couldn't wait. Without thinking, I reached out and snaked an arm around Anaya's waist and jerked her on top of my lap. She gasped and the sound forced my eyes open.

"Cash…"

I pulled her other hand up and placed it on the right side of my face. My skin instantly began to thaw. So good. I'd almost forgotten what being warm felt like. Her thighs set my hips on fire, the flames spreading all the way down to my toes.

Heat. Peace. Pain. I could barely breathe through it all.

"Please," I said. "Please, don't let go."

She slid her palms down my neck until they rested over the pulse throbbing just under my skin. She shook her head. "I won't."

Anaya pressed her forehead to mine and our breaths clashed in the one inch of space between our mouths. It took everything in me not to kiss her. She'd made it clear she didn't want me, but it didn't stop me from wanting her. I shuddered, gripping her hips, not wanting to let go. Not ever wanting this moment to end. Slowly, every part of me warmed. The blood in my veins. The bones and skin that held me together. All of it blazed with Anaya's essence.

"Thank you," I whispered against her cheek.

Anaya nodded, causing my lips to brush against her face. "Just…try to sleep. You need it."

I needed a lot of things in that moment. But having her molded to me like this, her heat filling up my insides, my hands on the swell of her hips…let's just say sleep was pretty far down the list.

"Like this?" I asked.

Her thumbs rubbed up and down my throat, causing me to squeeze her tighter. "Yes. Like this."

"Why does this feel…"

"Right?"

"Yeah," I said.

Anaya sighed and shook her head. Her braids created a tent around our faces. She smelled like the sea. She smelled… familiar. "I don't know," she said. "I…don't know."

Chapter 16

Anaya

"Rise and shine."

Cash groaned, pushing his face back into the pillow, and I frowned. I was risking a lot being here today. Especially after last night. Cash falling asleep cocooned in my warmth, his hands touching places that hadn't known another in a thousand years…it had been too much. Too close. But it had helped him. He had actually slept all night. I hoped today would add to that progress as well as give me the answers that Balthazar refused to give.

"Sleeping," he grumbled into the cool pillowcase.

I crossed my arms over my chest. "You can sleep when you're dead. Get up."

"How about you crawl in here with me to keep me warm instead? Fair warning, though, I can't be held responsible for what happens once you've entered my lair."

I could see half of his grin against the pillow and I couldn't stop myself from smiling, wondering exactly what he would do if I took him up on his offer. I shouldn't have been wondering things like that. Not when I would eventually end up trading him in for a ticket back to Tarik. I touched a fingertip to the back of his neck and watched him bow up off the bed as heat singed down his spine. He inhaled, and stilled as if he expected me to go on. I pulled my hand away.

"Come on." I sat on the edge of his bed and the sheets began to warm. "I want to show you something. It will make you feel better."

Cash rolled over and squinted up at me.

"Don't you have souls to reap?"

"Not at the moment." I yanked the blankets off him. "But that's why we should hurry. My time is limited."

Cash grumbled something under his breath and stumbled off to the shower. When he emerged, his hair was wet and spiky and he was wearing a green T-shirt that said *Kiss me. I'm pretending to be Irish.*

He caught me reading it and grinned, scrubbing his fingers through his hair to shake the excess water out. "You wouldn't be the first girl this shirt has worked on. But you could be the first dead one if you wanted."

I rolled my eyes. "Let's go."

A half hour later, I'd directed him to a small lake on the edge of town. Thankfully, we were alone. The water looked like a smooth glass mirror, reflecting the bright-green pine trees that bordered the rocky beach. The sky above us was bright blue and perfect, lending just the right amount of heat to the breeze sifting between the trees. Cash climbed out of his Bronco and approached me from behind, hands shoved in his pockets. Probably to keep them warm.

"So, what are we doing out here at the butt-crack of dawn?"

"We're going to try something to make you feel a little better."

I rubbed my arms and stuck a toe into the water. After a few moments, steam started to roll off the surface. Cash peeked over my shoulder and blew out a breath. "You're doing that?"

I nodded and kicked my sandals off, then stepped into the water, wading out until it lapped up around my waist. The bottom of my white dress floated up so that it felt like I was sitting on a cloud. Little green and orange fish rippled around me, curiously inspecting my fingertips hovering on the surface. I smiled and smoothed my hand in a circle around me and they scattered. When I looked up, Cash was standing on the beach, mouth half-open, looking uncertain. A shadow swirled up the base of a tree behind him, but I don't think he noticed. He was too focused on me, the look in his eyes tearing down the walls I'd worked decades to build up around my heart.

"Are you coming in?" I waded out a few steps deeper and leaned my head back to dip my braids in the now-warm water. Cash made a stuttering sound that I assumed was supposed to be words, then started yanking at his clothes. First his T-shirt. Then his jeans and shoes. My breath caught in my throat and I looked away, feeling warmer than usual. Once he was down to his boxers, he stepped into the water and swam out to meet me.

He shuddered out a breath. Steam rolled off the water that splashed up against his well-defined chest. He dunked his head under the lake water and popped back up with a laugh. He smoothed his hair back as water streamed down his face. Seeing him like this, laughing and alive, started the unraveling in my stomach all over again. I fisted the sides of my dress in my hands to keep them from doing something I'd just regret later.

"It's so warm!" He swam close enough so that we were only inches apart. Steam rose up between us. "How did you do that?"

I shrugged and treaded water. "I thought of it last night. I always wondered how far the heat could go if I let it."

Cash's gaze lingered on my face and he swallowed. "Pretty far I guess."

"I always loved the water when I was alive," I said, my mind wandering back to dangerous memories of days spent on the edge of the sea.

"Oh yeah?" Cash grinned. "Where did you live?"

I let myself sink a few inches so that the water coated my lips, then pushed myself back up. "Egypt. Near the sea. Our home was so close, the sound of the waves breaking onto the shore used to put me to sleep at night."

"Lucky," Cash said. "The only thing I ever remember putting me to sleep when I was a kid was Mom and Dad arguing. Then after she was gone it was just quiet all the time. The quiet almost made me miss the arguing."

My chest ached thinking about him small and alone at night. "I'm sorry."

Cash floated on his back while his arms made lazy circles in the water as if he hadn't heard me. "I always wanted to live by the ocean. I've never lived anywhere but here, but when I went to the beach with Em a few times, it always felt like home. I never wanted to leave."

Ignoring the way our legs brushed together, I tipped my head back to stare into the sky, wondering how long it would take for me to get called away from this. I didn't want it to end. But I knew it had to. Which reminded me that we were here for more than just this.

"Do you feel better?" I asked.

Cash smiled. "Yeah. I finally feel…warm."

"Good." I held one of my hands out and he just looked at it, confused. "I want to try something. Touch my hand." It was risky giving him free rein over me like this, but if he were really a shadow walker, I had to know. I couldn't have his fate ending up like the boy on the cliff who saw no other way out. That wouldn't be Cash.

"Okay…" He reached his hand up and I exhaled, letting go of my skin, embracing my elemental form. My shimmer exploded across the water's surface so that it looked as if we were surrounded by a thousand floating stars. Cash raised a brow and I nodded for him to go on. Slowly, he placed his hand against mine. Palm to palm. Blue sparks ignited between our wet fingers and a current swept though me with a jolt. In an instant, every part of me was thrust into being whole again. I blinked away the dizzy sensation sweeping over me. I was corporeal. And all from his touch. Cash laced his fingers through mine and squeezed.

"Whoa…what was that?"

I stared at our entwined hands, the blue shimmer keeping them linked. It looked like a ribbon swirling through our fingers, binding us at the wrist. "It was you," I whispered.

Cash exhaled a shaky breath and pulled me into him by my hand. Inside me, alarms were sounding. Too close. Don't let him get too close. With his other hand, his fingers danced down my side before curling around my waist to hold me in place. Before I could stop myself, I arched into his touch and closed my eyes.

"Why do I always feel like I've got fireworks going off inside me when I have you this close?" he whispered.

I shook my head. I didn't trust myself to say anything in that moment. Not when I couldn't think through the heat and want building up inside me with each careful stroke of his fingers against my hip. Tilting my mouth up to his was all it would take to give in to what the rest of me wanted. As if he could read my thoughts, Cash pushed the wet braids back off my shoulder and slid his fingers under my chin.

"Anaya...you're shaking."

I bit my lip and kept my eyes shut. If I opened them...I'd give in. And then I would never forgive myself. "I know."

"Look at me," he whispered. "Please."

How did he have this power over me? Why did he have to be so wonderful and funny and familiar? His thumb brushed a droplet of water off of my lower lip and he lowered his face...

"Ouch!" Cash jerked his hand away from my hip as heat bubbled up between us. My scythe. I'd been so caught up I hadn't even felt it calling. I placed my palm over the blade, attempting to calm the tumultuous emotions tumbling around inside of me. Everything about this was wrong. Tarik was up there waiting for me and I was about to let Cash touch me in ways only Tarik ever had. What was wrong with me? I still intended to turn Cash over at the end of this, so what was I doing with him? How could I want him like this and still claim to love Tarik? I had to get out of there.

"I have to go." I took a step back in the water and Cash followed.

"Don't run away again, Anaya," he pleaded. "You can't keep taking off on me every time we're standing on the edge of something important."

His gaze clashed with mine and connection blazed between us. He wanted me. It didn't have anything to do with escape this time, and it was terrifying. It was terrifying because I wanted him, too. The only way to fight this was to get as far away from Cash as possible.

"I'm not running," I said. "I just…I have to go."

"Wait." His brown eyes got wide as he watched the air ripple around me like a puddle of liquid pearls. I turned away and shut my eyes. Stepped into the warmth. I felt Cash's fingers close around my wrist, and the feeling of his skin on mine was so shocking and right I couldn't move. I didn't even have time to think about what it meant. Not when the light and warmth already had me in its pull like this. Stars winked across my vision. They swirled and spun and shimmered until it was all a blur. A blur that faded into a dark, dank basement that swallowed that perfect glow down its throat.

It took me a moment to sort through the dark to find them, though it shouldn't have. These girls didn't belong in a place like this. Dirty and bound. Limp and awaiting salvation. I couldn't wait to give it to them. I stepped forward and stopped when someone behind me gasped. I turned around expecting to see their captor, or maybe a person who had been minutes too late to help them. What I didn't expect to see was Cash.

Chapter 17

Cash

Anaya's eyes opened wide, so gold they cut right through the dusty dark around us. I couldn't let go of her wrist. Couldn't move. What the *hell* had just happened? One minute I'd been trying to decide if the feeling in my gut meant that I wanted to kiss the girl in front of me and the next I'm in...I looked around. A basement?

"What happened?" Anaya whispered.

I looked back at her. She looked fierce with her badass blade dangling from her grip. But she looked afraid, too.

"How the hell am I supposed to know?" I hissed, the water dripping from my boxers creating a puddle beneath me. "What did you do?"

"I...I don't know," she said.

"How can you not know?"

A girl whimpered across the room and Anaya closed her

eyes. She jerked her wrist out of my grip. "Not now. We'll worry about this after."

"After what?"

Anaya rolled her eyes at me and turned around.

I looked over her shoulder at the pretty redheaded girl in the metal lawn chair behind her. Her hair hung in dirty strings around her face. A rag, I'm guessing that was probably used to wipe up the floor, was shoved in her mouth. Her hands and ankles were tied with a bright-orange rope. Another girl with pixie-cut blond hair who looked a few years older was tied up beside her, already lifeless. There was blood streaming down the girls' wrists and fingertips, pooling under the chairs. Jesus…where was it all coming from?

I raked my fingers through my wet hair and stepped back, waiting for my bones to shake right out of my skin. "Holy hell, Anaya… What is this? W-we need to call the cops or something."

"It's too late for that," she said.

Anaya ran her palm over the younger girl's coppery hair and cupped her face in her hand as she knelt down in front of her. She ran her thumb over the dirt and mascara smudges. She whispered something to her I couldn't hear. Whatever it was seemed to calm the girl, because in seconds she looked boneless, limp with relief. Anaya stepped back and pulled the blade above her head, her arms arched like wings. Every part of her lit up like a firefly.

"Whoa, what are you going to do with *that*?"

"What you wanted me to do to you," she said softly, her voice like a warning, then swung. The blade sliced through air and flesh and blood. I couldn't watch. Couldn't listen to the sound of whatever she was doing—an awful ripping sound. I slapped my hands over my ears and shut my eyes. When she went to work on the second girl I could still hear it, despite my efforts to block it all out. This was freaking crazy. I had to be hallucinating. Stuff like this just didn't exist.

"Cash?" Warm fingers pulled one of my hands away from my ear. I cracked my eyes open and swallowed the fear in my throat. My belly felt full of it. Anaya stared back at me, her pretty lips tugged down in a frown.

"Don't be afraid," she said.

"I'm not."

Anaya raised a brow and folded her arms across her chest. "Really?"

I cleared my throat and looked around Anaya at the girl standing behind her. She looked scared, with wide brown eyes, hollow freckled cheeks, and hair that curled around her chin like the tip of a flame. She looked all shimmery and red like a firework. The other girl kept her distance, her back pressed against the corner as she rubbed her hands up and down her tattooed arms.

"What are you gonna do with them?" I asked.

She smiled. "Take them home, of course."

Anaya looked over her shoulder and dropped her hands down to her sides, gifting me with a view of her head to toe. The girl didn't look like death. She looked like a freaking goddess. My fingers twitched at my side for a brush. I needed to paint her. I needed those eyes on my canvas. They wouldn't seem real until I did.

"Why are you looking at me like that?" Anaya asked. I blinked away the stupor and stood up.

"Are you going to get me back home?" I said, remembering my little trip with Noah. God, I hadn't been ready for another trip like that. Even now my head was throbbing and bile burned the back of my throat. "*Can* you even get me back?"

Anaya glanced back at the shivering girls behind her. "I think so. Just take my hand. We have to take care of them first."

I flexed my fingers in and out of a tight fist. She wanted me to touch her. Trust her. She was going to show me what happened to the souls that Noah didn't get. I wasn't sure if I was ready to see that now. I didn't want to tarnish this image of Anaya in my head. And if what Noah said was true, the image wouldn't just be tarnished. It would be decimated.

The dark basement around me that smelled like sweat and death, and the sound of heavy footsteps on the floorboards above our heads, told me I didn't really have a choice. I took a deep breath and laced my fingers through Anaya's smooth, delicate ones. Did she really touch death every day? Her hand didn't feel that way. It felt warm and comforting, like she'd just pulled it out of a bucket of sunshine. It made me feel like I never wanted to let go.

I watched her slip her free hand into the open palm of the soul beside her. I guess she was a soul. She had to be. Her body was still bound to that filthy chair. Dead. Still. Cold. Oddly enough she looked happy to leave it.

"This might be a little disorienting for you. Take a moment," Anaya whispered to me.

"I don't need a moment," I said as I stared at the pale, limp girl in the chair. I felt like I wanted to puke. "Just get me out of here."

Anaya shrugged. "Don't say I didn't warn you."

The air popped like static electricity and a nauseatingly familiar pressure enveloped me. The world spun into a bright blur and I groaned. My insides tuned to ice while my skin felt like it was on fire. *Not again.*

Just like before, it all stopped before my mind could process that everything had gone still around me. I opened my eyes and had to blink to make sure I was seeing correctly. It was like gray gauze had settled over my vision, but when I let go of Anaya's hand and spun around, it was clear I wasn't seeing things. That's just what this place was—nothing. Anaya stepped into me, wrapping her fingers around my biceps, and I immediately began to thaw under her touch.

"Where are we?"

She nodded to a set of pewter gates just visible through the haze. "The Inbetween. I have to drop one off before we take mine home."

"But I thought you said you only delivered to Heaven?"

She looked over her shoulder at the blond girl with the torn purple shirt and shook her head. "We're a little shorthanded right now. I was called for both of them this time. She wasn't on my list."

I nodded and followed her through the gates while she spoke in soft reassuring tones to the girls. Part of me wished I would have waited outside the gates, but the other part was morbidly curious about this place that didn't really fit in the mold of the afterlife I'd grown up learning about. Not to mention Noah—I didn't want to just listen to his warnings, I wanted to see for myself.

Anaya walked us just far enough through the gates to pass the girl off to what looked like another reaper. It was far enough. I clenched my fists, which were vibrating with energy. It was the souls. It had to be. There were so many, wandering aimlessly over the dull gray land. A boy maybe a year or two younger than me stumbled by us, mumbling to himself as if we didn't exist. His eyes were nearly black, the whites barely visible. Dark veins that reminded me of Noah stretched up his arms and neck. He stopped a few feet past us and twitched, then grabbed the sides of his head and began to moan.

My breath caught in my throat and I tripped over my own feet backing away. "What the hell is wrong with him?"

Anaya stepped to my side and didn't waste any time tugging me away, back toward the gates. Once she'd shoved me though, she stepped in front of me, blocking me from the redhead's view.

"I told you there was more than a Heaven and a Hell," she said.

"What happens to them?"

"Some are reborn. Some go to Heaven," she admitted, looking sad. "The rest decay before they get that chance. Those that do turn to shadows."

I thought about the empty black pits that once were that kid's eyes. There wasn't anything there. He was empty. It was just like Noah said. He'd been telling me the truth.

"And this is where Finn took souls?" I pointed to the gates, shaking. "That's what he did *willingly* for over seventy years? He dropped souls off so that they could...rot? Turn into shadow demons?"

"Why does it matter?" Anaya folded her arms across her chest, her brows pulled together in frustration.

"Why?" I exploded. "Because that asshole is sleeping with my best friend!"

Anaya's eyes blazed, and for once I didn't think it was desire. She stomped forward and stuck her finger into my chest. It practically sizzled against my skin.

"That *asshole* is the only reason Emma isn't a shadow demon," she seethed. "She was one of the doomed. She was wandering this wasteland, rotting, and he risked *everything* to save her, to give her the life she's living now so that she wouldn't transition into one of them."

I fought to control my breathing. It was coming so fast and hard that it hurt. My head was spinning. What was she saying? That Em...*my* Em was almost one of those things? How was that even possible? Emma was good. No, screw that. She was better than good. She was a saint compared to me. So how in the hell did she ever even end up in this place? What kind of fucked-up system was this? I didn't have to time to grill Anaya any further. She glared at me once more before latching onto my wrist and the soul patiently waiting on us. Without warning the world fell out from under me. Light exploded around us and reality went spinning off into space. When it was over Anaya released me and I collapsed to my knees.

"Damn it, Anaya!" I groaned just before I gripped my knees and heaved, watching my breakfast empty onto the crystal clear floor under my feet. As quickly as it landed it turned to vapor and seeped into a midnight-blue sky, turning to sparks once it hit the night. I watched in awe as my breath fogged over the glass-like surface. My stomach rolled again with the impossibility of what was happening. Anaya rested a hand on my shoulder and sighed.

"I told you—"

I glared up at her and shook her hand off. "Really? You want to give me an 'I told you so' *now*?"

She sighed and took a step back. "Never mind."

"Where are we now? Hell? Not really sure how it could get any worse than the last place."

Anaya looked at me, considering, then held her hand out into the air and closed her eyes. The white mist around us clung to her fingertips like puppet strings, just waiting for her to tell it where to go. A small smile lifted her lips as she smoothed her hand through the air like she was wiping a window clean. The fog parted, clouds scattering at her command. I couldn't catch my breath when I saw it. A pair of enormous gold gates the color of Anaya's eyes glowed against the ice-blue sky. Three big lavender-tinged moons bobbed around a collection of bright-white clouds. A lulling hum vibrated through the air, sounding far away. She looked back at me and the smile fell from her lips.

"You need to close your eyes and look away when I take her in," she said, reaching out behind her to grab the dead girl's hand. The girl didn't hesitate. Just bit her bottom lip and clutched on to Anaya like she'd never let go.

"What?" I scrambled to get to my feet. "Why?"

"My eyes look like this for a reason," she whispered. "That place…it wasn't meant for the living to see. The purity of that place will burn you…blind you."

"Is my…" I cleared my throat and stared at the gates. "My dad's in there. Isn't he?"

Anaya looked away and nodded.

"I want to see him." I stepped forward.

"No." Anaya pressed her open palm against my chest to stop me, and my eyes gravitated to the warm spot pooling beneath my shirt where her fingers lay. I had to take a deep breath to stop my heart from pounding so hard she'd be able to feel it.

I looked up at her, needing her to understand. "You owe me this. You could have warned me. Let me say good-bye…

and you didn't."

"You can't pass those gates to get to the ones you love any more than I can." She pulled her hand away. "We don't get the luxury of good-byes, Cash. It's part of death. Accept it."

The hurt in her voice told me we weren't just talking about my dad anymore. Who did Anaya have behind those gates? She walked away like she was dismissing me…like this didn't matter. I was getting so sick of her walking away from me every time I got close, every time things got hard that my blood boiled. I balled my hands into fists at my sides. "Don't walk away from me, Anaya!"

She didn't turn around. Just walked hand in hand with the soul in tow, her braids swinging behind her.

"Turn around," she said. "And this time don't say I didn't warn you."

The gates parted and light exploded from the gleaming space between them. I threw my arm over my eyes and turned away as the most perfect heat caressed my back. I felt dizzy. Not right. I sank down onto my knees, feeling like somebody had wrapped my brain in cotton. I don't know how long I sat like that. Time didn't seem to matter anymore. But after what seemed like an eternity, warm fingers whispered across my skin. Through my hair. Anaya's voice was soft in my ears, but I still couldn't open my eyes.

"Cash."

I reached out in front of me, trying to grab hold of something familiar.

"You're home," she said.

Something jolted me out of it. The cotton freed from around my thoughts. Rocks ground into my back and I sat up, looking around the empty beach. My clothes sat beside me and afternoon sunlight glinted off the lake water.

"Anaya," I said, voice cracking, not sounding anything like me. "Ana—" I stopped myself. I didn't have to say her name. The emptiness around me, the cold engulfing me—it was all I needed to feel to know that she was gone.

Chapter 18

Cash

The room was spinning. Or maybe it was just my head. I blinked away a few of the purple spots that dotted my vision and squinted at the chicken scratch Mr. Reynolds had scrawled across the chalkboard. He was saying something about…the Magna Carta? I didn't know. Hell, I didn't even care. I was starting to lose count of the sleepless nights. One night of sleep with Anaya was not going to make up for the rest. Especially when she'd proceeded to drag my ass all over the afterlife.

It had been two days and I still hadn't fully recovered. Last night had been yet another night of tossing and turning, listing to the hisses echo across my room in the dark. After a certain point, could you even call it insomnia anymore? Could a person die from a lack of sleep? It sure as hell felt like it. It felt like my insides were turning black like a banana you've left out on the counter too long. It felt like those little shadow bastards were killing me without even touching me. Like they were just waiting for that last puff of life to leave me.

I was waiting for it, too.

A wad of paper hit my shoulder and I flinched. I picked it up, fighting the urge to fling it back at someone, but stopped when I saw it was Finn. His eyebrows were all scrunched together. It's how he looked when he was worried about Em, which was pretty much all of the time. I definitely didn't need the guy looking at me like that. Especially after Anaya told me about him saving Em.

He lifted his hand and motioned to the paper. I unfolded it and laid it in my lap, so Mr. Reynolds wouldn't get a bug up his ass about us passing notes. To be completely honest, I didn't want anyone seeing me read his note. What were we, fifth-grade girls, for Christ's sake? I unfolded it and searched for a part that wasn't marked out.

> ~~You look like you need to talk~~
> ~~We can talk if you want after school.~~
>   We've seen each other in our underwear, so I think I'm allowed to say this now. You look like crap.
>
>   Finn

I rolled my eyes. Nice. *Very astute of you, Finn.* A wave of dizziness swept over me. Consuming me. Swallowing my vision for a few seconds before spewing it back up all tilted and off-balance. Every passing second it felt as if the life were draining out of me, or rather like it was being siphoned out of me. I felt something wet under my nose and swiped the back of my wrist over my face. It came back red. I stared at the crimson smear on my hand for a few seconds. I was so used to having paint on my hands, it took a few seconds to register that it was blood. Like the real kind. Not the make-believe kind I splattered across my canvases. This was real. It was happening. I was dying.

I pushed out of my seat, swearing under my breath. The blood had dripped all over me.

"Something wrong, Cash?" Mr. Reynolds stopped, looking me up and down, his eyes going wide with alarm. I could only imagine how I looked right now.

"Um… Just a nosebleed, I think." I held my palm over my face. "Can I go to the bathroom?"

"Of course." He tossed me the hall-pass key and I clutched it like a lifeline.

By the time I got to the bathroom I was freezing. Not the kind of chill that came with January—the kind that turns you to ice from the inside out instead of the other way around. But at least my nose had stopped bleeding. I filled my palms with water and doused my face. Watched the red water swirling in little circles around the silver drain before washing clear and disappearing into darkness. I half expected a shadow to crawl up through the hole. When one didn't, I waited for Anaya's face to show up in the reflection over my shoulder. I forced myself to ignore the little pulse of disappointment that throbbed in my chest when she didn't.

I looked at my pale reflection in the mirror and pushed the dripping black hair that was falling over my forehead back out of my face. Finn was right. I looked like shit. How much longer was this going to last? What was going to happen to me when it was over?

"You don't belong," a voice said from behind me.

I spun around, fear crawling up my throat. My heart pounded in my chest, reminding me it was still alive and fighting. Adrenaline surged through my veins. There was a boy behind me. Maybe twelve, thirteen. His skin was too white. Purple bruises painted the hollow of his cheeks and under his eyes. A gaping gash split the side of his face. He looked like a character in a Tim Burton film.

"What do you want?"

He stepped forward and a dull shimmer rippled in the air around him.

"What are you?" He cocked his head to the side and shoved his hands into the pockets of his jean shorts.

I couldn't hold the laugh in. That laugh was the last of my sanity leaving my body, crawling across my lips to escape. "Me? What the hell are you?"

"You don't belong," he said again. His voice sounded like static. He sounded like a dream. Or more like a nightmare. Like I needed more of those while I was awake. I pinched myself just to make sure I wasn't passed out at my desk in Mr. Reynolds's class. God, what I wouldn't give to wake up in a puddle of my own drool on a cold desktop right now, but I didn't. This was as awake as I was going to get.

"I...I don't belong where?" I asked, pressing my tailbone against the sink. "What the hell are you talking about?"

The boy looked sad. His lips looked all blue, cracked and pulled down at the corners. He started to shake. "Not him," he whispered.

"What? What is it?"

His frightened gaze was glued to the spot over my shoulder as he stumbled back. Someone sighed behind me and I turned around to find Noah. His ash-blond hair was flipped down over one eye and a feral scowl curled his lips.

"Great." He leaned back against the row of sinks, shoving his hands into his coat pockets. "Now I'm going to have to chase him. Thanks for that."

I looked over my shoulder to find the kid, and he...was gone. Just like that. The air was empty and cold. Absent of anything but me, Noah, and the stale scent of cigarette smoke and Pine-Sol.

"Why would you chase him?" I asked, stepping away to put some distance between us, thinking about the terrified look on that kid's face the second he laid eyes on Noah. It was like he'd seen him before. The soul Anaya had taken hadn't looked like that. If anything she'd looked...grateful. Even the one being shipped off to the Inbetween had looked confused more than anything, but not scared.

He folded his arms across his chest and his sleeves rode up enough to see a spiderwebbed map of black veins.

"If you're here to help him, shouldn't he be chasing *you*?"

"She's getting to you, isn't she?" he said. "You get that you're falling right into the trap they have set for you, right? She lets you feel her up, tells you a few lies, and now you're second-guessing everything I'm offering you."

I clenched my fist and my knuckles cracked. I wanted to lay him out, but he was right. Anaya was getting to me. Hell, she was more than getting to me. She was consuming me.

"I'm not falling in anybody's trap," I snapped. "I'm just confused, all right?"

Noah nodded and kicked the back of his boot against the wall to knock what looked like a fine layer of ash off it. "You have questions? Ask them. I'm not here to lie to you, Cash. I'm here to help. I wish you could trust that."

There was something inside me telling me that trusting him was the last thing I should do, a whisper that was getting louder every minute I spent with Anaya. But was it enough? Anaya was the one keeping something from me. I could see it in her eyes, a painful regret that took over every time I asked her about my future. Every time I touched her. I couldn't stop myself from wanting her. That went beyond anything I could control, but trusting her? That was something else.

Noah, on the other hand, wasn't holding anything back. He was an open book. If he had the answer he would give it. And whether I wanted to admit it or not, we were the same. I may not know how either of us got to be this way, but here we were, like two halves of a whole. Even now, standing a few feet from him, something dark pulsed in my veins, turning the blood almost black under my dying skin. I wanted to believe that Noah was good because that meant I'd be good, too, but I didn't know anymore.

"I saw her take a soul," I admitted, looking up from my wrist. "It didn't look how you described it. It was messed up, but it wasn't all bad. There was another side."

Noah laughed. "Did she show you what they do to the lost? The ones like I take? The ones they let rot until they are nothing more than a starving shadow with absolutely no recollection of who they once were?"

I shook my head, not knowing what to trust or what to believe. There was more than one side to this.

"Yes, there is another side. A better side. But do you actually think that you are going to get to have any part of that perfect, pretty peace you saw?" He laughed. "No. If Balthazar doesn't destroy you once you're free from that body—and that's a big *if*—you won't be delivering happy souls to some peaceful, perfect existence. You'll be turning them into *that*."

Noah pointed to a shadow that was swirling out from under a bathroom stall, a sickening hiss seeping from its belly. Before I could look away, three more followed, churning the fear in my gut until it bubbled up into my throat.

"Every soul you touch will rot," he whispered, stepping closer. "You will be hated. You will be feared. You will be the very thing inside of you that you're trying to fight. Don't let one pretty face trap you into that kind of existence."

I didn't want to believe what he was telling me, but it made sense. Why the fuck did this have to be so hard? The feelings inside me that were building for Anaya, the connection that had nothing to do with attraction, it was twisting everything that should have been clear.

"I'm offering you friendship," Noah said, sounding deflated. "I'm offering you a kind of immortality they will deny you. The chance to do something good in this world."

Noah clasped a hand over my shoulder and the chill from his skin seeped through my T-shirt, bringing the brigade of goose bumps on my arms to attention. If it was possible, he was even colder than me. A bell rattled out in the hall, starting the countdown until students would start to rush through that door.

"Just think about it," he said. "I'll see you soon."

The touch on my shoulder disappeared and when I turned around, Noah was nowhere to be seen. Once again he'd left me not knowing what the hell to think or believe. Out of the corner of my eye, a flash of blue hovered behind an open bathroom stall.

"Hello?"

The kid who had taken off when Noah showed up crept out from behind its edge. "Is he gone?"

I nodded, not really knowing what to make of this kid who was obviously dead, or the fact that I was having a conversation with him. "Why are you afraid of him? He just wants to help you."

The boy vigorously shook his head and wrapped his little arms around his middle. "The souls that go with him never come back," he whispered. "He takes them down there."

I knelt down in front of him, not wanting him to be afraid of me. I needed him to go on. "Down where?"

His gaze drifted to the shadow demons that were now hissing and snapping behind me. The kid backed up and they inched closer. "Down to them," he finally answered before disappearing through the wall like a puff of blue smoke. The three shadows behind me zipped past in a black blur as they chased after him and I tripped over my own feet trying to stand up.

What had he meant that Noah took them down to them? As in, he delivered them to the shadow demons? That didn't make any sense. He couldn't know what he was talking about, could he? Maybe he had Noah confused with a reaper. You couldn't really tell the difference after all.

Right?

Fuck, I didn't need this. I needed to know who to trust. Maybe I couldn't trust any of them. Maybe I really was alone in this. I grabbed the sides of my head to try to make the thoughts slow down. They wouldn't. They just spun Tilt-A-Whirl circles in my skull over and over until they crept down my aching throat. Into my clenched fists.

Everything went black. A blinding, screaming black.

And when it was light again I was standing in front of a broken mirror. My fist was bleeding. My cheeks were wet. But at least the thoughts were gone. Everything in my brain was horribly blank, replaced by a hurt that wouldn't go away.

The bathroom door swung open and I turned away from the broken reflection of my face in the mirror. Finn stood gawking at me, his green eyes sweeping over the bathroom like he was looking for who could have done this. Like he couldn't believe that I'd done it myself.

"What happened?" he asked, walking over. Slow. Cautious. He pulled the gray sweatshirt he was wearing over his head and wrapped one of the sleeves around my trembling, bloody hand.

I didn't know what to say to him. I still wasn't ready to tell him about Noah, not when I didn't know whose side he was really on—or what side I needed to be on, for that matter. What I did know was that Finn was keeping something from all of us and I wanted to know what it was. Seeing the hard look in his eyes as he talked about Balthazar that night in Emma's room was enough to tell me that he knew exactly what this Balthazar guy was capable of.

Swallowing a lump of pride down my throat, I stared at my replacement. The guy who had everything I used to have. Emma. A life. A future. I wanted to hate him for it, but I couldn't. Not when him having all of those things meant Emma being happy. Even if that meant I didn't get to have them anymore. Finn took another hesitant step forward and laid a hand on my shoulder. I wiped my bloody hands on my jeans and shuddered out a breath full of want and loss and fear. Then I said three words I never thought I'd say to Finn.

"I need help."

Chapter 19

Anaya

I stood outside Cash's house in the sunshine. It felt right, here in the light. In the sun. Its rays clung to me, caressed my hair and skin, whispering goodness into my ears. I missed when this was all there was. Before I made this mistake that I'd give anything in the world to take away. I could feel Cash inside the house, his hurt and uncertainty tugging on the invisible threads between us. I finally gave in and stepped through the warm, wooden front door and into the empty hall.

There weren't any voices to follow. Just the sound of memories being packed away into boxes. The rip and press of tape sealing it all away. I found them in the den. Cash sat in a pile of books. Surprisingly, Finn was with him, taping up a box, as if he belonged there.

"You're sure you want to pack all of this away? Now?" Finn said, standing up. "We could wait, you know, until…"

Cash looked up when he trailed off. "Until what?" he said. "He's not coming back. You should know that better than anybody." He tossed a book into a box with a little more force than necessary and sighed. "Look, you said you wanted to help. So stop treating me like a fucking fragile little girl and help me already."

Finn nodded and unfolded another cardboard box for a pile of jackets that were stacked on the big oak coffee table.

"Besides." Cash ran his hand over the cover of a thick red leather-bound book. "I don't want Em or her mom to have to deal with any of this when…"

"I told you nothing's going to happen to you," Finn said, voice tense. "We will think of something. So just stop talking like that, okay?" His shoulders sagged with the weight of the lie. Cash just shook his head and opened another book.

I took a deep breath, feeling myself fuse together cell by cell until the warmth was so intense it consumed me.

When the room came into focus, Cash was staring at me, jaw clenched, fingers stretched tight and white around the binding of a book. I'd left things badly between us. Refusing to let him see his father, then disappearing and leaving him alone with no explanation. I touched the spot on my chest that ached with guilt.

"I need to talk to him." I spoke to Finn but didn't take my eyes off this boy who sat in front of me. His eyes trained on my face, filling me with something so familiar it stole what little breath I was allowing myself to take.

"No." Cash turned his attention to Finn, lips pressed together as a look of understanding passed between them. "I want him to stay."

I sighed. "Suit yourself."

Finn settled onto the arm of a shiny brown leather sofa. Cash stayed where he was, huddled in a pile of books that smelled like his father.

He shook his head, gaze fixed on his hands. There was a battle going on inside him. I could feel it. See it written all over his face.

"What's going on?" I sank down onto the floor in front of him. "Did something happen?"

"Do you know what I am, Anaya?" His brown eyes connected with mine and they looked so tired. "Because I do."

Shock fizzled through me. "H-how do you know?"

"How long have you known?" Cash growled. "How long have you known that I'm a shadow walker and how long have you been keeping it from me?"

Finn looked confused, but I could only shake my head. "I haven't known the whole time," I said in a panic. "I spoke to Easton and he…he showed me. I swear to you, Cash, I had no idea until a few days ago. I wasn't even certain until the lake, after you crossed over with me."

How did he know? Who had he been talking to who would have known, because I was certain he hadn't found this in one of his books. This kind of information wasn't even widely known in the afterlife, let alone the living world.

"Did you know?" I asked Finn, who was staring at Cash in disbelief.

"No way," he said. "How the hell would I have known?"

"Tell me what it means," Cash said.

"You're a soul caught between life and death. It's the only thing that would explain you being able to cross between worlds and force me into corporeality."

"And why, exactly, does that make me so important?"

I shuddered, remembering the boy shoving souls over the cliff in Umbria. "It means you can be used to collect lost souls. At least that's most likely what Balthazar wants you for. As for the shadow demons…"

"Yeah, I know," he sneered. "I'm up next on the buffet line. I get it."

"Cash," I stopped him. "No. They wouldn't want you for that. I mean they would, but you're too valuable. They'd use you as a poacher, rounding up lost souls to deliver to the weaker ones below."

Cash's brows furrowed together and he shook his head mechanically. "No…he would have told me," he whispered.

"Who would have told you?"

He ignored me, wringing his hands to ease the way they were shaking, if I had to guess. "Don't lie to me about this, Anaya. If you're just trying to scare me, to get me to side with you—"

"I've seen it," I said.

Cash gritted his teeth and looked away. Someone had gotten to him. But who? And what kind of lies were they filling his head with?

"How did I become like this? Why me?"

I swallowed, uselessly. "When I brought you back. Didn't take you. It must have triggered it. I thought…" I stopped and looked at him, bundled up in a black sweater, a burgundy scarf wrapped tight around his neck. A knit cap shoved over his raven-black hair even though it was obviously a warm spring day. His skin was pale. His eyes tired and dark. He didn't look alive. He looked like Easton had said. Straddling the line.

"I'm sorry," I choked out. "This shouldn't have happened. I didn't…I didn't realize how old your soul was. I didn't realize what you were or why Balthazar wanted you."

"How old my soul is? What's that supposed to mean?"

Finn stared at Cash with a little wonder in his eyes. "It means you've lived before. Lots of times. This isn't your first life."

Cash closed his eyes and shook his head. "No....*no*." He said through gritted teeth. "If I'd been through all this more than once, don't you think I'd remember something? Don't you think I'd be a little better at it by now?"

"No," I said. "You wouldn't remember. It doesn't work that way."

"But Em remembers a little. From before."

"That's only because I helped her see."

"Then help *me* see!" Cash stared at me, hope glinting in his eyes. "Help me see, so this feels real. So I don't feel like a complete nutcase."

I couldn't show him. I couldn't allow myself to see his past. I was already crossing too many lines, forming bonds that were going leave me in shreds when this was done. "I can't. I won't."

Cash buried his face in his hands and trembled. The ends of his burgundy scarf dangled over his knees. I looked up at Finn and he nodded. He didn't have to hear the words. He knew. At least we still had that between us. He stood and patted Cash on the shoulder, then walked out of the room. I soaked in the silence until I heard an engine roar to life outside.

Slowly, he pulled his face out of his hands. His dark eyes burned me. His lips, pressed into a hard line, broke me. I reached out and placed my hand over his. He just stared at it for a minute, but after a few shallow breaths he finally laced his fingers through mine. I knew he was only touching me for the warmth, but I'd take it.

"So is this the only reason you're here?" he asked, refusing to look at me. "To you, I'm just another soul to deliver. Only I don't get to go where the rest of your souls go. I get hand-delivered to your boss."

"It's not like that," I whispered. "I wanted to take you the first time I saw you. I wanted to give you that salvation. I still want to. You have no idea what this is doing to me, to see you like this. I wish I had a choice."

He shook his head like he didn't believe me.

"Cash?" I asked, softly. "How did you find out? Who told you? If someone has been speaking to you, I need to know."

He stared at our intertwined fingers, quiet, as his thumb traced circles over my wrist. "What does he have on *you*, Anaya?"

He lifted his eyes and my stomach sank with a sick feeling. Did he know this too? He couldn't. Nobody knew but Balthazar and me.

"If you don't want to be a part of whatever is happening to me, then what is Balthazar doing to make you do it?" he asked. "I know that babysitting a human probably isn't in your job description. So I'm asking again. What are you getting out of this?"

Guilt stabbed at my insides, screaming, *tell him, tell him!* I couldn't. I couldn't tell him that I'd agreed to deny him everlasting peace so I could be with my family, with Tarik, again. I pulled my fingers from his. I didn't deserve his touch. This wasn't right. God…this was so wrong. What was I doing?

Cash studied my face for a moment, no doubt seeing the lie before it even formed on my lips. He grimaced and pushed to his feet. The connection between us pulsed with pain and regret. "That's fine. Keep your secrets, Anaya. I'll keep mine, too."

Chapter 20

Cash

"Happy birthday," Emma said in a singsong voice as I opened the door. She leaned on the doorframe, holding a plate with an oversize piece of birthday cake sitting on it like a work of art. A little fondant replica of me stood atop the cake, with a T-shirt on that said *I'm kind of big deal.* I laughed and dropped the box I was holding on the floor.

"He's edible, too," she said when she saw me squinting to read the little Cash's T-shirt.

"Just like in real life." I grinned.

"Ha, ha." Emma raised a brow. "So, are you going to let me in or what?"

"You didn't have to do that."

"Oh yeah?" She breezed past me. "Since when? Because this is the first year I can remember that you didn't put in a request for the flavor you wanted three months ahead."

"Things are different now."

Now I was on my way out. I sat down on the bed with Emma and took the fork she handed me. She took the first bite and laughed around a mouthful of red velvet cake.

"You're right," she finally said. "Now you're actually old enough to do all of the illegal crap you do for fun."

"Well, thanks for pointing that out," I said. "Now it won't be as fun."

I gave up a laugh and took a bite of cake, wishing I could really taste it like I used to. It was probably going to be my last birthday cake, after all. But food just didn't taste good anymore. Everything left a stale taste on my tongue. Made my stomach churn with the want to reject it. I didn't let her know that, though. Instead I shoveled a second bite in. Em and I didn't have many of these moments left. I wasn't going to ruin it.

"How'd you know this kind was my favorite?" I said.

"Do I look like an amateur?"

"No." I smiled. "No, you do not." No. She looked like the girl I remembered before her dad died. Full of life and love and hope. She wasn't that girl hiding in the shadows anymore, snapping pictures of a life she refused to live. She was happy. And that made me pretty damn happy. The look on her face in this moment…this was why I couldn't hate Finn. He gave this to her when I couldn't. I hoped I'd get to keep these memories in the afterlife, whatever that might be. Because I wanted to remember her just like this.

"I got you a present, too." She tossed me a wrapped package. I grinned at her and tore it open and…laughed. I held up the black T-shirt. It said *I see dead people.*

"I think you know me a little too well," I said. "I love it,

Em. It's perfect."

Emma set her fork on the plate and sighed, her eyes lingering on the packed boxes in the corner of the room. I could hear the disapproval in her quiet sigh and she brushed crumbs off her lap.

"You're still going to leave, even after I made you cake," she said.

"Yep." I sat my fork down too and watched tears gather in the corners of her blue eyes. She wiped them away before they could escape.

"You don't have to," she said.

"I know I don't," I said. "But I need to." I couldn't have Emma seeing me like this anymore. I'd already made Finn promise not to let her see me when I got bad. And it was getting worse. Every minute that passed it was getting worse. And I didn't want these little shadow bastards near her. She'd already gone through a hell all her own. No way was I dragging her into mine.

"I'm eighteen, Em. And the house is in my name now that the lawyers are done." I kicked her tennis shoe with my boot. "There's no point in putting your mom and Parker out when I've got my own place."

Emma stood up and stared out the window. "This is crazy. *Your own place.* That doesn't even sound right."

"It's not like I have the luxury of being a kid anymore."

She sighed. "I know that."

"Then what's wrong?"

I stood next to Emma, wondering if this would be the last time. If it wasn't this moment, it would be one very soon. Every ache that throbbed in my body was a big countdown clock to my departure. Did she know it? Could she feel it, too?

"We shouldn't be talking about this right now. We should be talking about what skank you're going to take to prom, or which stupid Steven Seagal movie you plan on torturing me with this weekend, or that art festival you promised to take me to this summer. Not this…"

"Em—"

"I don't want you to leave me," she whispered. "I feel like you're giving up. I feel like I should be doing something, but I don't know what to do."

The double meaning in her words created a lump in my throat. Emma had been such a big part of me for so long, I wasn't sure what would happen to either of us when you took that other half away. I didn't want to know.

"I'm not giving up," I said. "I don't really have a choice. And this is *not* on you, Em. There is nothing you can do. There's not even anything I can do anymore."

I wrapped my arm around her shoulders. They felt fragile even under my weak grasp. Everything about this moment felt fragile. The ocean of unspoken words between us. The memories colliding and collapsing inside both of our heads.

The way my vision was going black around the edges. *Wait…*

I stumbled back and grabbed on to the white wicker dresser behind me when my legs started to give. The room tilted off-balance. Out of the corner of my eye a shadow demon perched on the nightstand, grinning. No…

"Cash!" Emma's hands were on me in a second, but I didn't need her. I needed Anaya. Was this it? *God please no… please don't let this be it. Anaya needs to be here.*

I wasn't sure when I'd made that decision, but in that moment, I knew without a doubt that it was her I wanted to see on the other side of this. Not Noah. Not a horde of shadow demons. Just Anaya and all her light, even if she was hiding something from me. Good or bad, I felt like I belonged with her. She felt like home.

"Not yet, Cash," Emma's words sounded choked. "Not now, damn it."

I vaguely noticed her fumbling with her phone to dial 911. Pain flared in my insides. The darkness spread across my vision, blocking out that last little bit of light I was clinging to.

This was it.

Well…shit. Happy birthday to me.

Chapter 21

Anaya

Watching Cash sleep was peaceful.

Watching Cash sleep knowing he might not wake up was torture.

I could have lost him. If he had died, the shadows would have… I didn't even want to imagine what they would've done to him. What they would have used him for. I felt sick just thinking about it. I walked through the dim hospital room, lit by monitors and the one fluorescent light that glowed above Cash's bed, and stopped at the door. I wanted to go back and crawl in beside him to keep him warm, but Emma's voice dueling with the doctors on the other side of the door stopped me.

"What do you mean you don't know what's wrong with him?" she said. "This is a hospital. You're a doctor!"

"You don't understand." The doctor's voice lowered as if

he were trying to coax hers to do the same. "His organs are failing. His lungs are filling with fluid. No human should still be alive and be at the body temperature he's holding. We know what's happening. We just can't figure out why. We're still waiting on some test results to come back, so you just need to be patient. Stay calm for your friend."

Finn murmured something to Emma I couldn't quite hear through the door. I wanted to step through, but I couldn't leave Cash. Not even for a second. I could smell the shadow demons lurking just beneath the surface. Hungry. Waiting.

"In the meantime…is there anyone you can call?" the doctor said. "Any family that might want to say good-bye?"

Emma made a choked sound and Finn's voice broke in.

"How long?"

"It's hard to tell," the doctor's gruff voice said. "Nothing about his condition is anything we've ever seen. And he won't allow us to operate. I'd say we're looking at a week. Maybe two if things continue to progress the way they are now."

Emma burst into sobs and I stepped away from the door. This didn't have to be happening. This could've happened quickly. He could be at peace right now. This was all because of me. How…*how* did I let this happen? How could I have been so selfish? I may be earning my way back to Tarik, but would I be the girl he remembered when I got there? Would I still feel the same when it was him standing in front of me and not Cash?

"You're late," Cash croaked from behind me. I turned around, but he didn't try to get up. He just lay there, buried in the hollow of a blanket.

"I know." He patted the spot beside him. I sank down onto the edge of the bed and did my best to produce a smile for him. "Happy birthday."

He rolled his eyes and pushed the hair off his forehead. "Yeah, real happy. I thought for sure this was it this time."

Cash stared at the door, lips pressed together, listening to Emma lose it in every way outside the door.

"I don't want her here," he said. "I don't want her to see me like this. She's already been through enough."

"I don't think you're going to get rid of her," I said. "Besides, she's stronger than you give her credit for. And she's got Finn now. She won't be alone."

Cash nodded and closed his eyes.

"You look a little better," I said, studying the hard edge of his jaw under the fluorescent light. They had taken the piercings out of his eyebrow and ears. I was guessing the one in his mouth was gone, too. Lying there in nothing but a plain hospital gown, he looked stripped of everything Cash.

He grinned, eyes closed. "Liar."

I placed my hand over his and a shiver vibrated through him. I started to pull away, but he reached over and grabbed my hand to hold it in place. "It feels nice."

I let my eyelids slide shut, ignoring the warmth starting to burn at my hip. The call of someone waiting for me to give them what I'd refused to give him.

"Anaya," Cash said. When I opened my eyes, his gaze was fixed on my face, his dark eyes begging for something unspoken. "I need you to show me."

"Show you what?"

"Everything," he said. "Something. Don't send me to the other side not knowing who I was. I want to know. I have a right to know."

"Cash…"

"I know you can. You just don't want to."

I sighed and stroked the back of his wrist with my fingers. "What if you don't like what you see? You have enough reasons to hate me, Cash. I'd rather not add another."

"I don't hate you," he said, sitting up. "Is that what you think? That I hate you for this?"

I ignored his eyes trying to catch mine and instead focused on a table across the room. Condensation slipped down the side of a pink plastic pitcher of water. "You should."

Cash grabbed my chin and forced me to face him. "I don't."

He took a deep breath, his chest swelling, rising with life. "And I won't hate you for whatever I see. No matter what it is. I swear."

I was on the verge of breaking. Of giving him what he wanted. How could I deny him? He deserved everything from me after what I'd stolen. I looked into Cash's wide brown eyes. So kind. A soul that kind couldn't have anything dark enough to be afraid of.

"What if I close my eyes and wake up as something else? Someone else?" he said, squeezing my warm fingers with his cold ones. "Show me. Please."

A beat of silence passed between us and I nodded.

"Okay," I said. "I'll show you. But I have no idea how many lives you've lived. I have no control over what you'll see. It's likely you'll see something that impacted you. Scarred your soul, so to speak. I can't promise that memory will be good."

"I don't care. I'll take it."

I leaned into Cash as he lay back onto the pillows. He was shaking. If I were him, I would have been shaking, too, with the impossibility of what I was about to show him. My palm was warm. Glowing with power. I clasped it over his forehead and he closed his eyes, shuddering out a breath.

"Are you ready?" I whispered.

Cash nodded.

"Just breathe," I said, just before we fell right into the pulsing heart of a memory a thousand years old.

I sat on the beach. Sand sifting through my fingers. My toes. A breeze ruffled my braids and the hem of my dress. The sun, just an echo from the day, was fading fast, sinking into the depths of the horizon behind the sea. I heard footsteps behind me and smiled.

"I've been looking everywhere for you," Tarik said. The wind caught his dark curls and tossed them into his eyes. He pushed them away and grinned down at me. "We're going to be late."

"I've been right here." I looked up at him, losing my breath. The chiseled line of his jaw. The way the sun reflected off his skin, making it a shade darker than honey. No wonder the other girls in the village hated me. That heartbreakingly beautiful smile was for me. Only me. I held out my hand and let Tarik help me up. He brushed the sand from my skirt, businesslike, efficient. I still flushed and felt a rush of heat flow through me. I laced my fingers through his and we headed into the village. The smell of warm baked bread wafted through windows. The cobblestone street was spotted with shiny slick dots of moisture. Tarik squinted up at the dark sky and sighed.

"I think we're about to get wet."

As the words left his lips, the rain started to pour. Sheets of it created a wet, blurry curtain between us and the world. I held up my hands and laughed. The water streamed down my skin, pounded against my open palms, and I loved it. Loved the sound of Tarik laughing beside me. His black hair plastered to his scalp. His white shirt becoming one with his skin. He yanked me under the ledge of a building and pressed me as close to the clay wall as he could get me.

"We're missing dinner," I said through a smile. Water from his chin dripped onto my nose. "Your mother will be furious."

He smiled and pushed the wet braids back from my face, securing them behind my neck.

"I think this might be worth her wrath," he whispered. Tarik closed the space between us and kissed me. He kissed me like he was dying and I was feeding him the oxygen he needed to survive. I'd never in my life been as consumed by another person as I was in that moment. I'd never been as in love as I'd been in that moment. Tarik's hands slid up the backs of my thighs and lifted me against the wall. The rain beat against his back as he pressed into me, sheltering me from the storm.

"I don't want to wait anymore," he whispered into my mouth. "I want you. I want to feel the way I feel right now, forever." He stopped to claim another kiss from my mouth and broke away when I whimpered.

"I love you, Anaya," he said, burning me with his gaze. Water streaming down his face. "Say you love me as much as I love you."

"I love you." I barely got the words out before his lips crushed against mine, stealing the breath in my mouth. He tasted like rain. He tasted like what I wanted the rest of my life to taste like. And I knew in that moment that I didn't want to wait any longer for him, either.

I gasped as the sound of voices approaching tore apart the memory and blew it from my grasp. I tried to sit back away from Cash, but his fist was closed around my dress, refusing to let me go. His eyes were so wide, his mouth half-open, the words refusing to come. Something inside the hollow of my chest was hammering. The memory. Remembering what it had felt like to be that alive. I looked up at Cash and jerked my dress from his grip.

"No…it can't be…" I bit my lip. "You can't be…"

I shut my eyes, trying to compose myself as the door closed behind the footsteps entering the room.

"Anaya…what was that?" Cash whispered.

"It's you," Emma said, angry and surprised. "Anaya. I remember you."

She stormed forward as if I were the enemy and not the one who had given her her memories of Finn back.

"What are you doing here?" She glared at me before her gaze flitted to Cash. "Why did you do this to him? This is all your fault! You get that, right?"

"Em, cool it," he said. "Anaya…was that real? That was you. That was *me*. I felt you." He reached out, dazed, and placed his hand on my leg, his eyes tracing over every part of me. "I…I…"

"Hello?" Emma threw her hands up. "She did this to you!

Are you forgetting about that part, Cash? Snap out of it."

"Emma," Finn said, placing a sturdy hand on her shoulder. His eyes, eyes that had seen beyond forever, looked at us with a strange kind of understanding. He pulled her back a little. "Don't."

Emma looked back and forth between Finn and Cash, eyes wide and disbelieving. Her watery gaze finally settled on me.

"You were supposed to take him weeks ago!" She held her hand out. "He is suffering because of you. How can you just sit there and let him *die*? Why? I just want to know why?"

She broke into sobs and I turned away. I let my gaze settle on Cash's face. His eyes. Tarik's eyes. *Oh my God...* I stood up, suddenly painfully aware of the demanding call of heat at my hip. "I can't...I can't do this now. I'm being called."

Cash just looked at me as if he didn't know what to say. I didn't know what to say, either. I still couldn't believe this. He couldn't be Tarik. He couldn't. Tarik was in Heaven. He was waiting for me. This had to be some kind of illusion. But...it wasn't. The memories never lied.

I turned to Emma and took a step forward until we were toe to toe. Her eyes opened a little wider, but she stood her ground, her pretty jaw clenched in fear or anger. Maybe a little of both.

"If anything happens to him while I'm gone, I will hold you responsible," I said, my whisper like venom. "If the life is gone from his eyes when I return, then I will bring the wrath of the Almighty down on the both of you." My eyes flicked up to Finn, who was reeling Emma into his arms, fire in his eyes like a challenge.

"Back off, Anaya," he said. "We'll keep him safe. You're

not the only one who gives a damn about him."

We all turned around when we heard monitors wail behind us. Cash threw his legs over the bed, jerking IVs out of his wrist.

"Cash, what are you doing?" Emma rushed over to help him.

"I'm leaving," he said, holding her watery gaze with his. "Are you going to help me or not? I want to go home, Em. I don't need this hospital. And I sure as hell don't need a babysitter, let alone three of them. Everyone needs to stop acting like I can't take care of myself."

I let one last look pass between Finn and me before I settled my fingers around my blade and gave in. He nodded once. I closed my eyes and dissolved into the light.

Chapter 22

Cash

"I wish you'd stay at my house, or at least let me or Finn stay here with you," Emma said, smoothing the comforter on my bed for the millionth time.

I put my hand over hers to stop it, and her eyes drifted up to meet mine.

"Em," I said. "I'm going to be fine. I'm not going anywhere. Not tonight anyway. You heard the doctor. He said I have a couple of weeks."

"Why won't you let them help? Operate? Something." Her voice dissipated into a pained whisper. "Anything."

I looked across my room at Finn, who was leaning, arms folded, against the doorframe, watching us. He looked tired. I rested my elbows on my knees and sighed.

"Finn, will you tell her?" I said. "Tell her it won't do any good."

He pressed his lips together and averted his green eyes to the stain on the tan carpet where I'd spilled paint a year ago.

"You don't know that," Emma said.

"He's in an expired body," Finn said softly, as if the tone behind the words would make it any better. "There is nothing anyone in this world could do to change that."

The thought of being alone should've scared the crap out of me. But being surrounded by people whose eyes only reflected the fact that I was going to die scared me even more. Fear swirled around in my veins, mixing and melding with the last bit of life that flowed there. Black and red. Death and life. My lungs made an attempt to keep up but it just resulted in me coughing until my stomach twisted into tense knots. When it subsided and I could breathe again, Emma was curled up beside me rubbing circles on my back. A tear slid silently down her face, leaving mascara tracks on her cheeks.

"I love you, Em," I whispered, squeezing her knee. "But I *need* you to go. I just want to close my eyes and forget that this is happening. Even if it's just for a night. Besides, I'm sure Anaya will be back soon."

"You trust her?"

I thought about that. I thought about all the reasons I shouldn't, and still, I found myself saying, "Yes. You should, too."

It only took a flick of my eyes to the shadow demon swirling up the leg of the nightstand to get Emma's attention.

"They're here, aren't they?" she whispered. "The shadows?"

I nodded. There wasn't any use denying it. Finn crossed the room, his eyes following mine to the nightstand.

Breathe. I shut my eyes and took a deep breath, then exhaled. I had to keep it under control. If I could keep them at a minimum, this wouldn't be as bad. One I could handle. If a swarm of the things decided to show up, I was screwed.

"How many?" Finn asked.

"Just one." *For now*.

He nodded, stepping back to the center of the room, beckoning me to follow. "All right. Enough of this. Get up."

"What?" Emma and I said it at the same time.

"Trust me," he said. Those should have been the two words that kept me in place, but my curiosity got the best of me. I slid off the bed and stood beside Finn.

"Now what?"

"Get the shadow to come over," he said. "There's still only one, right?"

I nodded, feeling sweat break out across my bow. "Why the hell would I want to do that?"

"You're not helpless, Cash. Open your hand and focus on the power there. If you're a shadow walker it will be there. You just need to tap into it."

I flexed my hand and looked up at the shadow that was inching closer with each frantic beat of my heart, like it was being lured in by my panic. It finally got close enough to wrap around my ankles and I couldn't stop myself from shaking.

"It's okay," Finn whispered. "What do you feel like you could do?"

"Finn…," Emma interjected, sounding worried.

I held up my hand. "It's okay, Em."

I narrowed my gaze on my fingers and a blue shimmer sparked from the tips. The shadow slithered up the leg of my jeans and without a second thought, I reached out and closed my fingers around its neck just like I'd seen Noah do. A screech rattled my eardrums and the shadow twisted under my grip.

It sizzled under my skin but it couldn't get away, turning from smoke to sludge under my touch. When I couldn't stand the pain anymore, I released it and it slithered out of the open bedroom door.

Finn stared at me, wide-eyed. "Did it work? You were able to grab it, right? Force it into a corporeal state like you did with Anaya?"

I opened my trembling palm and we both stared at the angry red burn. My fingertips were blistered and my palm looked like raw meat. I swallowed. "Yeah. It worked."

"That's…unreal," Finn breathed. "I've never seen anything like it."

"You haven't?" I gaped. "Then why the hell did you have me try it?"

"I was part of the afterlife for over seventy years and never met a shadow walker," he said. "But I heard stories. That they could force any kind of spirit out of elemental form. Souls, shadows…why do you think everyone wants you so badly? You're powerful, whether you want to acknowledge it or not."

As much as my palm hurt like hell, I laughed, the sound part relief that I wasn't completely helpless and part terror that I seemed to have one more thing in common with Noah. I still didn't know if that was a good thing or not. God, I wished I could talk to Emma about this, but I didn't have a doubt that if I did, Finn would know about it by morning.

"Is it gone?" Emma spoke up, her arms wrapped protectively around her middle as she searched my room for something she'd never see.

"Yeah." I smiled and my shoulders sagged in relief. "It's gone."

Emma's phone started to ring in her pocket. She slid her

finger across the screen to silence it and groaned. "It's Mom. I'll text her and tell her I'm going to be late."

"Don't," I said. "Seriously, I'm good now, guys. And I give you permission to wake me up ridiculously early as long as you promise to bake me something."

To be honest I doubted I would have been able to keep anything down, but I knew it would make her happy if I sounded like my old self.

Emma watched me for a thoughtful moment and then leaned up to plant a soft kiss on my cheek. "Call if you need anything. I don't care what time it is."

I nodded and waved to Finn as he grabbed Emma's hand and led her out the door.

After they were gone, I lay in bed, listening to the ragged sound of my breaths. They sawed their way out of my throat before dragging back in. The room was so dark I couldn't see my hand in front of me. Good. If the shadow demons were here, I didn't want to know it.

I couldn't get Anaya out of my head. Out of my bones and veins and everywhere in between. I couldn't shake that memory. Was it real? Had that really been me, with her? God, she'd looked…she'd *felt* so alive. I could still taste her, and the memory didn't even belong to me. Or did it?

My bedroom door creaked open and I tensed, fighting the urge to curl into myself under the heavy blankets. But when a breath of warmth entered the room, like a spray of invisible sunshine, I relaxed.

"I'll tell you the same thing I told Em," I said, watching Anaya's shimmer appear in the dark doorway. "I don't need a babysitter."

"I'm not here to babysit you." She stepped into the room,

skimming her fingers on the doorframe, and stopped once she was inside. The door clicked shut behind her. I sat up and cleared my throat. I didn't need her of all people seeing me like this. Weak. I took a deep, ragged breath, pushed the blanket off me, and stood up.

"Did you see what I saw?"

Anaya's gold eyes lit up as they trailed over my bare chest. My heart was starting to pound. It felt good. It felt alive. I took a step closer.

"Y-you should lie down," she said quietly.

"Answer the question."

She looked away. I took another step closer. Close enough to feel her warmth sparking off my skin. Close enough for those sparks to catch fire and blaze through my veins. My chest. All the places that made me weak for her. Only her. My heart was a jackhammer in my chest having her this close.

"Anaya," I whispered through the aching need that had taken up residency in my throat.

"Yes?" She didn't look at me. Instead she held her golden gaze on the half-open window, her profile like a work of art shimmering though the dark. The curtains glowed, brought to life by moonlight and a breeze that smelled like fresh-cut grass. I touched her chin with one fingertip and turned her face toward me.

"Tell me it was real." I let my fingertip smooth across her jaw, down to her collarbone. A line of blue sparks trailed after my touch, stitching Anaya back to life. "I need it to be real."

Anaya just looked at me for a moment while my fingers found their way into the braids that covered her neck. Then, slowly, she nodded.

"It was real." She placed her open hand on my stomach

and a sound escaped her throat, almost a whimper. "We...we were real."

That was the only signal I needed. After all of the waiting. The wanting. I slid my hand up into her hair more firmly and kissed her, pushing her back until the closed door stopped us. Until there was just my weight against her. Her softness beneath me. The sense that every ounce of Anaya was filling up the empty hole in my chest. Anaya gripped the waistband of my shorts in her fists, opened her mouth beneath mine, and everything dead and dying within me roared to life. My right palm slammed into the door behind her to keep my balance and I lost myself in the warm sensation of her lips. The taste of her tongue. Her fingers brushing the bare skin of my abdomen. She whimpered and suddenly she was pressed against me, knee to chest. Jesus...she was going to kill me. And I didn't care. Anaya's fingers slid up my stomach and I couldn't contain the moan that left me. I needed more of her, but one nagging little thought kept interrupting perfection. Was it me she wanted, or Tarik?

"I'm not him," I gasped, forcing myself to pull away from her mouth. I squeezed my eyes shut, trying to form a coherent thought other than *what does she look like under that dress?*

"What?" She looked dazed, her gold eyes creating a glow around our faces in the dark.

"I mean, don't do this because you think I'm Tarik." I took a deep breath and looked down at her lips. "Do this because I'm me. Because you want *me*. Not because you want who I used to be."

Her eyes lit me up. Drinking me in. Considering. One of her hands slid up my chest. She spread her fingers out over my sluggish heartbeat and closed her eyes.

"I want *you*," she whispered. "I wanted you before I knew."

I wanted her, too. I couldn't remember ever wanting anyone as much as I wanted Anaya.

I closed the space between us slowly, letting her lips draw me in with their next breath. Heat bloomed in my mouth, slid down my throat. I couldn't get enough. I pulled Anaya against my body, wondering how someone who wasn't alive could feel warmer than me. Maybe that just showed I was more dead than alive at this point. I didn't care.

I stumbled backward, tripping over my discarded jeans in the floor, keeping Anaya pressed against me all the way. The backs of my knees hit the edge of my mattress and my pulse pounded a little harder. I was never nervous when I had a girl this close to my bed. But Anaya wasn't just a girl. She wasn't a girl at all. She was…everything. I kissed her harder, needing to be closer to her than I'd ever been to anyone. Heart pounding out of control, knowing I was this close to having her after wanting her for so long.

"You even taste like sunshine," I whispered against her lips, pushing the white strap of her dress down her shoulder.

"Cash?" Anaya mumbled, sounding worried. She pressed her palm to my chest. I realized she wasn't breathing anymore. Wasn't kissing me back. I pulled away.

"What? What did I do?" I gasped for breath, trying to focus on Anaya and not the way the room was spinning out of control. I could hold it together. I would hold it together. For her. For this.

"Your heart…"

My eyes followed her gaze to where her hand glowed against my bare chest. My heart thudded, slowly, erratically, under her touch. I sucked in a breath. It felt like I was breathing through a straw. She frowned and dropped her hand to the blade at her hip, rubbed her thumb across the handle.

"You need to sit down," Anaya said, pushing me back onto the bed. She sat down beside me and ran her fingers through my hair as I tried to catch my breath. Tried to right the room that was spinning around me like a top. I felt sick. I buried my face in my palms and breathed into the hollow of my hands.

"This is so not what I pictured when I decided to try to get you in my bed," I said, my words muffled by my fingers. Anaya laughed and kissed my shoulder, her lips leaving a little imprint of heat on my skin.

I looked up at her, trying so hard not to be angry. To not be humiliated. It wasn't working.

"Sorry," I said, wishing I could kick my ass into gear and kiss her again.

Anaya shrugged and swept a few braids off her shoulder so she could tilt her head to look at me. "That was my first kiss in over a thousand years. I should probably pace myself anyway, don't you think?"

I shook my head. "No. I don't believe in pacing yourself."

"Maybe you should." She grinned. "Look at you."

I took as deep a breath as my lungs would allow and pulled her onto the bed with me. Her braids spread out like a halo across my comforter, shimmering even when there was no light to reflect from them. I leaned over her and pressed a kiss to her jaw. Heat sparked across my lips.

"I'm okay," I said, cursing my body for being weak. "We don't have to stop." Every nerve writhing under my skin was begging me to just give up and collapse. I couldn't do that. This wasn't me. This wasn't what I wanted to be. I didn't realize I was still, face buried in the warm hollow of Anaya's neck, until she placed her hand on the back of my head. Moisture blurred my vision.

"I'm fine," I said.

"You're not." Anaya slid off the bed and I scrambled to sit up. "You're not okay," she whispered, shaking her head. "You have no idea how close you are. I can *feel* it."

"It doesn't matter—"

"It matters!" Anaya's fingers balled up into tiny fists at her sides.

I raked my fingers through my hair, wanting to pull it out. "What do you want me to do, Anaya? Tell me. Because I'm open to suggestions here. I'm on my way out. There's no stopping it. We've been over this."

"There's nothing you can do," she said, smoothing her dress out where I'd wrinkled it. "It's something I have to deal with. I made this mess. I'll clean it up."

"What mess?" I narrowed my gaze on her. "What do you mean?"

"I don't have time to explain," she said. "I have to go."

"Someone's going to die?" I asked, my eyes lingering on her blade as it started to glow and pulse with light.

Anaya tilted her face to look up at the ceiling as if she were seeing right through it. She looked determined.

"Not if I can help it."

Chapter 23

Anaya

I let the heat blooming around me take me home.

Or as close to it as I was probably ever going to get. I stared at the gates, the ache of longing working its way up my throat. It would have been nice to see my parents again. But after today, that dream would be gone. A hum of peace danced on the breeze, sifting through my hair, tickling my ears. A gust blew a few braids into my face. Braids that still smelled like Cash.

"Anaya," Balthazar's voice echoed behind me.

I turned around. I couldn't even force the smile that I knew he wanted from me. A smile that would tell him that everything was going smoothly. That good little Anaya had logged another day of doing exactly what she was told.

"What is it?" His blond brows furrowed as he stepped forward. "What happened?"

"How much longer are you going to put him through

this?" I asked.

"We've already discussed this."

"Will you ever let him cross over?" I said, meeting his gaze. "Or are you going to make him your slave for the rest of eternity?"

He laughed. "Oh Anaya, love, you haven't gotten attached to your pet, now have you? The job was only to keep his soul safe. Not to grow a heart."

I closed my eyes. "Answer the question, Balthazar."

After a few beats of silence, he sighed. "No. I'm sorry, Anaya. He has a greater purpose than crossing over. He is too valuable to let his talents go to waste."

"I can't do it," I said, trembling. "The deal is off. I'll stay working as a reaper. But I won't put him through another minute of this."

He raised a brow as he came to stand beside me. Glowing embers flew around us like fireflies. The white fog that clung to Balthazar like a cape spread out around us, rippling with energy and power.

"Excuse me? You *won't*?" Balthazar laughed, a loud booming sound that echoed from walls that did not exist in this place. "Do you forget that I *own* you, Anaya?"

"When he takes his last breath, I will be there. And I'll carry him over. Not to you, but to the gates. Where he belongs," I said.

His fingers latched onto my wrist before I could get another word out. My warmth. The only thing that kept the feeling of life flowing through me slowly crept up my arm before Balthazar's steady fingers leached it away, leaving me cold. Afraid. His eyes turned into pale blue orbs that refused to release me from their gaze.

"Do you really wish to challenge me?" he whispered into my ear. His breath was like ice, melting against my heat. "Do you honestly think I would *let* you make me look like a fool?"

Fear bubbled up in my throat in the form of a scream. I swallowed it back down into the empty pit that I used to call my stomach. I shook my head and whispered, "No."

He leaned forward and my heat began to inch its way out of my lungs, across my lips. The look in his eyes said this was my end. I tensed and readied myself. I knew this might happen, but still...did my thousand years of perfect servitude mean nothing to him?

Shock stole the plea about to escape my mouth as Balthazar released my wrist and stepped away. He shook his head and looked to the gates as if they might open and provide him with an answer.

"You will do what I ask of you," he said calmly. Somehow this was worse than his anger. Like the calm before the storm. "You will do it, or I will have Easton find you a permanent home in Hell. A pretty plaything like you?" He looked over his shoulder. "Why, they would rip you to shreds fighting over who got a turn first."

I looked at my feet, wishing I could release the pain and fear gnawing inside me. Wishing I had tears that could carry it all away. Instead it swam circles in my chest, torturing me.

"This isn't right," I whispered. I was starting to think Balthazar didn't know what that meant. What we were putting Cash through was wrong.

He turned and raised a brow at me as if he were surprised that I wasn't submitting to him after his threat.

"Balthazar, please," I whispered. "I'm begging you. I can't go on doing this knowing..."

He sighed. The weight of the world was in that sigh. "Knowing he possesses Tarik's soul," he finished for me.

I looked up, unable to conceal my surprise. My betrayal.

"How long have you known it was him?"

He shrugged. The keeper of the afterlife. The second in command to the Almighty...*shrugged*.

"What would you like me to say? I always knew."

Anger started an inferno in my chest. Turned my vision red. I didn't give a damn about his threats in that moment. He'd *known*. He'd been toying with me for a thousand years!

"How could you not tell me? You let me think he was okay. That he had crossed. That he was waiting for me!"

"Anaya, be reasonable."

"Be reasonable?" I seethed. "I have been nothing but reasonable for you, for this job for over a thousand years! What did you think I was working for?"

Salvation. I had been working toward a salvation he had promised me. A salvation that included Tarik. I squeezed my eyes shut, trying to fend off the memory threatening to take me. Something in me wouldn't let me. Something in me said he needed to see. When my eyes flew open, I could feel the heat seeping from my pores. Rage started a slow, steady burn in my chest.

Balthazar narrowed his gaze on me. "Anaya?"

I didn't think about what I did next. Just grabbed his wrist. His eyes widened and I clasped my palm over his forehead. They'd told me when I'd been given this power that it was a gift. To be able to look into the past. To show souls something worth remembering when their days had come to an end. If this gift was ever going to be good for anything, it was going to be good for this. I closed my eyes against the light enveloping

Balthazar and me in a feathery white cocoon.

"See it!" I screamed. "See what you promised me!"

The world around us swirled into a thousand colors, blinding me with the past before depositing me in the dark.

I stood staring at my reflection in the shiny surface of my father's best blade. I did not recognize the girl staring back. Her braids were wet with the sea. Her eyes were tired and dull. There were no more tears inside this girl to cry. There was no more life in this girl to live. Not without Tarik.

My knees quivered, but my hand was steady with intent. Fingers gripping the blade so tightly it cut into my palm, giving me a taste of what was to come. Red droplets fell like rain onto the sand beneath my feet. I looked up to the sea that held Tarik. That held my father. Pain pulsed through me until I fell onto my knees, watching the waves rage ahead. I wanted them back. I wanted this pain to end. And if it couldn't…then I would join them. I didn't think about my mother in that moment. I didn't think of the breaths I was giving back or the life I was leaving behind. The decision was simple when you took the rest of it away.

"Take me, too," I whispered to the sea and pressed the blade into my chest. The pain was instant. Fleeting. Nothing compared to the loss of Tarik and my father. Wind whipped across my face. Raindrops pelted my cheeks. Life leaked from my body and onto the sand. I closed my eyes expecting dark, but then everything was light. I blinked at the boy holding my hand, smiling. He was dressed in white. Cloaked in light. He had to be an angel...

He laughed. "I'm no angel."

I looked him over, confused, and he grinned. "I've seen that look before."

"Tarik," I said, overwhelmed with hope. "You can take me to Tarik now?"

The boy with white-blond hair raised a brow at me. His strangely golden eyes glowed.

"I'm guessing that's someone you have waiting on the other side," he said. "And normally this is the part where I take you home. But there's someone who needs to see you first."

I nodded and followed him blindly into the mist.

A man waited where the fog cleared. Tall and strong as an oak. Hair like sunshine and eyes like the sea. A white robe flowed out from behind him and clouds gathered at his feet. He smiled when I approached.

"My, aren't you lovely," he said, waving the boy beside me away. "Thank you, Darius. You may go."

The tall man raised a brow at me when I didn't offer any words. "Aren't you going to ask me if you're dead?"

I shook my head and bit my lip. "No. I already know I am."

He nodded and walked in a circle around me. "That's right. You did this, didn't you?"

After he'd come full circle, he stopped and pursed his lips. "I could call you brave or stupid. I'm not sure which is more appropriate."

"Can I see Tarik now?" I whispered, fear eating away at my voice. "My father?"

"Did you think it would be that easy?"

I felt my brows scrunch together. Yes. I had. Why else would I have plunged a blade into my heart?

He laughed and settled a hand on my shoulder.

"Oh dear, what a mess," he said. "No, beauty. I'm sorry, that is not how it works. There are some rules that even I cannot bend. And taking a life is one of those rules. The punishment for breaking that rule is Hell."

"H-hell?" My voice quivered. "But it was my life to take. It belonged to me. No one else!" My heart, on the other hand, did belong to someone else. It was useless without him.

"No," Balthazar's voice turned hard. "Your life belongs to the Almighty. He has a plan for each. And, Anaya, dear"—he shook his head—"you've sort of made a mess of his plan."

"Please…" I managed to whisper through the fear that consumed me.

He studied me for a moment, and stroked his chin. "I have a compromise."

"Compromise?"

"You work for me," he said. "Curry souls to the afterlife as a reaper. A collector of sorts. Like Darius."

I swallowed. "You want me to be Death?"

A strange smile lit up his face. "Yes."

"Will it get me to Tarik?"

He glanced at the gates and smiled. "It will get you to the other side. Yes."

"Then I'll do it," I said, stepping forward. "I'll do anything."

When the memory faded I was shaking. Balthazar wound

his arms around me and let me fall limp against him. An unexpected gesture after our previous encounter. My chest heaved with sobs, but no tears ever came. This ghost of a body wouldn't allow that. What had I done? What had I given up? How many lifetimes had Tarik wandered this earth while I was so sure he was at peace? Balthazar stroked my hair and sighed.

"I could have been more…forthcoming, I suppose."

I pulled away from him. "You manipulated me into this existence."

"I didn't want to see you in an eternity of flames, Anaya," he raised his voice. "You fault me for saving you from Hell?"

"No," I said. "No. I don't fault you, but I am asking for your help now. I'm asking you to make this right. Don't doom him to the kind of existence I've been working to escape for a thousand years. Undo this. Let him live."

His face softened and the cloud base below him rose and bubbled until it took the form of a chair. Balthazar sat and a sigh escaped him.

"His body has expired. There is no help for him."

"Then stop the shadow demons," I begged, falling to my knees. "Send them away. Send him a guardian. At least give him some peace in his final hours. I can't protect him from this—"

Balthazar narrowed his gaze at me. "Have they touched him?"

I nodded. "Yes. They're getting more aggressive every day. And I can't be there every waking—"

"How close is he?" He stood and started to pace.

"He's close." My voice shook.

He nodded. "Good."

"What will you do with him?" I took a step back.

"He is a shadow walker," Balthazar said, the blue around his pupils burning like a flame. "You have no idea how valuable your human is. It's rare for a soul to cycle through as many times as his has, to collect that much energy. In a human form he has more power than you could dream of. He can walk freely between worlds. He can force a soul into corporeality for capture. He could waltz straight into the depths of Hell and fetch me a demon if I commanded him to. And he's going to be mine. He'll work for me, collecting the souls that flee from you. In time, we'll rid the world of all of the lost."

"You...you can't just use him like that," I said. "He's done nothing wrong. He has a right to cross beyond those gates. You would take that away. To use him?"

I couldn't believe what I was hearing. Were we no better than those of the underworld now?

Balthazar turned on his heel and stared out onto the horizon, hands folded calmly behind his back. "Yes. And you're going to help me."

Chapter 24

Cash

I sat on my bed in the dark. The laptop screen glared back at me as I trolled WebMD and Wikipedia. There were a lot of half-ass guesses to what was wrong with me, but none of them were right. There wasn't one article on what to do when you're living in an expired body. My gut told me the answer to that was to give up. There was no cure. No solution. Just a question mark on the door that would open to the afterlife. Which afterlife I was going to was just another thing I didn't know.

I slammed the laptop shut and leaned back into my pillows. The house was too quiet. Too vacant. No Dad snoring. No muffled sounds of *Seinfeld* coming through the bedroom wall that connected our rooms. Just me. My breathing. The wind beating the house.

And the hissing.

I tensed and sat up, my eyes searching the dark. It was

useless to even try to see them this way. The dark was their camouflage. My fingers twitched on the comforter, wanting to flip the light on, but I was afraid of what I'd see. How many were here this time? The hissing was getting closer. Louder. Goose bumps rose across my arms. Calm. Anaya said I had to stay calm. Get control. I inhaled a deep breath and let it sit in my chest, burning my lungs. It was too cold. I finally coughed and let it out. Another hiss echoed through the dark.

"Screw this." I leaned over to flip on the lamp.

Light exploded across the dark, but the shadows were quick to snuff it out. My hand flinched back as one slithered up onto the nightstand.

"Youuuu commmeeee."

I looked up at the large shadow standing at the end of my bed. It was a big black shadow of a man twice my size. It cocked its head to the side and held out a hand. Black smoke like fingers curled toward me, beckoning me to follow.

Fear closed off my throat. Where was Anaya? God, please let her come back. Now. Like right freaking now.

"What do you want?"

"Youuuuuuu," the shadow man hissed. Something dark and sludge-like dripped from the cavern of his mouth, and I jerked my legs up before it could land on my shin.

"Look," I said, gripping the comforter. "I'm not who you want. If you had any idea how much Jägermeister I've drunk in the last three years, then you'd know there's no way I could ever taste good."

"Come!" It shouted. That sound sent panic ripping through my chest. It was a deep growling sound that wasn't human or animal. I needed to get out of there, but I was cornered by a wall of hungry darkness on every side. Adrenaline surged through my veins, or maybe it was something else, something that made me believe I was capable of doing what I decided to do next. My eyes scanned the room. Jeans on the floor. Keys on the dresser by the door. I could do this. Pain ripped through my chest as I dragged in a breath of air, then two. Holding the last one in, I reached out and grabbed the shadow demon between me and the exit by the throat. Sparks flew and a blue stream of vapor seeped out of my veins, latching onto the demon, binding it to my wrist. It hissed, setting off a symphony of growls all around as I slid off the bed, taking it with me. A second shadow broke away from the rest and snapped at me. I grabbed it with my left hand. I felt dizzy. Electric. The sensation almost enough to numb the burning sting developing over every inch of bare flesh that the shadow demons touched. When I got near the door, I released them both along with the breath I'd been holding. And damn if the pain lighting up my world didn't choose that moment to explode across the surface of my skin. I ignored it. If I didn't, there would be so much more to follow. Instead, I grabbed my jeans off the floor and keys off the nightstand and darted out the door.

By the time I made it to Finn's, I had finally stopped shaking. I turned the ignition off and sat in the Bronco, staring up at his crappy little garage apartment. One window glowed with light despite it being two in the morning.

"Please don't let Emma be in there." I climbed out of the truck.

Wind parted the darkness and every time a gust of it

touched me, I flinched. Where the hell was Noah the freaking shadow whisperer? For someone who claimed to want to be my friend, he wasn't very concerned with me becoming a meal. I couldn't get Anaya's words out of my head. She said she'd seen it. Shadow walkers delivering souls to the underworld. Straight into the hands of the things I was running from. Is that what Noah was doing with the souls he *saved*? I didn't want to believe that. He had to be different.

Please don't let them follow me. Please.

I looked up at the stars peeking through the wispy gray clouds in the sky and prayed that whoever it was that Anaya worked for up there heard me. I pounded up the steps to Finn's apartment and pounded even harder on the door. It took him a minute, but when he answered he didn't look surprised. He just looked…tired.

"Can I stay here?" I asked. "I would have gone to Emma's, but I don't want to lead these things over there. And…I don't really know where else to go."

He looked me up and down and stepped to the side for me to enter.

"Are they here now?" he asked once I was inside. I shivered and rubbed my arms.

"Not yet."

"You're going to have to get your emotions under control if you want to keep them at bay." He closed the door and locked it.

"Easier said than done."

Finn flipped on a small table lamp.

"They thrive on the emotions you're putting out," he said. "Fear. Anger. Depression. It attracts them like moths to a flame. That's how they always got to reaps before we could.

They could smell the dying before I ever got the call."

"Well, I must smell like a freaking buffet then."

Finn laughed at that.

I shoved my hands in my pockets and looked around the pint-size apartment. A burgundy sofa that had survived some kind of garage sale hell and a dinged-up coffee table sat in the middle of the living room. Two mismatched bar stools were pushed up against the little kitchen bar. But it was neat and clean. The only things out of place were Finn's black-and-white Converse tennis shoes he'd kicked off on the way to the bedroom.

"It's a rat hole. I know." He plopped down onto the sofa and ran a hand over the cushion. "I'm saving up to get something better after graduation."

"Hey, looks fine to me." I sat down beside him and checked the room one more time. At least he was going to make it to graduation. "It can't be easy starting from scratch."

He laughed and leaned his head back. "You have no idea. It all just sounds like a fairy tale at first. But nobody tells you what happens after 'they lived happily ever after.'"

"Do you regret it?" I studied his face, trying to see what Emma loved so much. "Do you wish things had just stayed the same? I mean, it's got to be easier being dead than all this."

Part of me really believed that. Life didn't seem very easy any more. Not that it ever really had. But when you started blurring the lines between life and death, things got… complicated. I was never very good with complicated.

"No." Finn shook his head. "And trust me. The way things were before, being separated from her like that…I'll take this and more any day of the week."

I leaned up and placed my palms on the coffee table to try

to stop shaking. "Well, she loves you," I said, shivering. "I've never seen her love anyone the way she loves you."

Finn smiled at that. He grabbed a blanket from the back of the couch and tossed it over to me. I wrapped it around myself to try to lock in what little heat I had left.

"What about Anaya?" he said. "Don't tell me there's not something there. I've seen the way she looks at you. I've known Anaya for a very long time. She makes a point not to look at anyone like that."

I shook my head and stared at the carpet. "She doesn't love me. She thinks I'm somebody else. And to be honest I don't think I have the energy to be some guy she's been chasing for a thousand years."

"Wait...somebody else?" Finn sat up with interest. "Do you mean she knew you in a past life?"

I buried my face in my hands and groaned at how ridiculous and impossible all this shit sounded. "You know how you pointed out I must have lived lots of lives to get to where I am now?"

"Yeah."

"Well, apparently one of those lives was Tarik," I said. "As in Anaya's fiancé."

Shock showed on every inch of Finn's face. He rubbed his chin and stared at the carpet. "Maybe she's wrong."

"She showed me, Finn." I rubbed my palms together and pain throbbed under the tender red skin. "I saw her through his eyes. I felt her. He loved her. And now I don't even know what to think. Am I him? I don't feel like I am. I still feel like Cash, with all of my own fucked-up feelings tearing me up inside."

Finn pinned me with his tired gaze. "Do *you* love her?"

"How am I supposed to answer that when I don't even know who she's really seeing when she looks at me now?"

"That doesn't have anything to do with it." He laughed. "You either love her or you don't."

" I...I don't know how I feel." I swallowed the lie easily enough. The fact was, I knew exactly how I felt about Anaya. I knew because I'd never felt that way about anyone before. And it scared the hell out me. It scared me because there wasn't anywhere for this to go. She was dead. I was dying. The whole thing was so screwed up it made my head hurt. I wondered if this was how Emma felt when she started to fall for Finn.

Finn laughed softly. "Yeah. Whatever you say."

When I looked up, his eyelids looked heavy. He shook his head to keep himself awake.

"Why aren't you sleeping?" I asked.

Finn sat up and rubbed his face with his palms, then pushed his fingers through his hair. "I'm entertaining you, remember?"

"You're weren't sleeping when I showed up." I nodded to the bedroom light on. "Don't blame it on me."

Finn shook his head and sighed. "I...I have dreams. Nightmares."

"About what?"

"You can't unsee the things I've seen," he said. "You touch enough death and it's bound to come back to haunt you."

He sounded far away in that moment, even though he was sitting right next to me.

"I'm sorry," I said.

He looked surprised. "For what?"

"For being a dick." I leaned back into the lumpy couch cushion. "You didn't deserve that. If I'm being honest, I'm grateful Emma has you. You changed her back into a girl I've missed for a long time."

Finn nodded and closed his eyes.

"If you want, we can sit here and avoid sleep together," he finally said.

I laughed. "What, are we deciding to be friends now?"

Finn's mouth tipped into a lopsided grin. "Hell, no."

"You know…" I hesitated knowing this was going to come back to bite me in the ass, but in the end it felt right. There was too much shit between Finn and I that needed to be put to rest. And I was tired of being alone all of the time. I glanced at him out of the corner of my eye and sighed. "I've got two spare rooms at the house. If you don't like this place, I could use a roommate. If you can get past the shadow demons and yappy dog across the street, it's not a bad set up."

Finn chuckled and nodded. "Yeah…maybe."

I smiled and closed my eyes to the let darkness take hold of my vision. Finn might not be a reaper anymore, but maybe if I was lucky, those little bastards were still scared of him. It didn't last long. I sat up, shaking when a flash of cold consumed the room. My breath looked like fog clinging to my lips.

"Who the hell is this?" someone growled from the other side of the living room.

Finn sighed. "Scout, give it a rest."

Scout? My eyes opened wide when the air in front of the coffee table swirled into a smoky figure that little by little took the shape of guy. A guy who didn't look much older than me or Finn. He jerked his head to toss a few blond curls out of his eyes.

"Wait a minute…is this the kid from the fire?"

Finn nodded.

"Well, I don't care who he is—I want him out," he said. "Do you have any idea how many shadow demons are lurking outside this place right now?"

Finn laughed. "I'll tell you what. You can start kicking out guests when you start helping me with the steep-ass rent your drunk of an uncle is charging me."

Scout rolled his eyes and kicked over a half-full Coke can on the table. Sticky liquid expanded across the table before spilling over the edge onto the carpet.

"What the hell is wrong with you? You don't care when I have Emma over here." Finn stood up and stomped into the kitchen. He came back with a towel and started blotting up the spilled Coke.

Scout waited until he came back and laughed. "Yeah, well, I get to see Emma in a bra when I time my entrances right. She's better entertainment."

Finn dropped the towel and his jaw clenched. "You son of a—"

"Wait a minute!" I stood up and stared at the two of them, trying to form words. There weren't any. This was...this was fucking crazy. "What the hell is going on?"

Scout scowled at me. "Better question—what are you? Because if you were just a human, we wouldn't have a shadow infestation going on out there."

Finn held up his hands between us. "Stop. Scout's a reaper. As for Cash"—he looked at Scout—"he's a shadow walker. Anaya was supposed to take him at the fire. For whatever reason, Balthazar had her keep him here."

"Why would he do that?" Scout folded his arms across his chest, looking me over. "The body is expired. It's not like he's going to be walking around for long. Look at him, for Christ's sake."

"Hey, fuck you too, Casper," I snapped. Hearing that I looked like shit was the last thing I needed right now. Especially from some dead, pretty-boy asshole.

Scout snorted and walked around the table to look me over. A shiver rolled over my skin the closer he got. I stepped back until the backs of my knees hit the couch cushion.

Scout raised a brow and laughed. "I've seen one of these guys. Blond one a few years back. Stole a soul right out from under me. I'd thought he was another reaper at the time, but after the ass-chewing I got from Balthazar, I figured out he was something else. Although I think he was more pissed that there was one of you guys running for the other team."

Blond one. Noah. He was talking about Noah. "Maybe he was trying to save the soul from that hellhole of nothingness you were delivering it to."

Scout raised a brow and looked at Finn. "What hellhole? You must be thinking of Easton, kid. I don't deliver downstairs. I don't like to get my hands that dirty. I deal strictly with the Inbetween."

"No," I said, gritting my teeth. "I'm talking about you. I saw what happens to those souls. You talk about how much you hate the scum lurking outside your door. Why the hell do you help turn them into that, then?"

"Cash?" Finn leaned down to catch my gaze. "They don't all end up like that. Lots are reborn. And the ones that don't get that opportunity are there for a reason. There's something dark they won't let go of."

"What about Em?" I countered. "What could she have possibly done to deserve that?"

He seemed surprised that I knew but didn't dwell on it. Instead, a look of guilt flashed over his face. "She was doomed because of me. It was against the rules for us to be together, but I didn't care. I couldn't let her go."

"And that's why you did what you did to save her."

Finn nodded and Scout spoke up. "Look, we aren't going to tell you the system isn't flawed. It is. But it is what it is. There has to be some kind of order. Some kind of consequence or the world would go to shit."

I needed to tell him about Noah. I needed to tell Anaya. I was so done with all of the secrets. Nothing was what it seemed. And, for that matter, nothing was turning out to be the way Noah said it was. What kind of game was this guy playing with me? And if Anaya wasn't around when my time ran out, what exactly was going to happen to me? It had been hard enough just to escape my room tonight. And if I couldn't trust Noah, either, I didn't stand a chance. Damn it, I was so screwed. I wasn't going to escape this no matter how long I hid in Finn's apartment.

I stepped around the table and paced the room. My throat was closing up. I felt dizzy. God…was this shit ever going to end? I couldn't take any more.

"I can't…I can't…" I pressed my fists into my eyes and tried to catch my breath. I couldn't *breathe*.

"Hey." Finn settled a hand on my shoulder. "Sit down before you pass out."

I let him lead me over to the couch and fell backward into the cushions.

Scout leaned over to squint at me. "He's losing it."

Finn shot him a cold glare. "Leave him alone. He didn't choose this."

I couldn't even form words. My tongue felt dead in my mouth. Pain blossomed in my stomach and suddenly there wasn't enough air in the room. No, no, no! I needed to warn him about Noah. Maybe Noah wasn't working for the shadow demons. Maybe he'd gone rogue and was some kind of vigilante for the afterlife. Even as the theories spun to life in my head, I knew they didn't feel right. Something inside Noah was dark. I just prayed that same darkness didn't live inside me.

Chapter 25

Cash

My eyes were throbbing behind my closed lids. Pulsing in the thin veil of darkness that separated me from the rest of the world. I'd only been asleep for an hour, if that, when I felt it start to creep over my skin. The warmth. *Her* warmth. It was all I needed to feel for sparks to ignite across the dark, burning me into awareness.

I heard the blur of whispers in the next room. Quiet. Urgent. Clearly not wanting me to hear what they were saying. Screw that. I was over the secrets. I groaned and sat up, raking my fingers through my hair like a comb. It didn't help. I could see myself in the reflection of Finn's crappy TV. Disorderly black spikes stuck up in every direction on top of my head. Like it mattered anyway. I was at death's doorstep. I don't think anyone was expecting me to look my best.

Seven a.m. sunshine doused the dusty living room

through the sheer white curtains that covered the window. I crept across the room and stopped at Finn's bedroom door. I pressed my palms on the doorframe and leaned in to listen to the voices on the other side.

"I don't have another choice," Anaya whispered. "You have to help me convince him."

Finn laughed. "You honestly think he'd listen to me?"

"Yes."

Footsteps caused the floorboards to groan. "You're delusional if you believe that," Finn said. "Besides, this is beyond screwed up, Anaya. He has rights."

"According to Balthazar, those rights have been removed," she hissed. "Look. I realize this is unfair but it's the better of two horrible options."

Uncomfortable silence spread throughout the bedroom until it made its way around the doorframe, where it wrapped around me like a tourniquet. Strangling me. What options?

"You have no idea what they would do to him down there," she whispered. "I've seen it."

She'd seen what? Did this have to do with Noah? I wiped my sweaty palms on my jeans and stepped around the doorframe. Anaya spun around and her gold eyes turned into big flaming saucers. Finn barely glanced at me before his gaze found his sneakers.

"You've seen what?" I said. "What's going on?"

Anaya stepped forward, blending in with the sunshine around her, making her look almost human. "Cash…" She closed her mouth like she didn't know where to go from here.

"Tell him," Finn said, his gaze trained on Anaya. "Tell him what you want me to do."

She never broke her gaze from mine. Almost as if she

were hoping I'd pull the answers out of her without her having to say the words.

"Tell me what?" I stepped forward, shaking. Shaking so hard I could feel my bones rattling together. "No more secrets. Just tell me what the hell is going on."

"I need you to let him help you die," she said.

"What?"

"Kill you," Finn snapped. "She wants me to kill you."

I looked to Anaya, wanting her to tell me he was lying. She didn't.

"It's the only way I can save you." She stepped forward. "I don't want to watch you suffer anymore. I *can't*."

My feet took a step away from her without my brain telling them to.

"Tell him the rest, Anaya," Finn said. He folded his arms across the black T-shirt stretched over his chest.

She glared at Finn, then looked back to me. "If we do this now, we can assure I'm the one to collect you and not the shadows. And I can save you this way, Cash. I can get you to where you were meant to go. If we do this, I can get you across the gates before he finds out. He can't touch you once you're there. Neither of them can."

Her words were floating around in my head like balloons without the strings attached. I shook my head, hoping they'd fall into place and make some kind of sense. She wanted me to give up. *Die.*

"They?" My heart pounded and I rubbed my palm over my chest. "Do you mean Noah?"

Anaya and Finn exchanged a confused glance. "Noah? Is he the one who's been telling you things? Is he how you know what you are?"

Don't tell them. They'll destroy you just as quickly as they would me if they ever caught me.

Noah's voice echoed in my mind like poison. I pushed it out. Anaya didn't want to hurt me. She cared about me. Or maybe she just cared about some dead guy I used to be. Either way, I trusted her.

"He's like me," I admitted. "He's a shadow walker. He said I couldn't trust you. That if I went with you I'd be responsible for turning souls into shadow demons."

Cautiously, Anaya stepped toward me. "Cash, listen to me. He is dangerous. He's been feeding you lies."

"Why would he do that?" I said. "You said it yourself, I'm too valuable to be tossed aside as meat. What could he want me for?"

"He's been enslaved to Umbria for Almighty knows how long," she said, solemnly. I watched a braid fall across her face and she gently pushed it away. "He's recruiting you."

"I know." I stumbled back against the doorframe feeling weak and hating every second of it. "He helps souls escape. He gives them peace."

"Peace?" Anaya scoffed. "He delivers them to shadow demons in Umbria to be eaten! Open your eyes. See him for what he is. Maybe he was a good soul once. One with a heart and a conscience, but not anymore. He's a puppet. He's a puppet that's been sent to bring you in."

I braced my palms on my knees and breathed in through my nose, out through my mouth. I couldn't get enough air into my lungs. The room was starting to spin around me. Noah lied to me. He was going to use me just like this Balthazar guy wanted to.

"You can either be at peace with working for Balthazar,

or go through with my plan to get you through the gates. If you refuse both of these options, then the shadow demons *will* collect you. And what they use you for will be far worse. I promise you that."

This was a nightmare. I rubbed my cold palms over my face trying to scrub away the dumb look I could feel settled there.

"If you don't want to do this, you could always go along with Balthazar's plan," she said. "Working for Balthazar may not seem like an ideal eternity, but it's better than what's on the other side."

"Don't feed him that bullshit," Finn spoke up. He sneered at her from across the room, his eyes haunted. "Don't delude him into believing this life is anything more than a prison sentence. A nightmare. He'll just hate you for it later."

"Stay out of this, Finn!"

"I don't understand," I whispered, leaning my forehead against the doorframe. "Why the sudden urgency? You were fine with turning me over to your boss just a few days ago." I pushed away from the door, anger sending energy I didn't know I had into each of my limbs. I clenched my fists, betrayal thick in my throat. She still wasn't telling me everything. Even after all we'd been through together.

"I thought Tarik was in Heaven. And my family." Anaya's voice shook with the force of her words. Words that were about to decimate me. "He promised to allow me to cross if I protected you and delivered you when the time came."

My heart shuddered and throbbed and tore to pieces in my chest. I took a deep breath and winced when my lungs swelled with pain. "It was all bullshit, then?"

Anaya looked up, pain flashing across her face. "No!"

"But you weren't going to hesitate," I said. "Before you knew I had his soul…"

She was going to throw me to the wolves to get what she wanted. She didn't give a damn about me. All she cared about was some poor bastard who had been dead and buried for a thousand years. And I wasn't him. I didn't *want* to be him.

Anaya rushed forward. "Cash, wait. You don't understand—"

I backed out of the room and grabbed my shoes. I shoved them on. Didn't even bother to tie them. "Get away from me," I muttered.

Anaya touched my shoulder and I jerked away. "Stay away from me, Anaya." My words broke apart when I looked at her. I'd let her in. Let her see all of me. And this is what she gave me in return. I couldn't even swallow through the pain. "Whatever this was…it was just a lie."

"No, it wasn't." She sounded panicked as she followed me out the door and into the sun. "I didn't know. I didn't know what he wanted you for in the beginning. If there was another way, I swear—"

I climbed into my Bronco and shut the door to block out her words. No. I didn't want to hear her. I couldn't. Not now. I rested my forehead on the steering wheel and cranked the ignition until the engine roared to life under the hood. I wasn't sure how fast my Bronco could go, but I hoped it was fast enough to outrun death.

Chapter 26

Anaya

He hated me.

He had to after everything I'd done. Everything I'd asked of him. But I didn't know another way. And I couldn't stand lying to him another minute. Pulling my knees up to my chest, I looked out over Cash's backyard from the roof of his house. A few lights inside glowed with life, casting shadows across the clean concrete slab where Emma's house used to sit before the fire that had changed everything. The billowing clouds overhead looked like smoke as they rumbled and spat out little droplets of rain. The music vibrating Cash's studio walls cut off and I sat up when the door creaked open. Cash stepped out into the rain, not even bothering to shield himself. It pelted his scalp and within seconds his black hair was dripping over his forehead. His blue T-shirt turned to paint against his skin. I had to squeeze my eyes shut when the memory of Tarik kissing me in the rain swept over me.

"Are you going to stay up there all night?" he finally said. When I opened my eyes he looked so tired, worn down. I scooted to the edge of the roof and let my legs dangle over the sides.

"I didn't think you wanted me to come in."

"I don't." He pushed the wet hair out of his face. "But that's probably not going to stop you, now is it?"

He didn't say anything else. Just walked back into his studio and left the door open so the light could be swallowed up by the night. Another clap of thunder shook the house and a bright purple streak of lightning cracked the sky in half, illuminating a few shadow demons creeping around the walls of the studio. I stared at the open door. He was angry. But he wouldn't have left that door open if he didn't feel anything for me anymore. Some part of him still cared. Still wanted this. I hopped off the roof and headed for the studio.

When I got inside, Cash was peeling off his soaked T-shirt. He tossed it into the corner of the room and glanced up at me, shivering. His arms glittered with gold paint.

"You're cold," I said.

"No shit, Sherlock." He shook his head and sat on the bar stool in front of a canvas. "So, Dr. Kevorkian. You here to finish the job yourself? I bet that blade of yours would do the trick."

Something inside me cracked at the sound of his voice. So bitter. Angry. It didn't sound anything like the boy leaving whispers in the hollow of my neck. If I still had the ability to cry, I knew tears would have been streaming down my cheeks. Instead the pain all stayed locked up inside.

"I'm so sorry," I said, my voice shattering. Just like the rest of me. "I know you don't believe me, but I wouldn't have been able to do it even if you weren't Tarik—"

"I am *not* Tarik," he snapped. "I'm just me. If that's not enough for you, then I don't know what to tell you. Sorry for your loss, I guess."

I flinched as each one of his words struck me like a slap in the face.

"I know you're not!" I shook, balling up the sides of my dress in my fists. "I don't want you to be. And I'll find another way if that's what you want. Just please...*please* don't hate me."

"What happens to you, Anaya?"

"What do you mean?"

Cash stared at his canvas, at the half-painted portrait of a sad girl with golden eyes. He was painting me.

"I mean what happens to you if you don't follow through for him?" he said. "What happens if you do this? If you let me cross the gates without his permission?"

I swallowed, trying to force that annoying ache down my throat. It wouldn't budge.

"Anaya?"

"I'll be banished," I said. "To Hell."

Cash placed his hands on his knees and closed his eyes. He was shaking from the inside out.

"Well, that option's out."

"It doesn't have to be." I took a hesitant step forward. "I'd do it. I'd do it for you."

"For me...or for Tarik?" Cash said, so quiet I almost didn't hear.

He might as well have slapped me in the face. How could he think that? I had told him I'd go to Hell for him!

Didn't that mean anything? Had I loved Tarik? Yes. But the connection I felt now was to this boy. This boy who was so wonderfully different and right for me that being in the room with him tilted my world off-balance. "How could you even ask me that?" I whispered.

"It doesn't matter anymore," he said. "Whatever I do, I belong to someone else."

I just looked at him.

"If I go along with this, I'll belong to this Balthazar guy. If I don't, then I belong to the shadow demons just like Noah." He stopped and took a deep breath, turned around to face me. His eyes branded every part of me. "And everywhere in between, it feels like I belong to you."

"Cash…"

He stood up and stepped into me. My shimmer sparked off his skin. His breath fanned across my face. Sweet. Heated, despite how cold the rest of him was.

"I really want to hate you," he whispered and reached up to brush a braid off my shoulder. When the braid turned to vapor between his fingers, his jaw clenched. He focused on his fingers and the braid became solid in his grasp. I closed my eyes as Cash's touch forced gravity to take hold of my skin. It burned as it took on the form of something I'd left behind so many years ago I'd lost count. Once I was solid, Cash pushed the braid off my shoulder, letting his fingers slide over my shoulder blade, and I opened my eyes. He stared at the strap of my dress.

"Why can't I hate you?"

It was only a whisper. I never realized a whisper could hold so much emotion. Could sound so tortured. I couldn't stand a sound like that coming out of his mouth. So I did the only thing I could think of to make sure the sound didn't come out again. I leaned up on my tiptoes and pressed my mouth to his.

His lips were so cold against my mine that I wondered if I was burning him. I started to pull away to check, but Cash wound his arms around my back and crushed me closer. So close the air between us was lost. So close, I couldn't tell where I ended and he began. Vaguely, I realized our legs were moving. A clumsy dance that landed us on the sofa in the corner of the room. All the way, he never broke the kiss. That kiss worked like stitches. It was the only thing holding either of us together. Trapping the hurt inside. I was terrified of the pain that would spill out when it ended, so I didn't let it. Cash lay back on the sofa and I straddled his hips without him having to guide me. His hands slid up my thighs and gripped my hips. His mouth opened a little wider under mine and I gasped at the dull sensations that flowed through me, growing stronger by the second. He wasn't just forcing my flesh into existence. He was making me feel things I hadn't felt since a heart had beaten with life in my chest. My hands wandered over the smooth, hard lines of his chest, trying to memorize every dip and ridge and muscle. When my fingers brushed over his bare stomach, Cash groaned, his hips lifting to press into me as if he wasn't in control of his own body.

"Anaya…" My name rested like a plea against his lips and all I could feel was his mouth working its way down my throat. The fire in my veins. The electricity that his fingertips created. A blue ribbon of energy wrapped around us, binding us, and nothing had ever felt so right. Cash's hand worked between us and flipped open the button of his jeans, and a flare of heat exploded to life at my side. My blade. Oh God… I pulled away gasping, my palm glowing against his chest. He was so close the heat drained out of me in an instant, replaced by fear.

I looked down at Cash. My braids created a wall around our faces. My eyes the only light in our little safe haven. He reached up and cupped the side of my face, trying to catch his breath.

"This isn't how it's supposed to be. I'm not supposed to see it coming." His voice cracked. He knew how close he was. He felt it too. "I don't want to see it coming, Anaya."

"I know," I whispered.

His dark eyes searched my face. For what, I wasn't sure. He rubbed his thumb across my bottom lip, so soft it made me tremble.

"I'll go," he finally said. "I'll do whatever Balthazar wants me to do."

"Cash—"

"If it means I get to keep you," he said, pressing his finger to my lips to quiet me. "If it means we can have more of this. Then I'll do anything."

I sat up and placed my hands on his chest. He felt like ice under my palms. He felt like he was already dead.

"You have no idea what you're saying."

Cash followed me up, so that his face was only an inch from mine.

"For once in my life, I know exactly what I'm saying," he said. "I've never felt like this about anyone, Anaya. And it doesn't take a rocket scientist to see that this isn't going to work with me alive and you dead. It isn't going work if I'm in Heaven and you're in Hell. There is only one option that gives us a chance."

Cash's eyes swept over my face. His hand reached up to

tuck a braid behind my ear.

"I feel like I've been waiting for you for a thousand years," he whispered. "I'm taking that option."

I searched his eyes for some kind of doubt. Something that said he was only saying these words out of fear. Or desire. The only thing I could see was certainty. And love.

"You're sure?"

He nodded and tugged me down to brush his lips against mine.

"It's weird," he whispered against my lips. "Not even you can make me warm anymore. It must not be far off."

I pushed Cash back down onto the sofa and curled up beside him. Wrapped every part of myself around him, trying to lend him my heat. He wound his arms around me and closed his eyes.

"How is it going to happen?" he asked.

"When your body gives out…I'll reap your soul."

"With the blade?" He sounded nervous.

I laughed. "Yeah. But it won't hurt. It will be a relief. No more pain. And then I'll take you to Balthazar."

I waited for him to ask me what exactly Balthazar would want him to do, but he never did. I had a feeling he didn't really want to know. I raked my fingers through his damp hair and pressed a kiss to his temple.

"What happens if you don't get here in time?"

His voice carried the force of an atom bomb in the silence, even though it was only a whisper. I could feel him shaking, so I smoothed my hand over his arm.

"I'll get here in time," I said.

"You can't promise that," he said quietly. "I need to know what to do if you don't get here and they do. Noah's stronger than me. And he's good at what he does."

It took me a minute to find the words. I didn't want to say them, but he was right. It was unrealistic to think that there was no chance of that happening. Especially when the dead kept pulling me away.

"Then you do what they say." I closed my eyes and squeezed his arm. "You do whatever you have to do to stay safe until I can get to you."

He didn't say anything. Just nodded and blew out a shaky breath. A breath that sounded like it held enough fear for the both of us.

"Go to sleep," I whispered.

"I don't want to," he said. "I don't want to wake up as someone else. I'm not ready for that. I'm not ready for any of it."

"That's not going to happen," I said, trying so hard to sound confident. Honestly, I didn't know how this worked. I'd never met a soul that had lived as many lives as Cash. The only kind of souls that stayed in circulation that long were the ones that continued to search for something. They never felt resolved, so they continued on their path, life after life. Death after death. It was amazing he'd made it this long. And just when his journey was about to end...I kept him from it. I rested my head against his.

"You wouldn't be happy if I came out the other side of this Tarik?"

I turned his face so that my eyes could see his. "No."

"Why not?"

"Because...he's not you."

Cash wound around me a little tighter.

"Tell me what you were like," he murmured, sleep pulling

him under. "When you were alive."

I thought back, something I didn't let myself do very often. Usually the pain was too great. But now it wasn't so bad. The past wasn't nearly as scary when you had a piece of it in your present. I rested in the groove of his arm and smiled.

"My father was a fisherman," I said. "He even owned his own boat."

"Really?" Cash's cheek rose with his smile. "Did he ever take you with him?"

"Sometimes," I said. "But mainly I helped my mother. Sometimes I would burn the bread just so I'd have something to feed the birds on the beach after Father sailed away. I used to think if I fed them and sent them off with a prayer, that they'd keep watch over him. Keep him safe somehow."

"Did they?"

I swallowed the bit of pain that rose up my throat like bile. "No. One day he sailed away and never came back. The sea took him away…and it decided to keep him." I paused, wondering if I should tell him the rest. Cash's voice echoed in my mind: *no more secrets, Anaya.*

"It took Tarik, too," I said.

Cash went still beneath me. He didn't even breathe.

"We were going to be married," I went on. "So Father gave him a job on the boat. It was only his second trip out. He kissed me good-bye, promised he'd return, and disappeared on the horizon."

Cash turned to look up at me. "Then what happened?"

I closed my eyes and tried to focus on the good. Focus on the boy that fate had given me all over again.

"He died," I finally said. "And then so did I."

Chapter 27

Cash

Sometime before the sun came up, I woke up and Anaya was gone. My arm was draped awkwardly over my chest, like she was still there to support it. I could still smell her on my skin. Like I'd slept in a thunderstorm. Like I was still in a dream. I sat up and scrubbed my palms over my face to rub the sleep from my eyes. To wake myself up enough to realize what I'd done.

I told her I'd go along with everything. Embrace being a shadow walker. Work for Balthazar.

And I'd meant every word. Was being a slave to the man who gave Anaya orders to collect the dead what I wanted to do with my eternity? No. But not having to say good-bye to her…I couldn't help but believe the sacrifice would be worth it. I'd never loved a girl before. Not really. Not like this. But I loved Anaya. I loved her so much it was hard to breathe when she was around. It was even harder to breathe when she wasn't. And not just because my lungs were failing. I knew now that Noah wasn't someone I could trust. No way was I going to end up like him.

I finally managed to drag myself out of my studio and into the house. Every part of me ached. I needed a shower. And coffee. And probably a new heart and set of lungs, but that wasn't going to happen. With my recent decision, there wasn't really a point in fighting to get on a transplant list. I searched the house for Finn when I didn't find him in the guest room, and finally found him in the den sitting on the couch staring at the black screen of the TV. I kicked the leg of the couch to get his attention.

"You know, when I said you could move in here, I meant you could have a bedroom to sleep in, too."

"I know. I just couldn't sleep." Finn squinted up at me. "Where have you been?

"I slept in the studio."

"You slept?" He raised a brow.

"I had help," I said. The memory of Anaya pressed up against me in all the right places suddenly swept over me and I cleared my throat. "You want some coffee?"

"Yeah." He stood up and stretched. "And make it strong."

I brewed a pot of coffee, but by the time I'd had my second cup I'd given up hope for anything to warm my insides. I grabbed my burgundy scarf off the back of a kitchen chair and wrapped it around my neck, then shoved my black knit cap over my head.

"It's like eighty degrees out there," Finn said as he sank down into a chair and took a sip from his Bank of Lone Pine coffee mug.

"It doesn't feel like it to me," I said. "I feel like I just took an ice bath. That means it's gonna be soon, right?"

He shrugged, refusing to look me in the eye. "I don't know."

"Finn."

He sighed and looked out the little kitchen window that still had the blue floral-print curtains that Mom put up before she left. The sun had faded them but Dad never took them down.

"Yes," he finally said. "It won't be long."

I sat my cup down and stared at the table, waiting for the fear to take over. It didn't. I felt oddly…calm. I'm sure knowing Anaya would be waiting on the other side for me helped that.

"Thank you," I said.

Finn drummed his fingers on the tabletop like he was stalling. His jaw clenched.

"Spit it out," I said.

"What are you going to do?" He looked up at me.

"I'm going to let her take me to Balthazar."

Finn pushed his fingers through his unkempt hair. "She offered you an out. You should take it."

"I won't let her go to Hell for me."

"Being a slave to Balthazar *will* be Hell," he growled. "You have no idea what you're doing."

I pushed my cup aside and stood up. "I know what kind of hell I'll be in if I lose her. And honestly…that's all that matters right now. With what you've been through with Emma, you should get this."

He shook his head. "That's different."

I laughed and started down the hall. "Whatever you say."

"Where are you going?" Finn called out as I made my way down the hall.

"Studio!" I yelled back. If I stayed here I'd say stuff to him that I didn't mean. He was just trying to help. But I didn't need that from him. I just needed him to take care of Emma after I was gone. My fingers were twitching anyway. I needed to finish that painting of Anaya. Her eyes still weren't quite right. No matter how much I mixed and melded the colors, I couldn't find a perfect match for that gold. And I needed to finish this before everything went down. One of the things I loved about art was that you could leave your imprint on the world. The things that inspire you, make you tick, you can leave them behind for the world to see. And Anaya was too beautiful to keep to myself. She was the imprint I wanted to leave.

By the time I pushed through the studio door, my knees felt weak. Shaky. I stumbled into the room, my footsteps echoing off the concrete floor. Something wasn't right. I felt nauseous. The world was tilted at an odd angle, spinning circles while darkness blurred the edge of my vision. I braced my palms on my knees and sucked in a lungful of ice-cold air that left me coughing until I couldn't breathe. When I pulled my palms away from my mouth there was blood. Lots of it. My eyes swept over the concrete; wet red drops were splattered against the gray. I stood up, heart hammering in my chest, and wiped my mouth with the back of my wrist.

"Anaya," I choked out through the fear in my throat. She needed to be here. What was going to happen to me if I died when she wasn't here? What if she didn't get here in time? I heard the hissing behind me and panic throbbed in my gut.

I spun around and braced myself on the bar stool in front of my half-painted portrait of Anaya. Shadow demons. So many of them they just looked like one big black blur that bled into the darkness enclosing my vision. One of them broke away from the crowd and swirled around my waist like smoke, and I froze. Solid. Still. Like ice. My fear melting off me in a dripping sweat. The shadow demon slithered up my body until its bloody cavern of a mouth was an inch from mine. It smelled like death and rot and things I'd never smelled before. Things I never wanted to smell again. I couldn't breathe. I couldn't move. This was happening. I wanted to run, but I didn't think it would do much good. They'd just follow me. Find me. Take me. And then what?

Another shadow demon circled my ankle. Its tongue flicked out, black like tar, but it felt like a flame through my jeans. I winced at the pain and they went into a frenzy. Hissing and snapping. Inching closer to me by the second, but still holding back like they were waiting on a command. I half expected Noah to waltz out of the darkness, demanding order, but he didn't. What kind of control did these things even have without him here to fight them off?

Shit! They *were* going to eat me. No! I couldn't go like this. Anything but this. Forcing my body into action, I shook the thing off my leg, stumbled a few feet back, and tripped over my canvas. I hit the cold concrete like a sack of rocks. Pain exploded across my back. Crackled through my chest. I gasped for a breath that my lungs wouldn't allow me to take. Dust particles twirled through the sunshine spilling into the room through the still open door. I was paralyzed. By fear or the fall, I couldn't tell which. If I could just get out of here, I could stall at least. Anaya would come. She always came in time. I just needed…

A big black figure stepped over me, blotting out the light.

Its body was massive. But I couldn't find one feature in its face, other than the gaping hole of a mouth and the two swirling blacker-than-black pits where eyes should have been. It reached its hand out to me.

"It's time," it said, a low rumble that sounded more like a growl than a voice. Using my palms, I pressed against the floor to slide away from it. I didn't get far, though. It took another step forward and its disgusting minions inched closer.

"Not yet!" It growled at one of the demons that nipped at my hand.

Do what they want. Whatever they want. Anaya's voice rang out in my ears like a warning. It's what she had told me the night before. The advice she'd given me and promised me I'd never have to use. So much for promises. I took a deep breath that left my head swimming and sat up, slowly.

"I-I-I'll go," I said. "I'll do whatever you want." I couldn't believe these were my words, coming out of my mouth.

The shadow man standing over me grinned and something dark and disgusting dripped from its mouth and landed on the studio floor. "Good." Its voice rumbled through me like a clap of thunder, setting my insides on fire. It took a step back, motioning for the others to do the same and I sat up.

The walls stared to shake and my hands flew out to brace myself. The floor under my feet began to rise and bend and crack apart. The concrete buckled and a crevice opened up right before my eyes. I'd stepped out of the way just in time. Screams wafted out the darkness. I had to blink, hoping it would clear away what I was seeing. This couldn't be real.

"Go." The shadow man pointed a dark finger into the opening. I looked up at it and raised a brow.

"What?" I took another step back, only to met with a wall

of shadows. "You want me to jump in there?"

It nodded.

"No!" I held my palms up, trying to put some distance between me and the hole. "Hell, no!"

Damn it! Where is Anaya?

"Gooooo!"

I slapped my hands over my ears when its voice rattled my skull. A flame licked my back. No. A tongue. A nip at my calf. I stepped forward, trying to get away from the shadow demons closing in on me from behind. I didn't want this.

The concrete disappeared under my toes. Rock crumbled and spilled over the edge. No sound echoed up from the pit to indicate that it had landed. It was hard, but I forced myself to take a breath. Another. I looked over my shoulder at the shadows ready to claim me. Let them have me or see what was on the other side? It wasn't even a choice.

I stepped forward and the darkness swallowed me whole.

Chapter 28

Anaya

I stood with my toes touching the edge of the cliff and peered over the side. The van hadn't made it all the way down. A tangle of fir trees held most of it in place. The rest of it was littered along the mountainside. Hunks of twisted metal. Shards of glass and tattered strips of tire. A red leather handbag.

A body.

I knew she was dead. I could feel the pull. More than one, actually. The rest must still be in the battered church van. Sometimes I wondered where the feeling went. The urgency to preserve a person's life. Save them. That impulse had been gone for so long that I didn't even remember what it felt like. I was about to step over the side but stopped when I felt the heat melt up from the ground behind me. Screams erupted from the soil, then tapered off until they were muffled by the earth.

Easton.

I glanced at him over my shoulder and raised a brow. He looked like a six-foot block of midnight carved out of the bright blue sky behind him.

"Really?" I said. "A church van accident? How scandalous."

Easton ignored me and brushed himself off. I stepped off the drop-off and he followed me over the edge without a word. He squinted at the sun, frowning. He looked annoyed. But then again, Easton generally looked annoyed. I started with the woman laid out a few feet from the van. Kneeling down, I brushed the matted brown hair from her face. Her silver butterfly barrette was hanging on by only a hair, so I fastened it back into her curls.

"Time to go home, sweetheart," I whispered and reached for my scythe.

Easton brushed past me and headed for the van. "Why don't you stop whispering sweet nothings into her ear and get the job done already?"

"Well, aren't you just a ray of sunshine this morning?" I said.

Easton grumbled something and disappeared into the van.

I lifted my scythe, and as natural as breathing used to be, I let it drop. It tore into her flesh and when it came back up, a pretty soul came along with it. She stumbled into me and I gripped her shoulders to steady her. She looked back at the van.

"Do you understand what happened to you?"

She wrapped her willowy arms around her waist and nodded. She bit her lip like she might cry, but no tears ever came. They never would again.

"My friends?" she whispered.

Her friends. I sighed and looked for Easton, who was still rummaging around in the van. I didn't want to tell her. If he was here, it couldn't be good for them.

Holding up a finger for her to wait, I made my way down to the van. Easton came billowing out of the broken window like smoke and I took a step back. He stood up straight and had a soul in each hand. The man looked dazed. The woman looked terrified, her eyes trained on Easton like he was…well, like he was exactly what he was.

"Two of them?"

Easton rolled his eyes. "They're all yours. I'm just helping you."

I opened my mouth and closed it again. Easton never helped me with my charges. He'd taken on all of Finn's when they asked, but when it came to mine, he refused. None of this made sense.

"What's going on?" I followed him up the hill where the friends stared at one another, not knowing what to say.

"Nothing." He wouldn't look at me. His violet eyes stayed glued to the horizon. "Just help me get them over."

There was no telling what he was up to. I had a feeling it wasn't good. A nervous ache started a slow burn in my chest. I didn't need any more complications. My afterlife was beginning to be defined by them.

"You're sure nothing's wrong?"

Easton spun around. His eyes on fire. "Anaya! Open the fucking gateway already!"

I pressed my lips together to hold in the argument brewing. Balthazar had sent him. He had to. Easton was notoriously unhappy, but he'd never in over four hundred years spoken to me that way. I nodded and closed my eyes. I raised my palms and felt the world ripple like water around me. Warmth. So much warmth swirled around me like a melody you never wanted to forget. How could Easton hate this?

When I opened my eyes, the world had dissolved and given birth to beauty. I smiled at the group of souls, whose faces were lit up with wonder. Their age, their worries, their fear melting off them like candle wax.

"What do we do now?" Easton said. "Wave a magic wand? Hold hands and sing 'Kumbaya'?"

"You've really never taken a Heaven-bound charge?" I said. "How is that even possible?"

He bristled. "I have. Just not for a long time."

He shoved his hands in his pockets and ducked down in his black duster. His violet eyes scanned the blinding white terrain. He twitched and slapped at a dandelion fluff that landed on his nose.

"There." I pointed to the two towering gold gates. They pulsed with life. With peace. A few angels milled about the entrance. Dressed in white and exuding happiness. Two of them pointed at Easton and laughed. He started forward and I grabbed his hand to stop him.

"We're on the same team," I whispered.

He pulled his arm away from me, never taking his eyes off the angel boy with gleaming white hair and clear blue eyes that looked like they'd been made from the sea. "Tell them that."

"If you're uncomfortable, go," I said. "I've got it from here."

I motioned to the angels at the gates and they smiled at the group of souls I had in tow. Easton didn't say anything. But he didn't leave, either. I made quick work of getting the three souls past the gates, and when they were closed, I turned the full force of my gaze on Easton. He squinted when my eyes lit him up like fire.

"Are you supposed to bring me in?" I asked.

"What?"

"Balthazar sent you for me, right?" I stepped forward, fear thrumming in my chest. "I've done everything he's asked. I even got Cash to agree to turn himself over. What reason could he possibly have—"

"It's Cash," he said.

I stopped cold in my tracks. The heat drained from my cheeks. Throbbed in my chest and in my fingertips.

"What do you mean 'It's Cash'?"

Easton's shoulders slumped. "I heard they brought a new shadow walker into Umbria this morning."

"Did you see him?"

Easton sighed. "Anaya—"

I stepped forward and placed my hand on his chest. "Did. You. See him?"

He shook his head. "It's him. It has to be and you know it."

I couldn't move. It couldn't be him. It couldn't. Not Cash. Not *my* Cash. My hand fell away from Easton's chest and I backed away, trembling. Falling apart. I'd promised him I'd keep him safe. That I'd make it in time…

"I…I need to go check," I whispered. "I need to make sure. He could still be okay. It might not be him. What if you're wrong? What if—"

Easton grabbed my arm and pulled me close enough to feel the pain and darkness that ran through his veins. He kept his eyes on an angel walking by, but his words were meant for me.

"Do you really want to waste that kind of time?"

When I didn't answer he gave me a good shake.

"You know it's him," he said. "We both know. So we can waste time running all over Lone Pine looking for a guy who is not going to be there, or we can go get him. What's left of him, anyway."

Something inside me broke. I could feel the horror on my face when I looked at Easton.

"Joke, Anaya," he said. "It was a joke. We'll get him."

He ran his palm over my hair and grinned. I slapped his hand away.

"Has anyone ever told you that you have a very sick sense of humor?" I hissed.

"I'm pretty sure that *you've* told me that." He raised a brow and grinned. "On several occasions."

"Well, it's still true." I was trying to compose myself, but I wasn't pulling it off. I was breaking on the inside, and those cracks were starting to show all over my face. They had to be. Easton nudged my shoulder.

"Come on, princess," he said. "Let's go get your shadow walker."

Chapter 29

Cash

I knew I wasn't dead yet. If I'd been dead I wouldn't be able to feel pain. Unbearable pain. Pain like a living thing that held a grudge against my very existence. Pulsing and clawing its way through my insides. I'd never felt anything like it before, but I sure as hell felt it now.

When a bead of sweat trickled into the corner of my eye, I cracked my lids open and blinked it away. The heat burned my eyes. Scorched my skin. I tried to suck in a breath, but the sour, smoky smell made me gag.

"He's awake," a guy's voice said. It echoed as if we were in a cave. Once my eyes adjusted to the hazy dark, I could see that's exactly what this was. It sort of reminded me of the Carlsbad Caverns Dad took me to once when I was a kid. Rocks shaped like fangs jutted up from the floor and down from the ceiling. Like I was sitting pretty in an enormous set of jaws. Part of me was waiting for them to close in and chew me into tiny bite-sized bits of Cash.

A muted blue glow blanketed the walls, me, and everything in between. Something thick like saliva dripped onto my boots and jeans. I tried to raise my hand to rub the sting out of my eye but it wouldn't budge. I squirmed and looked down. My hands were tied behind me, crushed between a rock that felt like it had been pulled from a campfire and my back. I tried to stand up, but my legs wouldn't work.

"What's going on?" I said, peering into the dark. "Why am I tied up?"

Something moved in the dark. A flash of gray emerging from the writhing shadows that slithered along the walls. Finally, Noah stepped out of the darkness and looked down at me. His ash-blond hair dangled in wispy strands just above his cold, steel-blue eyes.

"They're afraid you'll try to get away," he said.

"From where?" I jerked on the ropes. "Where the hell am I?"

A hiss echoed through the cavern, sending a chill racing up my spine despite the heat. Noah turned around and squinted into one of the dark corners, his shoulders tense. When the hiss faded, he relaxed a little.

"Umbria," he said. "You're in the shadow land now."

"You're kidding me, right?"

He raised a pale brow. "Does it look like I'm kidding?"

I let myself look around the cave and swallowed. Smoke clung to the ceiling, where some kind of red liquid dripped to the ground around me. A drop landed on my cheek, so I rubbed it off with my shoulder. I stared at the red smudge and a fresh wave of fear crashed over me. Blood. It was raining blood. I gasped for a breath the room didn't want to give me. A breath my lungs didn't want to hold.

"It's just the blooderflies," he said. "They make a mess but they won't hurt you."

"Blooderflies?" My voice cracked.

He pointed to the ceiling, where you could see flickers of glistening red wings through the layer of smoke. Each one was small enough to sit in the palm of your hand. In the blue light, you could see right through their bloody, liquid wings to the veins pulsing inside.

"They sleep up there," he said. "They'll leave soon."

I shook my head and closed my eyes. Maybe if I closed my eyes tight enough it would all go away. Maybe I'd wake up to the credits of some horror movie where stuff like this belonged. Because it sure as hell didn't belong in reality. "Why did you do this to me?"

Footsteps squished and squeaked across the wet floor. When I opened my eyes, he was kneeling in front of me. "Because I need a replacement."

"What?" I jerked on the restraints. "You said you wanted to help me! I trusted you!"

"Stop taking it so personal," he said. "You're a good kid, Cash. But I'm done here. I've put in my time. You think I want to live out the rest of eternity being some kind of delivery boy to these things?"

"If it's so awful, why do you do it?" I gasped, my lungs fighting for air. "Why don't you leave?"

"You think I'd be here if it was that easy?" He glanced back at the shadows lurking behind him. "Around here, it's feed or be eaten. Those are your choices. There is no third option."

Choice. Looking at the desperation in Noah's eyes, I could see that's exactly what he thought this was. He thought he could bring me in and get a ticket to go roam the Earth, free as a bird. He was fucking delusional. Why would they let him go when they could have two of us? Noah watched me with a crazed, empty look in his eyes. There wasn't going to be any convincing him. Not today. Probably not ever. I needed to come up with something else. I needed to stall him.

"So why not go to work for Balthazar?" I finally asked.

Noah stood and paced in front of me, biting his thumbnail. He laughed humorlessly. "After the things I've done?" He raised a brow. "No, thanks. I don't need a one-way ticket to Hell."

"I can help you. Anaya can help you."

Noah's cold glare snapped up. "Stop begging. You sound pathetic. And if you expect to last longer than a day down here you're going to have to toughen up. Now, what's it going to be? I suggest you decide quick. They're not fond of waiting."

I stared at the glistening rock between my dead legs and felt my jaw clench. Sweat dripped into my eyes. Or maybe it was blood. I didn't care. I'd made my choice. Hell, I'd even made peace with it. And this wasn't it. Apparently that didn't mean much to the scum that had dragged me down here.

"I'm not even dead yet," I said, reaching for some way to stall. "Don't I have to be dead to do whatever it is they want me to do?"

Noah sighed and sat down beside me. He stared at his boots, which were coated in ash, and played with one of the laces. He avoided looking at the crowd of shadow demons creeping out of the corners, filling the room until there was barely space left to breathe. How the hell could he be so calm?

My fingers balled into fists against my back.

"It won't take long. There's no way a human body could survive more than a few days down here anyway," he said. "They just collected you now because they knew that piece of reaper ass you've been tapping was going to bring you in if they didn't."

"Don't talk about her like that," I growled, feeling the sound that came out of me burn my throat. If my legs had worked, I would have done more than growled at him.

Noah chuckled. "Defending your dead girlfriend's honor should be the last of your worries. Because after that body of yours gives out…there's no escaping this place."

I rubbed my forehead on my shoulder when another bead of sweat trickled into my eyes. Noah finally looked up and acknowledged the horde of shadow demons inching closer. Slipping across the slick red floor. The big black one that looked as close to a man as one of them could get broke away from the crowd and stared down at us both. It growled something I didn't understand to Noah.

"What's it going to be, Cash?" He cocked his head to the side to look at me, giving me a glimpse of the black vein etched into his neck. "Are you the pizza? Or are you the delivery boy?"

"What if I don't want to be either?"

Noah laughed and combed his fingers through his hair. "Then they'll choose for you."

I looked past Noah, at the deceiving soft blue light rippling through the cave. The room was packed with shadow demons, their darkness dueling for dominance. They hissed and snapped at the blooderflies that fluttered around in a circle, creating a bloody cyclone before being siphoned out into the hazy twilight beyond the cave opening. Fear closed up my throat when they turned their attention back to me. Howling and writhing with the need to feed. My legs tingled and I managed to pull them up to my chest, pressing as close to the rock behind me as I could get. None of this sounded appealing. But the thought of letting these things devour me made me want to vomit. And Anaya…what would they do to her if she came down after me? Did she even know I was gone yet? I couldn't imagine her in a place like this. I didn't want to.

"She'll come after me," I said. "You know she will."

Noah stepped in front of me and lowered himself until his face was level with mine. "Is that supposed to scare me? Do you have any idea how many shadows are outside this cave?"

Fear crept up my throat and I jerked on my restraints. There were more? This cave was packed.

"One little reaper would be nothing for them. A snack," he said. "They'd shred her piece by piece. Devour her. But first…" He grinned. "I think first they'd play with her. Is that what you want?"

No. The fear in my throat was everywhere now. In my chest, making it even harder to breathe. Not Anaya. What was my plan here? To just sit around playing nice with these things, waiting for her to walk into a trap? No freaking way. I couldn't let her do that. I wouldn't. Even if that meant being like Noah. Maybe if she believed there wasn't anything good left inside me, she'd leave it alone. Forget about me. It was a chance I was going to have to take.

I closed my eyes and took as deep a breath as my lungs would allow. "Teach me how to be a delivery boy."

"I hope you have a strong stomach," Noah said as he grabbed me by the wrist and pulled me up out of the bubbling black puddle in the ground that looked like an oil spill. I couldn't stop shaking. Convulsing. What the hell had I just seen? If that place wasn't Hell, then I didn't want to know what Hell was.

"Strong stomach? Are you saying it gets worse than that?" I looked over my shoulder where the pit had been. All I saw now was wet, glistening pavement.

Noah snorted. "You have no idea."

Around us, abandoned buildings with windowless faces stared back us. They lined the desolate street. The only things that looked alive were the streetlamps buzzing overhead. There wasn't so much as a rat. But a city wasn't far off. Even from here, you could smell the smog, hear the sirens and signs of a bursting metropolis. I wondered if I yelled for help if anyone would hear. I doubted it.

"Where are we going?" I stumbled behind Noah, grabbing my chest. It hurt to breathe. Noah stopped at the steps of an abandoned brick building. The insides looked charred, the walls crumbling. Noah closed his eyes and took a deep breath.

"Do you feel it?"

"Feel what?"

He pointed ahead, where a pale blue color flashed in one of the windows. "Them."

Another blue blur flickered behind the broken glass and a cold sensation pricked at my insides like needles. I took a step closer and the pinpricks hummed under my skin. Holy hell… "I do feel it."

"Good." Noah glanced at me and took the concrete steps two at a time. "Let's go fishing. You'll normally try to lure in a bigger group, but for your first time we'll just take a couple."

I stumbled up the steps after him. Noah dissolved right through the door, leaving me standing on the other side. Looking around the abandoned street, I pushed the door open and stepped inside.

"Noah?"

"Shhh." He hissed from behind me. I spun around in the dark and he held up a finger to his lips. I nodded, wishing I knew what the hell we were doing here. Or where we even were. It didn't look like it was anywhere near Lone Pine. I'd been to places like LA and New York with Dad before. This place might fit into one of those places, but how the hell had we gotten that far so quick? A flash of white zipped past us and Noah nodded toward a dark hallway. The orange glow from the streetlight outside spilled in through the broken windows. I stepped over shattered glass and chunks of molded drywall. Fear throbbing in my chest almost as hard as the pain.

"Grab him!" Noah shouted. I looked up in time to see a white glow split the darkness in the hall. Without thinking, I reached out and grabbed on to it. It felt like a burst of electricity crackling through my fingers and I winced as the force of it shot up my arm. Someone screamed and suddenly, cold flesh wriggled under my fingers. It was…a kid. He was just a kid. He looked up at me, his face pale and gaunt. His curly black hair dangled just above his big brown eyes. He couldn't have been more than fifteen. He looked like he belonged with the skater kids at school who took over the park every Saturday afternoon. He didn't look like he should be dead.

"W-what are you gonna to do with me?" he stuttered.

"I…I…" I didn't know. What *was* I going to do with him? I knew what they wanted me to do, but could I? Looking down into his innocent eyes, I didn't think so. I may have been a lot of things in my life I wasn't proud of, but this...

Another scream erupted in the silence and we both looked up. Noah. He came pounding down the stairs, a girl behind him. He had a fistful of her long brown hair in his grip. Her face was twisted up in a scowl. She swung out, trying to connect a punch into Noah's side, but he jerked out of the way and chuckled.

"Let go!" she shrieked.

"If you wouldn't have run like that, maybe I wouldn't have had to grab you by the hair in the first place," he said.

His eyes landed on me and they brightened. "Look at that. You got one on your first try. Aren't you just an overachiever?"

I stepped out of the hall, shaking, but keeping my grip on the kid. Everything in me was screaming to let him go, but I couldn't seem to make my fingers follow the direction. "What are we doing with them?"

He rolled his eyes. "You know damn good and well what we're going to do with them. Unless you're willing to take their place." He raised a brow.

The kid wriggled under my grip. My heart pounded so hard in my chest I could feel it in my toes.

"Well, are you?" he asked again.

I thought about those things at the foot of my bed at night. Trying to get to my soul, right through my skin, the day of Dad's funeral. They'd do that and worse to Anaya if she went down there trying to save me.

I couldn't let that happen.

For a moment I let myself linger with her memory. The way her lips tasted, the little sounds she made when I kissed her. Her smile, warm and sweet against my skin. If I did this, she'd hate me. Memories would be all I had left. I took a moment to mentally lock them all away with the piece of myself I'd never give to the shadows, then steeled myself for what was to come.

I looked at Noah and shook my head. The fear thrumming in my chest for the girl I was pretty sure I was in love with wouldn't letting me answer any other way. A satisfied look spread across his face and he nodded.

"Good," he said. "Let's get this over with."

Chapter 30

Anaya

Ash rained down from the sky and the heat of the underworld swallowed me. Easton stepped up beside me and looked out over the barren wasteland to the skull-lined cliffs.

"How are we supposed to get him out of there?" I asked, watching shadows scream and dive from the cliffs.

Easton narrowed his gaze as if trying to find a way in. "I don't know. But we better come up with something soon. He's not going to last long down here."

The memory flooded over me in an instant. The pain. The moment when I realized Tarik was never coming back. I couldn't go through that again. There would be no escape from it this time. No blade to take me away. He'd be gone. And I would have to live with the absence of him…forever.

I forced the panic exploding to life in my chest down until it was just a faint throbbing in my gut. We would get him out.

We had to. I hadn't found him after a thousand years only to lose him now. Not like this.

Easton nudged my arm and walked out ahead of me, his boots crunching in the rocks and ash. "Let's go."

I hurried after him, one hand on my scythe. I didn't know how much it was going to help me against a horde of shadow demons, but I held on to it anyway. Ready to destroy anything that got in my way. When we were close enough to the cliffs to see the flaming shadows leaping up from the waves, Easton grabbed me and pulled us behind a skull. My shins hit the thick ice base and I winced. It…burned. I stared down at the red slashes marring my skin.

"You okay?"

I looked up at Easton, trying to conceal my horror. I could feel pain in this place. It stung and throbbed and reminded me of the end of a life I didn't want to remember. The memory of the blade slipping between my ribs almost caused me to cry out, but I held it in. They could end me here, just as easily as I'd ended myself. "I…yes. I'm fine. How do we know where to find him?" I placed my hand on the stone to brace myself and looked down the coast at the endless row of skull caverns. "He could be anywhere. Where do we even start?"

Easton stared into the flaming horizon where Hell beckoned him. He was ignoring a call. I could see the pain written all over his face. The scythe smoking at his side. Here, where we became flesh and blood, it had to be burning him right through to his skin.

"Easton?"

"We need a diversion," he finally said, wiping the sweat from his brow with the back of his wrist. "There's no way we're going to get inside to search. And even if we do…we won't make it out. We need something to draw them out. We need to empty those caves."

A shadow slithered around the side of the cavern as if drawn by our scent and we froze. My fingers curled around the pearl handle of my scythe and Easton placed his hand over mine to stop me.

"You'll attract more of them," he whispered. The shadow swooped down until it hovered right in front of my face, hissing, wanting a taste. I inhaled and the black scent of death swirled down into my lungs. It burned like fire and my eyes watered. Even when my body had been living, I'd never felt anything like this. Everything inside me screamed for self-preservation. Telling me to run away and never look back. But I couldn't give in to that fear. There was too much on the line. Easton squeezed my hand and I shut my eyes. I couldn't look at it, this thing that had Cash. I wanted to destroy it. After an excruciating moment, an awful shrieking sound escaped the shadow's throat and it whipped around the skull and dove into the frothy gray sea. I sagged against the skull and Easton blew a long breath out, releasing my hand.

"Is he worth this, Anaya?" Easton stood up. "If he is, we'll do this. But we are about to reach the point of no return. In fact, I can't promise you any of us will make it out of this. So I'm going to ask you this once, do you love him? Do you love him enough to face the possibility of this being your end?"

Easton stood in front of me, waiting. He'd jump in feet-first whatever I decided. I knew that. I knew it because whether he wanted anyone to know it or not, Easton had a heart. So did I. And it belonged to Cash. "I love him. I won't leave him here. But you should go. I don't expect you to risk yourself for this."

Easton stepped back and rolled his eyes. "I don't bow out from a fight. You should know that about me by now."

"What I know is that you don't give a damn about some human. No matter who they are. No matter what's on the line."

"*You're* on the line here, Anaya!" He glared at me. "Don't you get that? Don't you get how valuable this kid is? How badly Balthazar wants him?" he said. "If we don't bring him back from this…*you* will play Balthazar's price."

"And you are willing to risk yourself for that? For him?" I asked, my voice shaky.

He sighed and scrubbed his fingers through his black hair. "You. I'm willing to risk myself for *you*. Don't get some preconceived notion that I give a damn about the human. I don't."

Despite the heat and the pain and the danger of the place around me, I smiled.

"But you give a damn about me."

Easton caught sight of the look on my face and groaned. "Don't you dare tell anyone I said that. I'll leave your pretty little ass down here if you do."

"You're a good friend, Easton," I said. "Thank you."

Easton ignored me and bounced on the balls of his feet as if he were pumping himself up for what came next. "I hope you're ready to do this." His violet eyes narrowed on the cliffs, determined.

"What are we doing?" I said, panicked. "We…we don't even have a plan."

"Yeah we do. The distraction thing."

"That's not a plan, Easton! That's an idea. A suggestion."

Easton ignored me. "Whatever happens, just make sure

you get in and out of those caverns before they come back," he said. "I'll do my best to keep them out, but I won't be able to hold them off for long."

I reached out for Easton, but he slipped through my fingers. "Wait! You never said *you* were the distraction."

Easton spun around and a lopsided grin lit up his face. "Worried about me, Anaya? You should know better than that."

He turned and ran, his duster flying out behind him like a wave of smoke. "Dinnertime, you little bastards!" He disappeared into an ash cloud and a few black blurs zipped after him. On the other side of the cliffs the shadows screamed with need.

"Anaya, run!" His voice echoed from somewhere I couldn't see.

My legs jumped into action at the sound of his voice, and my breath sawed in and out of my lungs, burning my throat. Fear pounded in my chest like a drum. I ran, watching the black shadows pour out of the eyes and nostrils of the skull cavern closest to me. It looked like a continuous gush of oil, spilling out onto the land before it separated into a thousand black pulsing forms. I paused only long enough to wait for the stragglers to make it out, then wrapped my fingers around the mouth of the skull and pulled myself into the darkness.

Once I was inside, I pressed my back against the warm, wet wall and swiped at the tears running down my cheeks. I hadn't been able to cry in a thousand years. And I didn't like the fact that I could now. Easton was out there. For me. How could I let him do that? How was he supposed to make it out?

I shook the thoughts out of my head and stepped away from the wall. I couldn't worry about that now. If I didn't find

Cash, Easton was risking everything for nothing. The thousand years that had led us to this moment would be for nothing.

"Cash!" I slipped in something thick and wet and caught myself on the wall. In the dim blue light, blood dripped down from the ceiling like rain. I pushed my wet braids out of my face and unsheathed my scythe, moving forward. Only forward. Never looking back.

"Please be here," I whispered into the darkness. "Please be alive."

The cave finally opened up into a wide room. Stones like fangs lined the walls. The sounds of my breaths echoed in the hollow place. He'd been here. I could feel the memory of him, the essence of him. "Cash."

Something splashed behind me and I spun around shaking. I refused to let fear overwhelm me. I didn't have time for that. When I couldn't find the source of the sound, I walked the perimeter of the room, keeping my wrist over my nose to block the smell. I was halfway around when I saw it. Silver ropes that looked as if they were made of some type of flexible metal lay unraveled on the ground next to a stone. And beside them, Cash's bracelet. The little scrap of hemp and beads he never took off, even to shower, lay saturated in a puddle of blood. A whimper escaped my throat and I stumbled back into a set of hands so hot they scalded my skin. Fear surged through me and I raised my scythe, turning around.

Easton grabbed hold of my arm and frowned. "Slow down, princess. It's just me."

His black hair was plastered to his scalp with sweat, and somewhere along the way he'd shed his long black coat, leaving him in a plain black T-shirt. Pale white scars looked like spiderwebs crawling down his biceps out from under the sleeves of his shirt. I was a little shocked. Most of us chose to shed the scars of our life, symbols of our death. Yet Easton had kept his.

"Are you okay?" I finally managed to ask.

He nodded. "Yeah, but we need to go."

Trembling, I spun around and snatched Cash's bracelet up from the ground and slid it onto my wrist. "He was here," I said.

Easton's jaw clenched as he looked down at the bracelet. "And now he's out there."

"What?" My freshly beating heart nearly stopped. "Is he alive?"

Easton grabbed my hand and started tugging me out of the cave. "Not for long. It's feeding time out there."

Chapter 31

Cash

The world fell out from under me.

The fall felt endless. Monumental. It felt like whatever was waiting for me on the other side was going to determine the rest of my eternity. I wasn't ready to face it. My feet hit the ground with enough force to buckle my knees, and ash billowed up around me in a cloud of gray. The soul wriggled, trying to break my grip on his arm, but I held tight. I didn't want to be the one holding him. Bringing him to this place. But I didn't know what else to do. I tried to stand, and pain exploded through my kneecap when I put weight on my leg.

"Damn it," I gripped the soul by the back of the T-shirt and stumbled onto my other leg. He laughed, nervously. I started to think he'd finally snapped, but then I saw him looking at my T-shirt.

"The shirt's a little bit of an understatement, don't ya

think?" I glanced down. It was the shirt Em had gotten me. It said *I see dead people.*

I shook my head and turned my attention to the shadow-infested cliffs. "You have no idea."

Noah approached me, his fingers wrapped around a fistful of the girl soul's long brown hair, and shook his head. She didn't even yelp. She just looked lifeless. "Don't worry. Once you get rid of that body, it'll get better. Right now, it's slowing you down, but you'll be amazed at how powerful you'll feel when it's gone. It feels like you're shedding a suit of armor."

Better? Noah was full of shit. There was no "better" in this place. He'd just drunk too much of the devil's Kool-Aid. Convinced himself that this wasn't wrong. I looked into the kids' eyes, wide with terror, and I felt sick. This wasn't okay. Dead or alive, this wasn't any kind of existence. Not one I wanted to live, anyway.

"Come on." Noah pulled the girl behind him. She followed, limp and resigned to her fate. There wasn't any fight left in her. Mine was another story. He ground his heels into the ash when I pulled him forward and whimpered.

"Please don't," he whispered. "I can tell you don't want to. You're not like him. You could let us go if you wanted. You could."

I could…but where would he go? I slowed my pace behind Noah and glanced up at the black swirling hole in the sky that had deposited us here. My heart pounded against my ribs. As far as I knew, that was the only way out. And I had no idea how to get up there. Ash landed on my face, soft as snowflakes and hot as hell.

"Please!" he cried. "We didn't do anything wrong! We just weren't ready to go yet. But we'll go now, wherever you want.

Just not here, please…"

I jerked on his shirt and shut my eyes. "Will you shut up? Please? I'm trying to think."

Even if I could get them away from Noah, how was I supposed to get them back? They may be dead, but they'd never last down here. An afterlife of wandering the Earth as a ghost was one thing, but this was something entirely different. Who would even *want* to last down here? We were close enough to the cliffs now to hear the hisses and screams. The waves crashing against the rocky cliffs in a deadly rhythm.

"So, how do we get back up there?" I asked, picking up my pace. "You know, Earth? Life? Whatever the hell it is."

Noah shot me a suspicious glare over his shoulder and a gust of wind plastered his ash-blond hair against his forehead. "Why do you want to know?"

I shrugged, trying to play it cool. "I'm supposed to be learning the ropes, right?"

He stopped and I almost stumbled into his back. He stood a few feet from the cliff edge, staring out over the sea. Rocks crumbled and spilled over the edge from the pressure of his boots. I imagined him as a painting in that moment. Wishing he was, so I could control the outcome with my fingers and brush. "Don't do this."

"Don't do what?" I asked. "Learn? I thought that's why we were here."

He shook his head and spun around. "Don't try to play me. You think I'm stupid? You think I don't know what you're thinking?"

I took a step back, putting pressure on my leg, and winced. "You have no idea what I'm thinking."

Noah's steel-blue eyes narrowed on me, and his fingers

released the girl, who fell into a crumpled weeping pile of soul to the ground. "Yes, I do. I've stood where you're standing. I've faced the uncertainty. And let me tell you something. Down here…" He spread his arms wide to motion to the wasteland of death around us, and his gray coat rippled out in the wind. "There is no room for a conscience. There is no place for the things you are feeling. So turn them off."

I balked. "Turn them off? Do you hear what you're saying? They're *kids*."

"That doesn't mean anything here. They are souls. It's my life or theirs. I choose me."

"Your *life*?" I laughed bitterly. "Noah…you're dead! This isn't a life. It's not even an afterlife. It's a fucking nightmare!"

A life was the feel of a charcoal pencil between my fingers. A paintbrush in my hand. Kissing. Laughing. Cheap beer and good music every summer at the lake. Eighties action movies with Em on a Friday night. A life was what I wanted with Anaya. Not this.

"Stop making me out to be some sort of super-villain!" He seethed. "I'm helping them. If it weren't for me they'd spend eternity as one of these things. I'm giving them an out."

Behind Noah, shadows were clambering up the cliff's edge, as if drawn in by the scent of the souls we'd carried in. The girl curled into a ball and chanted something that sounded like a prayer under her voice. In that moment, I thought of Anaya. Of the girl in the dirty basement. I'd been horrified at the time, but she'd saved her. Given her peace. This girl…she deserved peace, too. And not the sick, twisted kind Noah offered. If I didn't do everything in my power to give it to her, if I gave in to this darkness consuming me, what did that make me?

I didn't know anything about my past lives. About Tarik or any of the other people I might have been over the last thousand years. But I didn't think any of them would have been the kind of guy who would've given in. Anaya wouldn't have loved me if that had been the case. All I knew was who I was in this life. In this moment.

Since the fire, everything had been leading up to this. My fate. Only I got what most people didn't—a choice. I didn't want to be like Noah. I'd done too many screwed-up things in my life already. I refused to end it like this.

There was only one way to be that guy *and* protect Anaya. I had to die.

"Take them back up," I said.

Noah jerked the girl by her arm and she yelped. "I take them back and *they* are going to want a replacement. And I'm not putting myself on the menu."

"I am." I stepped forward and my head spun. My vision started to go black around the edges. Everything in me hurt and I was suddenly so painfully aware of it that I couldn't freaking breathe. "I want this to be over, Noah."

"You're crazy." Noah stepped away from me like I was a virus that might infect him. With truth. Guilt. Things he'd obviously made himself numb to long ago.

"I'm not crazy." I released the kid I was holding and he took off so fast he was nothing but a blue blur in my peripheral vision. Noah cursed under his breath and held himself back from going after him. "I'm just…tired. I'm so fucking tired it hurts. You're going to have to find a new replacement because I am not going to be like you. I can't. I'd rather be dead."

Noah's eye widened and he slowly wrapped his arm

around the girl's neck to drag her back toward the cliff edge. I was going to have to stop him. I followed after Noah, gritting my teeth as I put weight on my leg and fought through the pain. I may not have a badass scythe like Anaya, but I had something else. I flexed my fingers, feeling the power pop like fireworks under my skin. It was all I had. That, a bum leg, and a body that was past ready to quit. I couldn't let it quit. Not yet.

I didn't even think about what I was doing. What I was risking. I plowed into Noah and the air whooshed out of my lungs on impact. The air around us sizzled and my skin burned where we touched. He dropped the soul he'd been holding and she screamed, scrambling away from us. Noah grunted, pulling me down with him, and rolled me onto my stomach.

"Stupid human!" he growled. "You have no idea what you're playing with. How long do you even think they'll last out there?" Noah grabbed me by the back of my neck and shoved my face over the edge of the cliff. Shadows howled and sprang out of the crashing waves in flames. They slithered up the side of the cliff, and my heart felt like it was in my throat.

This was it.

I couldn't breathe. I pushed back, but Noah's grip on the back of my neck forced me back down. And let's face it—by this point, I had the strength of a baby bunny. There wasn't any fighting him. Even the hum of electricity under my skin was staring to fizzle.

"You're a real asshole," I growled, spitting ash out of my mouth. "You know that, right?"

"Look at it, Cash," he said. "It's your fate. It's your end. There won't even be a soul left when they're done with you. Just skin, bones, blood, and the pathetic memory of a kid who's too stupid for his own good."

Sharp rocks from the cliff edge dug into my hands. If I could have painted this moment, it would have been a bitter black. A painful red. I gritted my teeth and focused on staying in place. I focused on Anaya's light. A bright gold hope. Weak or not, I wasn't going down without a fight.

"If that's my fate," I said, "it's yours, too."

With one last burst of energy, I reached back, grabbed on to Noah's arms, and pulled. The second my palms left the rocks, our weight sent us tumbling over the edge. My stomach dropped as the ground underneath me disappeared. I reached out on instinct, my fingers finding a sharp shard of stone jutting out over the edge. Something jerked on my ankle and Noah grunted below me.

The stone sliced open my palm and blood trickled down my forearm. A few droplets fell into the horde of shadow demons below us, sending them into a frenzy.

"You idiot!" Noah shouted. "Do you have a death wish?"

I wrapped my other hand around the stone and winced. "I'm going to die anyway, remember?"

"It doesn't have to be this way." Noah squirmed, obviously searching for something more reliable than me to grab hold of. But there wasn't anything there. The cliff side was too sheer and slick. "We could be a team. You could still be with your reaper."

I looked down at Noah, swinging beneath me. He was wrong. I could never be like him and still be with Anaya. That's not who she loved. And she deserved better. A shadow leaped up from the darkness, nipping at Noah's ankle, and a flame swirled up his leg, wringing a scream from his chest.

"Cash!" His fingers were slipping loose. My fingers were

slipping, too. "Do something. Pull us up!"

"I can't." I couldn't. I could barely hold on. There wasn't anything left in me. And those freaking shadows were closing in. Piling up on top of one another to reach us. "I can't…"

I shut my eyes and took a deep, painful breath, wanting Anaya's voice to be the last memory in my mind.

Just breathe.

I thought about her heat. I remembered her smile on my lips melting into a scorching, earth-shattering kiss. I inhaled and imagined the scent of thunderstorms and dreams. I wouldn't let these things go. They were going with me. I let one finger slip free. Another. My left hand dropped to my side.

"What the hell do you think you're doing?" Noah cried.

"Letting go." My right hand opened and…

I felt weightless for an instant, falling…

Then hot fingers wrapped around my wrist, jerking me to a halt. I opened my eyes and blinked up at a guy with black hair falling into his violet eyes.

He grinned. "Need a lift?"

Chapter 32

Anaya

I crawled across the ash and lay down next to Easton, reaching for Cash. Tears were drying on my face. My legs burned. Seeing him go over the edge like that…I'd thought I'd lost him. I never knew I could move so fast. His dark eyes connected with mine and he exhaled with what I could only imagine was relief. Every wave below him that crashed into the rocks sent a spray of shadows and flames up the side. The other shadow walker clung to a groove in the rocks below him, screaming as he shook a shadow from his leg.

"Grab on," I said, holding back a relieved sob. He was alive. Cash nodded and swung his other arm up to clasp my hand. Easton and I both crawled back, pulling until Cash came up over the edge and collapsed. His breaths were weak and wheezy. His skin so pale it blended with the ash in his hair.

He took a moment to catch his breath. "You shouldn't be

down here. It's too dangerous. You should have left me. Do you have any idea what these things could do to yo—"

I touched the side of his face to shut him up and smiled. "Like I said before, I don't take orders from humans."

He grabbed for my hand. "I love you, Anaya. I'm sorry if that freaks you out, but I do. And I don't want to die without saying it."

His voice was drowned out by coughs. "Shhh…" I smoothed his hair back over his forehead and lifted his head into my lap. I pressed my lips to his and lent him some of my heat. When I pulled away he shook his head.

"I'm not going to make it back up there."

"Yes, you are." I sat up and nodded to Easton. "Help me with him. You are not going to die in this place."

Easton slipped his arm under Cash, but once he was up Cash waved him off, determined to stand on his own. Stubborn. He braced his palms on his knees and looked around. "There were two souls…we brought them here. We need to take them back. And Noah…"

"No way," Easton spoke up. "I'll hunt down your two souls and get them to where they need to be, but I'm not risking my ass for the other one. He can rot down there for all I care."

On the other side of the cliff, Noah's screams had gone silent. I couldn't bear to look, so I just shook my head. "It's over for him. And we need to get you back if you want a chance to say your good-byes. I want to do this right. I don't want you to have regrets in this."

He nodded, face grim. "You're right. I…I need to see Em. At least one more time."

I bit my lip and held my hand out, ready to lead him to his end. To his next beginning. Cash reached out, and then his eyes widened.

"Like you said, pal," a ragged voice said from below us. "If I'm going down, you're going down with me."

Cash let out a small grunt of surprise and then he was falling back, Noah's pale hand wrapped around his ankle as he crawled up over the cliff's edge.

"Cash!" That scream lasted only a moment, but it felt like an eternity. Shock and horror registered across his face as his arms pinwheeled and his feet came out from under him. In an instant Easton appeared beside me, scythe drawn. He leaped after Cash, out over the edge, and I grabbed on to Easton's ankle to stop him from going over, too. Cash groaned, body caught midfall, as Easton's scythe pierced his chest. He gave one hard tug and Cash's soul ripped free from his body falling over the edge, taking a screaming Noah with it.

Refusing to think about what had just happened, I crawled back, pulling Easton with me. Once we were up, Easton stood and stumbled back, scythe hanging at his side in his white knuckled fist. "Anaya…I-I."

He didn't finish. I was too shocked to feel the pain, but I knew it was there. Cash's soul slowly climbed to his feet in front of us, dazed, shimmering with a thousand facets of light. Shaking, he raised his hands and stared at his palms.

"I'm sorry," Easton whispered. "There wasn't…it was the only way."

I nodded and swallowed the lump of unwelcome pain in my throat. I knew that. "Cash?"

He looked up and met my gaze. I couldn't tell what he was feeling. He looked…numb.

"I…I'm dead." He looked over his shoulder at the sea of shadow demons feasting on his former flesh and Noah's soul.

"I'm really dead. This is real."

I stepped forward, and as I'd done for so many others, took his hand and said, "This is the only the beginning."

Chapter 33

Cash

For the first time, I didn't feel sick after the disorienting process of Anaya pulling me over to the other side. In fact, I didn't feel anything. I was dead. I looked down at my hands again, shimmering like a freaking Christmas tree, and swallowed. This had to be a dream. No…a nightmare. I'd wake up any minute, Emma kicking my ass to get me out of her bed before her mom woke up and found me. Then we'd go eat pancakes and I'd spend the day sketching and playing *Guitar Hero* while Em tried to make me study for some lame calculus test. Life would be normal again. Death would be something we wouldn't have to think about for another sixty years or so.

"Cash?" Anaya's voice was soft and sweet, breaking apart the panic inside of me like glass. "Are you okay? Please, say something."

I didn't know what to say, so I just nodded and stared

up at the big pewter gates in front of us. On the other side, souls milled around the entrance, stealing curious peeks at us. Probably wondering who the reapers were dropping off next. Anaya practically glowed in this place. Her big golden eyes held mine with so much worry that I wanted to grab hold of her and never let go. Pretend all of this wasn't happening.

Easton and the hooded guard spoke in hushed voices for a moment and then the gates parted, allowing us entrance. I knew Anaya had prepared me for all of this. It's not like I didn't know what was going to happen, but son of a bitch…I was *dead*. How was I supposed to feel about this? How did they expect me to react? I didn't know. All I felt was this strange buzz of electricity trying to break past the barrier of numbness sweeping through me. Nothing hurt anymore. I didn't even feel like I needed to breathe.

Anaya grabbed my hand and pressed herself against my side, close enough to whisper against my ear. My whole body ignited and my hand instinctively wound around her waist. I glanced down at my jeans and thought, *Nice to see you're still with me, sir.*

At least not *everything* was numb.

"You don't have to do this," she whispered low enough for only me to hear. "I'll take you to be with your father. All you have to do is say the word."

She kept her face pressed into my neck, her lips at my ear, as my fingers squeezed her hip. I waited for my heart to pound out of my chest with the weight of what she was asking me, but it didn't. Everything inside stayed silent. Hollow. She was offering me Heaven, but somehow it didn't seem like it. Stuck in a place where she would never be, knowing that she would likely be punished with the unimaginable for putting me there…it sounded more like Hell. I shook my head and pressed my lips into her braids.

"No," I said. "You're not getting rid of me that easy."

She smiled against my neck and her lips left the warm imprint of a kiss just below my ear.

Easton cleared his throat and fidgeted, looking uncomfortable. "Can we get this over with, and then can you two please get a room?"

I followed Anaya through the gates and grinned at Easton. "You know, you'd probably be able to get that stick out of your ass a whole lot easier if you found somebody and got a room yourself, East."

He scowled at me as the gates swung closed behind him. "I'm not a direction. It's *Easton*. And some of us have jobs to do. Contrary to what you've seen, the afterlife doesn't revolve around getting laid."

"Boys!" Anaya snapped her fingers at us. "Game faces. And you…" She stalked toward Easton and stopped at the toe of his boots. Towering over her as if she were a little girl, he groaned.

"What did I do now?"

Anaya reached up and wrapped her arms around his neck. Easton froze, looking uncomfortable, then hesitantly hugged her back before breaking contact and stepping away.

"Thank you," she whispered. "But you're done. I'm not letting you go in there and get involved. You've already risked too much."

Anaya placed a kiss on Easton's cheek and smiled. Easton looked a little flustered, and I wanted to punch him in the throat to wipe the look off his face. I didn't, though. The smoking blade at his hip, the scary-looking scars on his arms, and the fact that he had saved my ass might have had a little to do with that.

"It's…no problem." He scratched the back of his head and looked back and forth between us. "Just don't expect me to bail you out again." He turned his attention to me. "And you. Take care of her, or I'll haul your ass back downstairs myself."

He took two steps back, then disappeared into a swirling black pit beneath him. Anaya took a deep, shaky breath and looked past me to a gleaming building in the distance. Its mirrored walls reflected the nothingness around it, making it hard to spot.

"Come on," she said. "He's waiting for us."

"What's going to happen?"

"I…I don't know exactly." I followed on her heels, staring at the glass floor under my feet as we walked. Stars swirled around beneath us, like fish under a glass-bottom boat.

"But I'm going to work for this guy, right?" I said. "Like you."

Anaya nodded. "That's the plan."

She stopped at the steps to the mirror building and I skidded to a halt behind her. A man stood on the steps, a strange smile on his face. A glint in his silvery blue eyes. His white robe stirred with a breeze that I couldn't feel.

"Well…this is a nice surprise," he said, stepping down to circle us. His gaze left cold electric shivers rolling down my spine. "I'll be honest, Anaya, I didn't think you were going to pull this off. But I have to give credit where credit is due."

"I didn't pull anything off," she said. "He wants to do this."

"Good," he said, spinning on his heel and starting up the cold marble steps. "Then this should be easy enough. Follow me."

Anaya kept a safe distance from me as we followed through the halls. Images flickered and flashed across the walls. It looked like a thousand flat-screen televisions all broadcasting death. On one cube of color a man fell backward off an airplane platform. His head cracked against the runway below. A tiny glow of a girl gathered up his soul and the image faded into another. The next screen over showed a man choking on a hunk of lobster. He fell over in his chair, tearing down the HAPPY RETIREMENT! banner behind him on his way down. I blinked at the screen, unable to keep up with the images. Everything about this place screamed death.

"So…you're Balthazar, right?"

He laughed and spared me an amused glance over his shoulder. "Yes. Am I not what you expected?"

"To be honest, I didn't know what to expect," I said.

I shook my head, trying to break my gaze away from the wall of dying faces. One by one they flashed across the wall. Some in pain. Some in peaceful sleep. It all would have made one hell of a painting. A terrifying one, but still. I reached out and ran a finger across the image of a girl's face and the image rippled like water under my touch.

Balthazar cleared his throat, breaking my attention from the wall. Anaya stood beside him, patiently waiting for me to take it all in.

"Please, come in." Balthazar held his hand out and ushered us into an office. Inside, the walls looked like they were made of stars. Balthazar took a seat behind a big glass desk and motioned for us to sit.

"Tell me what you already know, Cash."

I exchanged a look with Anaya and folded my hands in my lap, feeling like I was in a job interview. Which was really screwed up, considering I was dead. "Um…you want me to work for you."

He nodded. "Yes. But it's so much more than that. I guess you could say, I want your help in cleaning up our earthly streets. A bounty hunter of sorts. Only you don't collect any bounty at the end of a job."

"What do you mean?"

"We have an epidemic." Balthazar swept his hands over the glass-top desk and an image rippled across the surface. An image of a soul terrorizing a family. A girl sat huddled in a corner as the soul with big dark eyes and pale gold hair flung a chair across the room. It splintered against the wall and her shriek bounced off the walls like a siren. "Lost souls. Souls that have escaped their reaper. Souls that have managed to escape the Inbetween and have an ax to grind, like Maeve. The soul that terrorized your human friend."

I waved him off. "I know who Maeve is." I caught a glimpse of Anaya's surprised expression. "Em told me."

Balthazar nodded. "I can't have them down there wreaking havoc. It throws everything off-balance."

I shrugged and leaned back in my chair. "So why not let the shadow demons have them if they're such a problem?"

"Because they are not all bad. But that doesn't matter," he said. "They have no place among the living. I need you to collect them, bring them here for sorting. We have a system. And that system does not cater to helping those of the underworld grow stronger."

I thought about the horde of shadows I'd dangled above just hours earlier and shivered. I didn't want to help them get stronger, either. "So, why me? Why all this trouble to get me here?"

Balthazar laughed and leaned across the table. "You have no idea how rare you are, do you? How special?"

"Look." I scratched the back of my head. "I may be a lot
of things, but special isn't one of them. I did have a girl once
tell me I was a special kind of asshole, but I don't think that's
what you're talking about here."

"Your soul is over a thousand years old. It's been recycled
over and over, each time gaining more strength. For a soul to
recycle that many times and end up sitting in front of me is
unheard of. You have the strength to walk between worlds.
Corporeality means nothing to you. You, Cash, are a valuable
weapon."

I didn't feel like a valuable weapon. I still felt like me. Like
a kid who got drunk on Friday night and got by high school on
a C-minus average.

"Will you hurt them?" I thought about the kids from the
abandoned building that Noah and I had collected. "The souls
I bring in?"

Balthazar raised a brow. "Why do you care?"

"Because I'm not a monster." I laughed. "Look, I've seen
what they do with them on the other side. If that's what we're
talking about, you can count me out."

He studied me for a moment, tapping his knuckles on the
glass as if he didn't know what to make of me.

"They will be sorted. Some will stay in the Inbetween.
Souls like you've just seen will go to Hell. They will be put
back in the place they belong. That is all."

I nodded. "Do I get to have a life?"

Balthazar laughed. "A life? You do realize you're dead,
son. Anaya explained that much at least, I would hope."

I rolled my eyes and Anaya's warm hand rested on my arm.
I glanced down and laced my fingers through hers. The energy
buzzing under my skin was almost too much. Like fireworks

bursting in my veins. But when she touched me it calmed, almost soothed by her warmth. "That's not what I meant."

Balthazar sighed and leaned back in his chair. "Come here."

Anaya and I looked up at the same time. "Why?"

"Because you need to go through transition. Did you think this was it?"

I laughed, incredulously. "Well…yeah. I'm dead."

He raised a brow and electricity crackled in the air, forcing me up out of my seat. I came around the desk and he stood up to meet me. "You may be powerful, but there is one thing you need to remember." He leaned in so close that his breath created ice crystals along the shoulder of my T-shirt. "I can end you," he whispered.

Shaking, I laughed, then swallowed the sound. "So, I shouldn't be expecting a Christmas bonus then?"

Balthazar stood back up with a smile and rested his palm over my shoulder. The cold jolted me with a shock at first and I looked over at Anaya, who was standing next to her chair. She looked afraid. I tried to smile and shook my head mouthing, "It's going to be fine."

But it wasn't. The cold grew more brutal by the second and a burst of pain exploded through me. The energy simmering just beneath my skin was popping through my pores, light seeming to tear my skin to shreds. My back bowed with the force of it and I groaned. Balthazar squeezed tighter and a fire ignited, swimming through my veins. A loud ringing sound vibrated my eardrums and somewhere in the muffled background I heard Anaya scream, "Stop!"

Balthazar laughed and I dropped to my knees. Fireworks burst like bruises behind my closed eyelids and then…nothing. Everything was dark.

Chapter 34

Anaya

A light swirled behind me, pulling on me like a rip current, glinting from the silver gleam in Balthazar's eyes. I knew that light. I'd seen it thousands of times. But it had never been for me. Not once. I knelt down beside Cash and ran my palms over his eyelids, his lips...my palms rested against his chest and I left them there. It slowly rose with a breath, then fell flat again. I pressed my face to his heart and a faint beat thumped against my cheek. I gasped, my fingers searching and touching all the places that showed signs of life.

"Oh my God..." I looked up at Balthazar. "Is he alive?"

"Not exactly." He waved in two angels and signaled for me to step away. They smiled with delight and wonder, and they lifted an unconscious Cash into their arms and carted him out of Balthazar's office.

Panic ignited in my chest watching him go. I reached out,

but curled my fingers back into my palm and stepped away when I saw the look Balthazar was giving me.

"Where are they taking him?"

"To a safe place," he said. "He is regenerating. He'll need a little time to rest."

I clutched my hands against my stomach to calm the nervous feeling churning there. "Regenerate?"

He nodded and sank back down into his seat, nonchalantly flipping through a stack of gold papers. "Yes. He'll need certain abilities that you don't have to do what I'm asking of him. Things only a soul with his power would be capable of."

Unable to ignore it, I glanced over my shoulder at the glowing porthole of light behind me. The force of it blew my braids out in every direction. I pulled them over my shoulder to hold them there. If it wasn't for Cash…"W-what it this?"

Balthazar slid the stack of golden papers across the desk to me with a silver-tipped pen. Light swirled and glowed around their edges.

"You have a choice."

"What choice?" It was never a choice with Balthazar. It was always an exchange. An order. Free will didn't exist here, and I made sure that I never forgot that.

"Heaven awaits you, Anaya." He nodded to the swirling light behind me. "I am a man of my word. You brought me the boy. Ensured that he was cooperative. All it will take is a few steps into that light to collect your reward. Your redemption."

I looked down at the hemp bracelet still around my wrist and swallowed. I'd only wanted Heaven when I knew Tarik would be there. Did I still want it? Did I want to put a world of impossible between us again for everlasting peace? My mother and father were there. After so many years, did they assume I was in Hell? Were they in pain over me? This could be a chance to give them that peace.

My finger grazed over the bracelet and I closed my eyes, letting my mind fill to the point of bursting with everything Cash. Sleepy and paint-spattered in the mornings. Warm and trembling, with his mouth touching mine, his kiss promising to make me feel alive and free. He'd sacrificed his eternity for me. No questions asked. He just had that much faith in me. Not Tarik. Cash. I owed it to him to have that much faith in him.

"What are you waiting for?" Balthazar's voice interrupted my thoughts. "This is what you've been working a thousand years to achieve."

I opened my eyes, aching with memories and want, then sank down into the chair across from Balthazar. I stared at the gold papers and pen. "What is the other option?"

Balthazar smiled, no doubt counting on this. "It's a contract. Another thousand years of servitude. After those thousand years, *if* you can find me another shadow walker, I'll grant you and your mate the freedom you desire."

I almost groaned. Another thousand years of collecting the dead. But Cash would be there. I couldn't lose sight of that. And this wasn't just about me. It was about him. A thousand years and we could both be free. We could be together. I touched the contract hesitantly.

"Another thousand years of collecting the dead," I said. "That's it. No tricks this time. No hidden truths?"

Balthazar leaned forward, folded his arms across the desktop, and smiled. A sunrise of color ignited under the places where his skin touched the glass. "Collecting the dead? Oh, no, Anaya. You'll be doing something much more important than that."

Chapter 35

Cash

The whir of the heating and air unit and the cool gust from the ceiling fan brought me back to life. I didn't open my eyes right away. Still hovering in that place between nightmare and reality, I was sort of afraid to. I opened my hand and let my fingers explore the expanse of cotton sheets and rumpled comforter. The cotton disappeared and they slid over smooth warm skin. I stopped, praying it wasn't a dream, and allowed my eyelids to peel open. Anaya sat on the edge of my bed, smiling down at me. Early-morning sunlight came pouring over her in slices through the blinds. All at once everything came rushing back. The heat of the shadow land, the cold pain crackling like electricity through my body, me being…dead. I shot up, breathing hard, and patted myself down. I didn't feel dead. I didn't quite feel like myself but… I shoved back the sheets and peeked in my boxers.

"Thank God," I breathed.

Anaya laughed from beside me. "Of all the things to thank God for."

I scooted back and combed my fingers through my hair, feeling the reliably messy spikes stand right back up like they always did. "Hey, after everything that's happened, it wouldn't have surprised me if the little guy hadn't made the journey. And we're a team. We stick together."

My gaze wandered down the length of Anaya and I couldn't go another minute without touching her. Yeah, I needed answers. But at the moment, she was all that mattered. I reached out and snaked my arm around her waist to pull her close, but my arm passed right through her. My brows pulled together and I reached for her knee, but my fingers swirled into smoke the instant our skin touched.

"What the hell?" Shaking, I pulled my hand up and stared at the back of my wrist. My skin had a slight shimmer to it, nothing like Anaya's but it was there. Sort of a silvery blue embedded beneath my tan skin. "What's going on, Anaya?"

"You are going to have to concentrate to regain corporeality," she said. "Balthazar says it won't take long before you'll be able to stay solid without even thinking about it."

I narrowed my gaze on my fingers and felt a little zing of electricity rush through to the tips. When I reached out this time, they closed over Anaya's perfect satin skin. I didn't move. Just stared at the way a swarm of blue sparks ignited where our skin collided.

"Son of a bitch…I really am dead."

Anaya reached out and tipped my chin up with her fingers. "Not completely. You're somewhere in between."

"What's that supposed to mean? What did he do to me?"

"He reanimated you," she said. "Once you learn to control your abilities, you'll be able to walk among the living fully corporeal, heartbeat and all. But you also have the ability to lose that for easier passage between worlds. Balthazar says you'll have a better chance at nabbing escaped souls if they are under the impression you're just another oblivious human."

I sighed, trying to wrap my mind around it all. "Why can't you do that?"

"You're a very powerful soul. Most of us don't have even an ounce of the power it takes to pull something like this off."

I nodded. "So...I'm still sort of alive. But if I want I can do stuff like walk through walls."

"Yes."

Okay. This was freaky as hell, but I could live with it. It's more than I'd hoped for. I could still have a life. See Emma again and tell her I was okay. That everything had worked out. She might not look at it that way, but I'd seen the other side. I'd seen how this could have turned out. Sitting here in my bed, with a heartbeat in my chest, and the hottest girl in the universe at my side...yeah, it definitely could have been worse. Suddenly, I felt lucky. I felt...good. I took a deep breath and my lungs swelled without hurting. They just tingled and hummed with artificial life. I wrapped my arm around Anaya's waist and pulled her close enough so that our thighs touched. My other hand rose and she touched her palm to mine, lacing our fingers together in a perfect weave. I had to focus to keep it that way, but it didn't take much.

"Look at that." She smiled. "Already getting the hang of it."

I glanced down at her hip, looking for her blade...it was gone. So was the brown leather belt that usually held it in place for her. My eyes connected with hers and I realized they were different too. A rich deep brown with flecks of gold swirling in the depths. A smile lit up her face.

"Where's your scythe?" I touched her face, her lips. "What happened to your eyes?"

She placed her hand over mine and pulled it away. "I got a promotion."

"What kind of promotion?"

"I'm your guardian," she said. "The shadows aren't going to forget about you. Especially since you're one of the only two shadow walkers left in existence now. And while this body and these abilities may seem like a gift now, they are only going to make you more vulnerable to those of the underworld. Balthazar said you were much too valuable to be on your own. So I signed a contract to be your personal guardian."

"And he let you do that?"

She shrugged and snuggled in close to me. "He didn't think he'd be able to keep us separated anyway, and there is no rule saying we can't be together now that you're technically not one of the living."

I started to smile but stopped. "I thought you were going to get Heaven for turning me in."

Anaya's hand slid up my chest, over my collarbone, and into the hair at the nape of my neck. I shut my eyes, burning for her by the time her lips touched my ear.

"Heaven isn't the forever I was working for, Cash," she whispered. "You are."

I pulled back to see her face, and the energy between us felt raw and electric. I wanted her more than anything. And there wasn't anything stopping me from having exactly what I wanted. Not anymore.

My lips didn't need any help finding hers. They knew the way there, as if it was a well-worn path to home. Alive, dead, in Heaven or Hell, Anaya was home. She was everything. I wrapped my arms around her tighter, my palm finding the small of her back. She opened her mouth under mine and I groaned, pushing her back onto the bed. Anaya's arms wrapped around my bare back and my hands slid up her sides, wanting to feel something other than the cotton dress covering her.

"Please tell me this comes off," I said against her lips.

Anaya laughed. "If I want it to, it does."

I kissed my way down her neck to her shoulder and nudged the white strap over with my thumb. She arched underneath me and I just about lost it. "Please, tell me you want it to."

Anaya hesitated for a second, long enough for me to wonder if I'd gone too far, and then the sensation of her skin against mine sent all my rational thoughts out the window. My hands itched for a paintbrush, or maybe that was just an itch to touch her. Anywhere. Everywhere.

I leaned back a little to look at her and my heart pounded out a frantic rhythm in my chest. It may have been new, but it was getting a workout. I touched a fingertip to her chin and let it slide down the smooth, tan column of her throat.

"I want to paint you someday," I breathed against her neck. "Just like this."

Anaya wriggled under me. Her lips found my jaw. And that was it. I was a puddle of worthless goo in her hands. I probably wouldn't have been capable of holding a paintbrush in my hand by that point. "We have at least a thousand years to work on that. But how about this time, you kiss me instead."

My stomach fluttered and I smiled against her mouth. "Now that I can do."

Chapter 36

Cash

I stood in the empty hallway of Lone Pine High School. It felt so small. So insignificant after everything I'd been through. I wasn't here to go to class anymore. Now I was here for the escaped soul that wandered the halls. There was no telling how long he'd been here. But I knew he was a kid. The same kid I'd seen in the bathroom that day, back when nothing made sense. I hiked my bag up over my shoulder and looked behind me. Anaya leaned against the lockers, arms folded across her chest. She'd traded in her white dress for a pair of jeans and a white tank top that made me want to fall to my knees. Her braids were gone, replaced by one thick, loose braid she kept pulled over her shoulder. She said it was time for a change. I was still convinced she was just trying to distract me. Next thing I knew she'd be in a bikini, then I'd never get any souls collected.

"I'm right here if you need me," she said.

I nodded and headed down the hall, letting the prickling cold sensation guide me. It felt like a glittering rope of energy, stretched out in front of me, tugging my chest. I passed Ms. Abernathy's AP lit class and stopped at the blue metal door that led to the men's restroom. It was where I'd seen him before. My heart pounded in my chest and I crossed my fingers that this went down the way it was supposed to. It's not like there was a vo-tech course for shadow walkers. Sure, Anaya had given me some tips on how to handle souls, but I still didn't exactly feel prepared. I pushed through the door and the room exploded with cold. The energy crackled across my skin like sparks. He was definitely here. I looked up in the mirror and there he was, standing behind me. I spun around, slowly, and dropped my bag to the floor.

"Why are you here?" he asked. He was so dim; he looked like a faded image flickering in and out of existence, reminding me of the old black-and-white movies Dad used to watch late at night when he thought I was asleep.

"I'm here to help you," I said, unsure what he would want to hear. Also, praying that what I said was true. "It can't be fun, being here all alone all the time."

"Is the other one here?" He peered around me looking for Noah.

"No." I shook my head. "He's not coming back."

He looked unsure, but finally shook his head and dropped his gaze to the floor. "You could stay with me. We could play." He looked up at me, hopeful. "I know some games."

I nodded. "How about I take you somewhere you don't ever have to be alone again. Someplace where there are other kids to hang out with. People who care about you."

He shoved his hands into the pockets of his worn-out-looking overalls. "No shadows?"

I shook my head and extended my hand out to him. "No. No shadows, buddy. You don't have to be scared of that anymore."

He nodded and placed his hand into mine. A sudden jolt of energy connected us and I grabbed on to the sink to catch my balance. I looked down at our arms and a blue light swirled beneath our skin, linking us together.

"What's that?" He sounded nervous, a tremble in his voice.

"I…I don't know." I grinned, trying to make him feel better. "I'm kinda new at this."

He nodded and I tugged him along with me out into the hall where Anaya waited. We emerged and she smiled warmly, taking his other hand and whispering sweet things to him. When we passed the half-open door to the yearbook room, I stopped, tugging us all to a halt. I checked my watch. Emma had yearbook this hour. And I still hadn't seen her. Hadn't explained. The sudden urge to see her, knowing she was so close, wouldn't let me take another step.

"What is it?" Anaya asked.

"It's Em," I said. "I need to talk to her. Can you…"

Anaya touched my arm and nodded. "I have him. Just don't take too long."

I kissed the corner of her mouth that lifted with a smile. "Thank you."

I eased into the room and quietly shut the door behind me. Emma was across the room, huddled over a computer and a stack of prints, her blond hair dangling over the back of the chair. I wondered why she didn't turn around until I saw the earbuds to her iPod hanging out of her hair. Six months ago, she never would have done that. Been that oblivious to the world around her. Six months ago she didn't feel this safe. I smiled and rubbed my chest where it ached a little. I hadn't thought I'd get this. A chance to talk to her again. I walked up behind her chair and listened to her humming the tune to a song from one of those indie bands she'd always liked. She stopped and I realized she must have seen my reflection in her computer monitor. Emma spun around in the chair, nearly knocking it over, and then she was in my arms, crying all over my shirt.

"I'd be crying, too, if I listened to crappy music like that," I said into her hair. She half sobbed and laughed, then slapped my arm. I squeezed her tighter, feeling more like *me* than I'd felt in weeks.

"I thought you were dead." She sounded muffled against my shoulder, holding on like she was afraid I would disappear again if she let go. I pulled away and wiped the tears off her cheeks with my thumbs.

"I'm okay. That's all that matters."

She got quiet and her eyes searched my face. She reached out and touched my cheek, then grabbed my hand and stared at the faint shimmer breaking through the pores of my skin.

"What happened?" A tear leaked down her cheek. "Are you…"

"Not exactly." She looked like she was going to pass out, so I pushed her down into the chair and sat on my knees in front of her. "I'm sort of both now, Em. Alive and dead. And I work for your boyfriend's old boss now."

She slapped her hand over her mouth, then pulled it away long enough to whisper, "I'm sorry. This is my fault."

"No, it's not. This is what was supposed to happen to me."

She shook her head, lip trembling. "You don't believe in 'supposed to.'"

I held her hand until she looked me in the eye. "I know it might not seem ideal to you. Hell, it probably seems like a nightmare, but it's not. I'm happy. I have a heartbeat." I pressed her hand to my chest to let her feel it. "I've got breath in my lungs. I have this moment with you, and the chance to have more. And I'm in lov—" I stopped, feeling weird telling her about it. Her brows pulled together and she looked over my shoulder to where Anaya peeked through the little window in the door, then disappeared again.

"Anaya?" She turned her attention back to me. "You're in love with Anaya?"

I glanced over my shoulder and couldn't hold back the dopey smile. I laughed and scratched the back of my head. "Yeah. I guess I am."

Emma just stared at me for a minute, then laughed and hugged me. "Oh my God…you love a girl. Cash Cooper loves one, *singular,* girl. And a reaper girl!"

"Hey, she's not a reaper anymore," I said, grinning like an idiot. "She's sort of my guardian now. It's her job to watch out for me. We're a team."

I didn't tell her Anaya wasn't the first girl I ever loved, because it didn't matter now. We were all right where we were supposed to be. It finally felt like all the pieces were in place. For the first time since all this started, I felt like I could really, truly be happy for her the way she deserved.

"So…things can go back to normal now?" She sounded too hopeful. I couldn't let her have that kind of hope. I wrapped my hands around hers and stared at our fingers.

"You're back, right?"

"For now," I said softly, as if the tone of my voice would soften the blow. "I'm not really alive anymore, Em. My body isn't going to age. And I have this job now…"

She swallowed and her eyes watered. She looked away from me like she was trying to study the collage portrait of this year's senior class on the wall. It didn't take long to find the image of me and Em, my arm slung around her shoulder as we both grinned like idiots. It had been taken before all of this had even begun, and it felt like a lifetime ago. "What does that mean? You're leaving?"

"Not yet, but I don't want you to get used to this," I said. "I'll still be around when I can, but it won't be like before. I'm going to be busy. I've got responsibilities now. But you've got Finn. And he is a good guy. Like, a seriously good guy. You won't ever be alone."

She sniffled. "I know that. But you're my best friend. I don't want to say good-bye to you."

I nudged her chin with my hand. "Hey, it won't be a good-bye. It'll never be a good-bye for us. Okay?"

Emma nodded and sighed. "You realize prom is next week? It's going to blow if you're not there."

I sat back on my heels and an image of Anaya in a hot prom dress, pressed up against me in all the right places as we danced, flashed behind my lids.

I cleared my throat and smiled. "I'll be there. Besides, who's going to spike the punch if I don't go?"

After I explained everything to her and let her grill me, I promised I'd see her again and made my way back out into the hall. Anaya was sitting in the middle of the hall with the kid. They'd found the deck of playing cards that had been in my backpack for like a year.

Anaya smiled up at me, gathering the cards and putting them away. The kid actually looked...happy. I decided right then and there it was impossible not to be happy around Anaya. Heaven hadn't given Anaya her light—she'd been born with it. She'd died with it. And now she infected any soul that she touched with it. She was so beautiful it almost hurt to look at her. She stood up and grabbed my hand.

"Everything okay?"

I smiled and brushed a tendril of dark hair out of her face, tucked it behind her ear. "Perfect. Well...it'll be perfect if you say you'll go to prom with me next week."

Anaya rolled her eyes and tugged me down the hall.

"Oh, come on," I groaned. "Give me one last reckless night as a teenager, then it's serious shadow walker time, I swear. You could wear a hot dress and I can wear a tuxedo T-shirt. We can pretend to be humans and spike the punch and dirty dance all over the gym. If Balthazar throws a hissy fit, I'll tell him I was scoping out a soul."

Anaya laughed and pulled me down to kiss my jaw. Heat much more powerful than the kind running though my veins throbbed in all the right places. "Now, how could I say no to that?"

"That's just it. You can't." I grinned. "You love me too much."

My gaze drifted over her face, which was overcome with emotion. Her fingers coasted over my throat and she nodded. "You're right. I do."

My heart thudded in my chest and I wasn't sure if the Almighty himself could have pried me away from her side in that moment. Out of the corner of my eye, I saw the kid watching us and figured it was probably best if I didn't kiss her senseless right there in the hall. It made me in that much more of a hurry to get this soul to where he needed to be, so we could be alone.

"I love you, too." I gave her a quick kiss, then held my hand out to the kid waiting beside us and guided him through the silvery light to the afterlife. I was going to give him peace. A second chance. And for the first time in my life, I finally felt something I don't think I'd felt in a thousand years.

I felt complete.

Acknowledgments

First, a big thank-you to my editors Heather Howland and Kaleen Harding for helping me bring Cash and Anaya's story to life. This book would not be what it is without either of you. And an extra hug and thank-you to Heather Howland for my beautiful cover and for being a source of support and inspiration. I am so thankful to have someone like you in my corner. Also big thanks and hugs to the entire Entangled Teen crew.

To my fabulous publicists Jaime Arnold and Heather Riccio, I'm pretty sure you ladies wear superhero capes. To Melissa West, Rachel Harris, Trisha Wolfe, Lisa Burstein, Mya Smith, and Kelly Hashway. Thank you for your constant support. I don't know what I would do without you!

Huge hugs and thanks to my incredible street team! Raizza Cinco, Ali Byars, Angela Copa, Lea Krnjeta, Taherah Abbas, Iris Hernandez, Amy Fournier, Vi Nguyen, and Eileen, you girls rock!

To my amazing friends, Molly Mclean, Ashley Ward, Amber Bunnell, and Carolyn Lambeth. You girls are my rock! Thank you for keeping me sane.

And finally thank you to Jared and my beautiful boys, Colten and Caden. My world would not spin without you.

*Go back to the beginning with Finn and Emma
in the first book of the Kissed by Death series…*

inbetween

*"A captivating whirlwind of death, revenge, and true love.
I want a reaper of my own!!"* - Jena from Shortie Says

Since the car crash that took her father's life two years
ago, Emma's life has been a freaky—and unending—lesson in
caution. Surviving "accidents" has taken priority over being a
normal seventeen-year-old, so Emma spends her days taking
pictures of life instead of living it. Falling in love with a boy
was never part of the plan. Falling for a reaper who makes her
chest ache and her head spin? Not an option.

It's not easy being dead, especially for a reaper in love
with a girl fate has put on his list not once, but twice. Finn's
fellow reapers give him hell about spending time with Emma,
but Finn couldn't let her die before, and he's not about to let
her die now. He *will* protect the girl he loves from the evil he
accidentally unleashed, even if it means sacrificing the only
thing he has left. His soul.

Prologue

Finn

"Tell me again. How did you miss the mark?" I shoved my hands in my pockets and pressed my lips together to keep from grinning. "I swear, Anaya, this is the last time I follow one of you Heaven reapers anywhere."

Anaya and I walked down a two-lane strip of asphalt that glistened with puddles of leftover rain. Somewhere in the distance, a second round of clouds let out a hungry rumble. Anaya silently kept pace beside me, the gold band around her biceps glinting with each feather-soft footstep.

She turned her nose up into the air. "I never miss a mark."

"Then would you mind explaining why I'm walking up a mountain to get to our reap? We could've just flashed there."

She squinted at her surroundings, hesitating. I knew we

were close, but it was way too fun messing with her to let this one go. "It's okay to admit you're losing your touch," I said. "I'd be happy to take the lead on this one."

Anaya held up her hand, ignoring me. "Do you hear that?"

I stopped, listening to the mangled wail of a horn in the distance. As if pulled in by the sound, a black blur, like a cloud of ink, whipped past us before disappearing around the bend.

Shadows. Scavengers from the outskirts of Hell. Souls that weren't chosen to start again, had escaped their reaper, or hadn't earned their way into Heaven, so they'd been left to decay and rot. They were soulless beings that craved the scent of death. The taste of a soul.

I hated them. But I hated the memories they brought back even more.

Every shadow that blurred across my vision was a cold reminder of Allison, the love of my afterlife. What I'd done to her. What I'd almost let her become. Her name tumbling around in my skull made my chest ache.

But I couldn't change it. I'd never be able to change it. I'd pushed her into a world where we'd never be together again and nearly gotten myself banished to Hell in the process. The shadows would never let me forget it. After fifteen years of penance, Balthazar wasn't likely to let me forget it either. A sick feeling started to brew in my gut, so I shook it off and watched another black blur zip past us. At least they always led us to our targets.

"See." Anaya smiled and skipped ahead. "We're here."

Sure enough, around the last bend, a candy-apple-red Camaro lay upside down, crumpled like a discarded Coke can at the tree line. The horn blared, the sound careering off the rock wall and slamming back into the cliffside forest where it splintered into a thousand echoes between the branches. If I had to guess, the car had taken a similar journey. A ringlet of white smoke seeped from under the ruined hood and twirled up into the air.

"Looks like we have a winner." Anaya pulled her pearl-handled scythe from the leather belt she wore around her white dress, and twirled it in her hand. The twelve-inch blade, with its efficient, palm-sized handle, gleamed like it had never been used.

I glanced down at my sad excuse for a scythe with its plain iron handle and dingy blade. Heaven's reapers got all the perks. I may have been a slave to the Inbetween, but I was still a reaper, for God's sake. We were supposed to be the stuff of nightmare and legend. You'd think they'd at least give me a decent scythe. "Hey, what do you think the chances are of me scoring one of those?"

"Keep dreaming, Finn."

I stopped, leaving a few feet of distance between the car and me. Whoever was in there wasn't ready for me. Not yet. A slow warmth, an ache, spread through my chest, and drove sparks through my veins. Not the impatient icy burn I would have expected from a reap at all.

That…was different.

Anaya strolled past me, the shimmery brown plaits that hung down to her waist swaying behind her. "Look at the bright side," she said. "At least they did away with those awful cloaks."

She gripped the scythe and looked to the heavens. Her lips moved around the words to a prayer, one she'd never let me hear. Then, with a graceful sweeping motion, the blade of her scythe sliced through the car. She tugged once, twice, and yanked her glittery prize from the wreckage. Anaya shoved her scythe back into the leather belt at her hip and pulled the man to his feet. The shadows were on him in an instant, hissing and swirling like smoke around his legs and waist, just waiting for us to make a mistake. They were desperate. Hungry. Of course, their reaction wasn't really a surprise. Balthazar had loaded the territories with reapers, cutting off their food supply—souls rarely slipped through the cracks anymore.

Anaya turned around, tucking the soul behind her, and swung out her scythe. The shadows shrank back before dissolving into an oily spot on the pavement. She scowled and shoved her scythe back in its holster. "Vermin."

Vermin. I'd almost doomed Allison to be vermin. I couldn't look away from the dark spot on the pavement.

"Emma?" The soul babbled, rubbing his head. His eyes swam dizzily in his skull as he tried to regain his bearings. "Emma. You have to help Emma. Have you called an ambulance?"

I closed my eyes, trying to block him out. I didn't want to know her name.

"It's going to be fine, sir. She's going to a very…nice place. Don't worry." Anaya looked up at me, her odd golden eyes begging me to back up her lie.

I couldn't give him what he needed. What he needed was to hear that his daughter was going to live a long, happy life. All I offered was death. I wouldn't lie to him. The fact that I was about to take his little girl to the Inbetween was bad enough.

If she ever decided she was ready, that is. I glanced back at the car, waiting for the icy pull to kick in. Something still didn't feel right about this.

"Dad!" a girl's broken voice cried from the inside the crumpled car.

"Help her!" the man cried, trying to scrabble toward the car. Anaya easily held his shimmering form back. "For the love of God, she's only fifteen years old. You should have helped her first."

Now the pull kicked in. Except, *this* pull was dizzying and familiar in an unfamiliar way. And getting stronger by the second. My head spun with the force of it. Something was wrong here. Nothing about this felt like a standard reap. But I'd swear I felt this before. Once…

Memories pulsed through my mind in blinding flashes as I inched toward the vehicle. Soft-as-satin lips, warm whispers against my neck, smiles like the sun… The pull intensified, like a pounding in my chest, and my knees buckled. I knelt down to the broken window. Something like hope surged through me, followed by a cold rush of fear. I could only think of one other time that it had felt like this. Back when I'd peeled the soul from a frail, bloody body, packed in snow. The day that had changed me forever.

No. It couldn't be her. Not again, and not like this. Blond hair lay matted with blood against the girl's cheek. I reached through the window and traced the path of a tear that had fallen from her closed eyelids, my fingers scattering like mist. Her skin was petal-soft, deadly cold. A warm spot pooled in my hand where we touched, then traveled up my arm, down my neck where the heat exploded in my chest. Connection throbbed beneath my ribs. Certainty pounded in my temples.

Allison…

I jerked my hand back and scrambled away from the car.

It was her. After all these years…*it was her.*

"What's wrong with you?" Anaya sounded annoyed.

"Dad?" the girl whimpered again, weaker this time. Or maybe that was the gray, gauzy feeling that was suffocating me. Fifteen years. Fifteen years of wondering if I'd done the right thing, and this is what I find? A girl halfway to death, clutching a bloody backpack? *No. No. No!* I shut my eyes and focused, touching my scythe to be certain. It wasn't there. No burning pull. No clawing need to take her soul. She could still be okay. Unless—

"Finn?" Anaya crouched down in front of me. "I don't know what is going on with you, but if you are incapable of handling this, I will."

I blinked until Anaya's blurry face slowly came into focus. I bolted upright. "Is she yours? Are you here for both of them? Because it's not me." A cold, throbbing panic took up residency in my chest. When she just stared at me, confused, I snapped. "Answer the damn question, Anaya!"

Realization slowly replaced the confusion in her eyes. Anaya shook her head and stared up through the spiky treetops where a crow swam across the turbulent lavender sky. "It's her."

It wasn't even a question. I couldn't hide this. Couldn't shove the secret into the dark safety of my pocket and walk away. Anaya knew.

She glanced back at the car, and then her gaze settled on me. "Walk away," she said, her voice just a whisper of breath. "If you have any sense left in you, you'll walk away from this and forget it happened, Finn. Don't screw this up. You've worked too hard to go back now."

I still had *some* sense. I must have, because part of me

knew she was right. That I should walk away right now before this went any further. I blinked at the car, trying so hard to ignore the pull tugging me to her, warm and urgent like the need to breathe. The pull telling me I was here for a reason, even if that reason wasn't to take her soul. I didn't admit that to Anaya, though. Instead, I nodded, not trusting the words tumbling around in my mouth.

Anaya wrapped her fingers around her charge's hand and smiled at him. The air behind her rippled like a silk curtain, then erupted with light. His eyes went wide as he glanced at Anaya, then to me.

"I'm…I'm…" He stopped when Anaya patted the back of his hand, the word *dead* hanging among us.

"Yes," she said.

"And my daughter?" His shimmer dimmed as he watched the car teeter ineptly on the cliff's sharp drop-off.

"I'll take care of her," I said. "I swear."

I swallowed, realizing I meant it. What were the odds that I'd find her again like this? What were the odds that out of all of the places in the world she could have been reborn, she'd end up in California? I'd reaped this territory for years, and she'd been right under my nose. There had to be a reason.

Anaya shot me a sharp look, but didn't get a chance to follow through with her usual rant. Glittery tendrils of light reached out and wrapped around her and the soul in tow. A gust of balmy air exploded from the porthole, blowing Anaya's braids in every direction. It fluffed her white skirt until she looked like she was floating on a cotton mushroom top, then spun them around until they were just a swirl of blinding color.

When they were gone, the wind died, and the light

dimmed and dissolved into the murky blue twilight.

Something cracked.

The tree that held the wreckage in place swayed. I looked up. A brilliant flash of red bounced on a branch, as if begging it to snap.

Maeve.

The soul whose second chance I'd stolen fifteen years ago when I pushed Allison through the portal in her place.

And all at once, I realized what fate wanted me to do.

"Don't!" I scrambled for the car. It wobbled on the one tire that hadn't gone flat, threatening to go over any second and take the girl inside with it.

"I knew following you around would eventually pay off." Her voice echoed through the treetops, followed by a mocking laugh. "I realize this is bittersweet, so I'll let you say a quick good-bye before I kill her and ruin your sad excuse for an existence."

I wriggled through the window, closed my eyes, and gave into gravity. Cells connected. The air sizzled. I flexed my fingers, only a breath away from being fully corporeal.

No.

I stopped myself, fighting the urge to slip my arms around Allison's limp frame, and pictured Balthazar, the second in command to the Almighty, ruler of reapers. He'd feel me go corporeal and would know I'd found her again. I punched the ceiling and let my skin scatter like sparks against the gray felt. I couldn't afford that kind of hell right now.

She groaned and something like relief flooded me. Yes, definitely still alive. But not for long. The tree swayed again, this time allowing a little of the car to slip through its hold. I glanced out the window and watched a few rocks spring loose from the cliff and roll to the bottom.

"Finn, come out of there," Maeve sang. She bounced again, rocking the car. "Just give in to this and we'll call it a day. She was going to die anyway. You'd just be doing your job."

She was *not* going to die. I wouldn't let her.

"Come on, Allison." I leaned in close and watched her eyelids twitch, then crack open one at a time. Thank God. "I know you're scared, but I need you to trust me."

Her eyes darted back and forth, wide and afraid, before settling on me. "Who are you? Where's my dad?"

When she leaned up to try to see in the front seat I moved in front of her to block her view. "He's fine. Don't worry about him right now," I said, softly. "I need you to get up. See that window?" I pointed to the upside-down broken window and she nodded.

The car lurched again.

"You need to crawl through there. And you need to do it fast."

She tried to sit up, then winced and fell back. "I can't. It hurts."

I plastered a smile on my face and had to force myself not to touch her, to brush the hair out of her face, to grab her arm and pull her the hell out of there. "Yes, you can. You're tough. I can tell."

She shook her head. "No, I'm not. Really. I didn't even make it through one week of softball before I sprained my ankle."

I laughed in spite of myself. "I have a feeling you're a lot tougher than you give yourself credit for. Now come on." The car rocked and I tensed. "Get out of the car."

She looked into my eyes for a long moment, then pushed herself up and inched toward the window. I crawled out first, coaxing her to follow.

The car shifted. Groaned. I heard more rocks break loose from the cliff to tumble over the edge.

"You're making this unbearably complicated, Finn. Really, why not just pull her out of the car and get it over with?" Maeve taunted, a smile behind her words. "You're already dead—what else could Balthazar possibly do? Oh…well I guess there is Hell. But other than that?"

Pushing Maeve's laughter out of my head, I focused on Allison. "Come on, pretty girl," I said, fear thrumming in my chest. "You can do this. You *have* to do this."

The gash bleeding through her blue jeans snagged on the broken window and she sobbed.

"Don't stop. I know it hurts. But you can't stop." We were so close. Another few feet and she'd be free. I kept my eyes on her, trying to figure out a way to distract her from the pain. "You know, one time I broke my leg," I blurted out.

She sniffled and looked up at me.

"I'd climbed this big tree on my dad's farm. I didn't tell anyone where I was going, so when the branch broke, I knew I was in trouble. I had to walk all the way home on that leg just to get there before it got dark."

"Why didn't you wait for somebody to look for you?"

"Coyotes. All I could think about was how I used to hear them howling at night. Our neighbor used to find his cattle torn to shreds."

She scooted a little farther out. "Didn't it hurt?"

The car groaned and tilted underneath us. Allison gripped the seat, her eyes wide.

"It hurt like hell, but it was a lot better than ending up like the cattle."

She squeezed her eyes shut and wiggled the rest of the way through the window, into the pine needles and dirt on the side of the road. She crawled forward a few more feet and collapsed. Her cheek pressed against the wet pavement as she fought to catch her breath.

A loud *crack* split the silence, and the car lurched forward, its weight breaking the tall bone of a tree. Within seconds, it rolled off the side and into the chasm below, a chewed-up red spot swallowed by the dark.

Maeve's scream ripped through the mist that had started to fall, and in it, I heard her cry for revenge. I'd worry about that later. For now, I looked down at Allison.

I watched her breaths make foggy shapes as they puffed erratically into the night. Her lashes blinked away the tears that were running across her cheeks. No. This wasn't Allison anymore.

"Emma," I whispered as a beam of headlights curled around the bend in the road. "You need to flag down the car that's coming around the corner. You're going to have to get up."

"My leg…" She looked up, tears in her eyes. "Why can't you do it? Why aren't you helping me?"

Guilt tied my insides into knots, making it hard to look at the girl reaching up for my help. I couldn't give it to her no matter how badly I wanted to. Balthazar and his damned rules!

"I can't. I'm so sorry." I took a few steps back until she lowered her hand. "But you can do this. You're tough. Remember?"

Her gaze swung to the lights glistening on the pavement

and she pushed herself to her knees. I took my chance. I let myself fade. Dissolve into the mist around me that was calling me home.

I watched Emma wave her arms at the slowing car. She was safe. Alive. I closed my eyes, laughing with relief. I'd done it. I'd saved her. Except…

I looked up at the broken tree where Maeve had balanced only minutes ago. There was no way I could walk away now. Not when I'd led Maeve to her.

Damn it. This was bad on so many levels. I watched Emma collapse against the man from the car as he wrapped a jacket around her shivering shoulders. Warmth spread through my chest. Yeah…*bad* wasn't a strong enough word. Disaster was more like it. And I didn't care. She was worth it.

"I'll keep you safe. I swear it." I repeated the promise I'd made to her father, then closed my eyes and let the wind catch me and toss me into the night.

Like what you've read so far? Pick up

inbetween

available online and in stores everywhere!